JED HAD TO DIE

TARA SIVEC

Cover Design by Tara Sivec
Edits by Erin Garcia
Interior Design by Paul Salvette, BB eBooks
bbebooksthailand.com

For any woman who has a significant other like Jed. I hope someday you find your Payton and Bettie, and bake that man a blueberry pie.

Table of Contents

"Honesty may be the best policy, but it's important to remember that apparently, by elimination, dishonesty is the second-best policy."

—George Carlin

CHAPTER 1

Coffee: Because crack will get you fired.
—Coffee Mug

"I LOVE YOU more than anything. You're strong, wonderful, and amazing. You never let me down, and I'm so blessed to have you in my life, Cecil," I whisper, tightening my arms and putting a little more feeling into my hug of gratitude.

"I'll take *'What You Should Have Said to Your Boyfriend When He Proposed'* for two-hundred, Alex!"

With a sigh, I drop my arms from around the Cecilware Venzia espresso machine and turn to face the woman leaning against the counter with a smirk on her face.

"You're hilarious, Bettie. Remind me again why I hired you?"

Bettie pushes away from the counter with her hip and runs her palm lovingly down the side of the espresso machine.

"Because I'm the only one who loves Cecil almost as much as you do, and I'm the only employee at Liquid Crack who can understand what you're saying when you lose your shit and spray your southern accent all around this place," she muses with a shrug.

She's right, but I refuse to give her the satisfaction of admitting it. Bettie Lake is the exact opposite of me in every way, but for some reason, we click, even if she annoys the shit out of me sometimes. I knew within the first ten seconds of meeting her when she came in to interview for a manager position three years ago that I would hire her, no matter what her experience was. After spending the day interviewing people who didn't shy away from telling me they hated coffee, but didn't mind working in a coffee shop, I was ready to flip tables when Bettie walked in. With her poker-straight jet black hair chopped off right at her chin, short, chunky bangs with hot pink streaks, a nose ring, and tattoos that covered both arms, her chest, and the side of one neck, she flopped down in the chair across from me and said, *"Coffee. Must. Have. Coffee,"* and it was love at first sight.

Platonically, of course. I don't swing that way, even though my ex-boyfriend now assumes I do just because he can't understand why anyone wouldn't want to marry him. But I'll get back to *that* later.

Liquid Crack is my baby. My one true love. Well, aside from Cecil, but without Liquid Crack, I wouldn't have Cecil.

Don't worry, he understands.

After running from my hometown of Bald Knob, Kentucky as fast as I could when I graduated high school, I moved to Chicago and spent the next four years working my ass off getting a Business Management degree from Loyola while working two jobs and saving every penny I made to open my own coffee shop. Five years after I graduated from Loyola, Liquid Crack opened its doors in Lincoln Park, one of the most popular neighborhoods in the city.

Much to my amazement, people flocked to my little shop when word spread fast that I sold the best coffee in the city, and ordering your favorite cup of Joe didn't require you to know how to speak Italian to get the size right. When you come up to the counter at Liquid Crack, your size choices are *I'm Okay*, *My Head Hurts*, *My Eye is Twitching*, and *PEOPLE ARE ABOUT TO DIE*.

That last one is the extra-large, obviously.

It's not as confusing as it sounds because I don't have ten thousand different types of caffeinated drinks on the menu. I only use Kona beans from Hawaii, and you can pick from black coffee, espresso, or a latte. Period. No hazelnut-mocha-choka-froo-froo-with-extra-whip nonsense here. Sometimes I'll have a flavor-of-the-day if my distributor is running a special, but that's as close to froo-froo coffee as I get. When you come in to Liquid Crack and you're having a bad day, all you have to say is, "People are about to die," and within thirty seconds, you've got yourself an extra-large cup of the nectar of the gods.

Coming in at just around a thousand square feet,

with the original red brick walls and hardwood floor of the building it's housed in, Liquid Crack doesn't have tables and uncomfortable wooden chairs. It's filled with mismatched couches and high-back comfy chairs I found at flea markets. Even though my shop is right in the heart of downtown Chicago and frequented by all the business people who work close by, this is not the type of coffee shop where you come to do business. When you sit down on a couch in Liquid Crack, you sit there and enjoy the coffee in your hand like a proper human being. You don't power up your laptop to finish a spreadsheet, talk loudly on a conference call, or conduct a performance evaluation. You order your drink to go, or you sit down and forget about your troubles for a little while. It's perfect. It's cozy, and it's all mine.

The bell above the door chimes and I lean around Bettie to smile at the incoming customer, my cheery disposition momentarily faltering when I see who it is.

"Payton, I need two *My Head Hurts* and one *People Will Die*, ASAP. Oh, and I hear congratulations are in order! Benjamin just told me the good news."

Bettie snorts and I grab the hand-towel draped over my shoulder and whip it against her ass as she walks by me to get started on the order.

"Hi, Mark. And I'm not sure what Benjamin told you but-"

Mark, who works with my ex at a brokerage firm across the street, holds up his hand and cuts me off when his cell phone rings, bringing it up to his ear and talking so loudly I'm sure people back home in Kentucky can hear him. Leaning over to the register, I grab the framed sign sitting next to it that says, "*Anyone caught working will be shot or sold to the circus,*" and hold it up right in front of his face.

He wisely ends the call with a sheepish shrug as Bettie comes up next to me, humming the *Jeopardy* theme song under her breath while she sets the cups of coffee on the counter in a to-go container.

"Sorry about that, Payton. I forgot about your crazy no work rule," Mark apologizes as he picks up the cardboard tray. "I hope you go easier on Benjamin when he's in here. My man needs to work a hell of a lot more to pay for the big, fancy wedding you two are going to have."

He gives me a wink and starts backing away, the phone ringing in his hand again and his booming voice filling the quiet space when he answers it. He moves faster across the shop until he's out the door, all before I can say anything to him.

"You can take those coffees back to the firm and shove them up Benjamin's ass! Or better yet, bend over and shove them up your OWN ass for insinuating I need a man to pay for anything!" I shout across the shop, getting a few weird looks from the handful of customers sitting around and enjoying their coffees.

"That was nice, but it might have been more effective if you said it TO him, and not yelled it across the shop like a crazy person after he was already out the door," Bettie laughs.

"He's the third person today to come in here and congratulate me. What the hell is Benjamin thinking?" I mutter, heading over to the sink to start cleaning the pile of dirty mugs.

"I believe his exact words when he came in yesterday were, *I know you really meant to say yes, you were just surprised. As soon as you start wearing that gigantic ring the size of the Sears Tower that I've been bragging to everyone about how much it cost, it will sink in that you're going to be Mrs. Benjamin Montgomery!*" Bettie says in a deep voice. "I'm paraphrasing, of course. He actually said the dollar amount out loud, but I've blocked it from my mind. Even just the idea that you have a piece of jewelry that costs more than my car shoved into the back of your nightstand drawer makes me want to stab you in the face."

I sigh, turning off the faucet when the sink is full of water and soap bubbles, wondering how on earth I'm going to convince Benjamin that I meant it when I told him I didn't want to marry him. I moved to a big city like Chicago because I was tired of living in a small town where everyone knew your business. And also because the only place that sold coffee was the one, full-service gas station on the town square and they wouldn't know what fresh coffee beans were if a bag smacked them in the face.

"I don't know how many different ways I can inform him it's over," I complain to Bettie with a sigh, rinsing off a blue coffee mug that says Washington, D.C. on it, under a picture of the White House. "With Benjamin lying to everyone he knows and telling them that I said yes to his proposal, and most of those people being customers of Liquid Crack, it's like living in Bald Knob all over again when they come in here."

That thought makes me shudder even though I'm up to my elbows in hot water. There are a multitude of reasons why I haven't been back to my hometown since the week after I graduated, and the gossip mill is just one of them. I love the hustle and bustle of a big city, I love the noise, I love that everything you need is within walking distance, and I love that you can stroll down the block every day at the same time and never see the same people. If Benjamin would just accept the fact that I don't want to marry him, I wouldn't be standing here on the verge of getting hives at just the thought of Bald Knob. I love Chicago, but Benjamin and his denial are starting to ruin that for me.

"You know every time you say *Bald Knob* I picture a town square with a giant stone statue of an old guy with his dick hanging out. And people flocking to the statue to touch his 'bald knob' for good luck," Bettie laughs, making the same joke she always does on the rare occasion that my hometown comes up in conversation.

I ignore her, lining up all the now-clean coffee mugs on a towel spread out on the counter next to the sink and taking a step back to admire them.

"Did I tell you Benjamin wants me to get rid of all my coffee mugs and order matching ones for the stores?"

She gasps, grabbing a hot pink and blue mug with the word *Dallas* written across the center in white, hugging it to her chest.

"I'm so glad I didn't let you know I was starting to feel bad for the guy. Let's kill him. I know people who can make it look like an accident," Bettie tells me in complete seriousness.

"You felt bad for him?" I ask in shock, wiping my wet hands on the apron tied around my waist as I turn to look at her.

Yes, I zero in on *that* instead of her comment about killing my ex-boyfriend. If one more person walks in the door and asks me about my wedding, I won't care about making his death look like an accident.

"Only for a second. I mean, you've been with the guy for five years. He was here when you opened Liquid Crack, and even though he's a pompous asshole who wears entirely too much hair gel, you dumped him when he proposed, the same day you signed the papers to franchise this place," she reminds me.

When she sees my eyes widen with guilt, she quickly sets the coffee mug down and rests her hands on my shoulders.

"I said *only for a second*," Bettie repeats. "Any man who wants to get rid of coffee cups you've been collecting since you were a kid deserves to be dumped. And castrated. Possibly poisoned with a side of head-and-eyebrow shaving while he's sleeping."

While it's true that I broke up with Benjamin when he proposed, a few hours after my final meeting with the lawyers to sign the paperwork to make Liquid Crack a franchise, I didn't want anyone thinking I said no because of my business and where it was going. I said no because I didn't want to get married. To anyone. I said no because growing up in Bald Knob, you had two choices – get married to someone you'd known since birth and start popping out kids, or get the fuck out of there and get a life. I chose option two and I learned how to be a strong, independent business woman. I loved Benjamin and we had a pretty good relationship, up until the franchise discussions started six months ago. He wanted to change everything that made Liquid Crack what it is today. He wanted to make it uniform and corporate and just like every other coffee shop franchise all over the world. We'd done nothing but fight about it for months and his proposal honestly did surprise me at the time. I thought we were on our way to ending things and here he was planning for our future.

The coffee mug fight right before I left to sign the papers was the final nail in the coffin of our relationship as far as I was concerned. Every single mug in this place that people use when they stay to drink their coffees are mine. Growing up in a small town, I had nothing but time on my hands to dream about my future and all the places I wanted to go when I was finally old enough to leave. Anytime someone I knew went on vacation, I always asked them to bring me back a coffee mug. In a place where everyone knows your business, it didn't take long for the entire town to know about my coffee mug collection and help contribute to it over the years. When it was my turn to travel, and when I finally had the money to do so, I kept up with the tradition, always grabbing a mug from the airport gift shop on my way out of town.

I love that my shop doesn't have boring, matching coffee mugs. I love that when you come in, you never know if you'll be drinking out of a London cup with Big Ben on it, or an Orlando one with Mickey Mouse ears.

"So, if Benjamin wanting to do away with the mugs gets him castrated and poisoned, do I even want to know what would happen to him if I told you he wanted to change the name of the shop?" I ask, taking a step back when her nostrils flare and she growls low in her throat.

"Excuse me? Can I get a triple, Venti, soy, half-sweet, non-fat, Caramel Macchiato? With extra Caramel drizzle?"

Bettie and I turn to see a twenty-something woman standing on the other side of the counter and looking up at the menu board in confusion. I knew as soon as the first couple of words left her mouth that this wouldn't end well. The majority of young women who frequent Liquid Crack are college students from DePaul. Some of them are normal and order their coffees like the smart, college-educated people they are, while others are like *this* chick. They speak every sentence with an upward inflection, like every word out of their mouth is a question and they have no idea what the fuck they're doing.

"We should go for drinks later?"

"I just bought these new jeans, but I'm not sure they look good?"

She's probably confused because there are only three items on the menu and she's assuming everything else is just written in invisible ink. Or the NorthFace jacket, black leggings, and Uggs she wears year-round have officially turned her stupid.

Bettie leans across the counter on her stomach and looks down at the girl's feet, then pulls herself back and turns around to face me when she speaks. "You are a disgrace to coffee. Go away before I yank off those stupid Uggs and beat you with them. IT'S ALMOST JUNE! NO ONE WEARS FUR-LINED BOOTS IN THE SUMMER!"

With her back to the confused college student, Bettie lifts her arm and points to the door.

I know you're probably thinking that as her boss, and the owner of the shop, I should apologize profusely to the customer, offer her a free coffee and make Bettie apologize.

Well, you would be thinking wrong.

I mirror Bettie, holding my arm out and pointing to the door without saying a word. Miss Venti-Soy-Blah-Blah-I-Can't-Read scurries away and out of the building, wisely realizing the chick with all the tats could easily vault over the counter and make good on her Ugg-beating promise.

Bettie and I share a high five when the bell rings above the door as she exits. As weird as this may seem, this is another reason why Liquid Crack became so popular. We taught an entire generation of college students and hipsters who live in this area how to appreciate a plain, simple cup of coffee. We aren't complete assholes, though. After living in Chicago for twelve years, I can spot a tourist as soon as they walk through the door. Bettie was born and raised in Chicago and can smell them from a mile away. They get a free pass when they come in here and a warning not to pull that Starbucks shit again if they decide to come back. For everyone else, they better learn how to read or get the hell out.

"I don't know if it's safe for you to tell me what Benjamin thought you should change the name of this place to. I'm feeling very ragey this afternoon," Bettie says, grabbing an empty Traverse City, Michigan mug a customer slides across the counter and taking it over to the sink.

"Brewlicious, Coffabulous, or Roastacular," I mutter, cringing and scrunching up my face in disgust with each name I speak that Benjamin insisted would work much better for a franchise than Liquid Crack.

The coffee mug slips from Bettie's hands and splashes into the sink of water when she whirls around and presses her hand over her heart.

"Was he abused as a child? First the coffee mugs, and now the Frankenstein-like mash-up of two perfectly good words to make new, horrible ones. Why does he insist on doing that? Every time he calls you *fantabulous*, an inch of his dick disappears," she complains, crossing her arms in front of her.

Bettie's outrage makes me feel much better about my decision to end things with Benjamin, even if he hasn't gotten the memo yet. I haven't even told her all the other things he suggested I change and argued with me about, going so far as to call the lawyers and investors on his own with the hopes that they'd agree with him. Lucky for me, they didn't. They knew what made Liquid Crack special, and they weren't about to change it.

"Forget Benjamin and his *freaktastically* disappearing dick. You are now the proud owner of a coffee franchise and you don't need him," Bettie reassures me as my cell phone rings from its shelf under the counter. "And better yet, you'll be so rich and famous when Liquid Crack*s* start opening up all over the world that you'll never have to set foot in that podunk town you grew up in ever again!"

I laugh as I grab my phone from under the counter

and bring it up to my ear, my smile slowly falling when I hear the sharp, southern twang on the other end of the line. As the woman speaks and my mouth drops open in shock at what she says, I silently wonder if Bettie cursed me by mentioning that podunk town, when I realize I might be setting foot back in that place a lot sooner than "never again."

CHAPTER 2

Recorded Interview
June 2, 2016
Bald Knob, KY Police Department

Deputy Lloyd: We have a witness who gave us
a written statement that they heard you
say, and I quote, "Let's kill him. I know
people who can make it look like an
accident." Are you telling me you never
threatened someone's life before?

Bettie Lake: I threaten people's lives
every day when they don't know how to
order a simple cup of coffee. That doesn't
mean I'd really kill anyone.

Deputy Lloyd: We're not accusing you of
killing anyone, Miss Lake, but it's a
little too coincidental that the day
before the victim was murdered, you were
overheard by a witness in Chicago talking
to our prime suspect about knowing people
who can kill someone and make it look like
an accident.

Bettie Lake: It was a joke. And we weren't even talking about killing this guy, we were talking about killing another one. Shit! I didn't mean that. Strike that from the record!

Deputy Lloyd: Miss Lake, this isn't a courtroom. You can't strike things from the record. And I'll remind you one last time, this interview is being recorded.

Bettie Lake: I just want to state on record that if Benjamin Montgomery winds up dead tomorrow, I had nothing to do with it. As a matter of fact, if anyone I know or have ever spoken to gets murdered, I had nothing to do with it.

Deputy Lloyd: According to our prime suspect-

Bettie Lake: Payton didn't kill anyone either, stop calling her that. If she's your prime suspect, maybe you people should stop rubbing the knob on that stone statue and get to work trying to find the real killer.

Deputy Lloyd: That's the second time you've referenced a stone statue. Do you know anything about the murder weapon that was used?

Bettie Lake: I thought he was poisoned? Oh, my God. I can't do this without coffee. Someone get me some coffee before I ki-ick this table over.

Deputy Lloyd: Were you going to say kill?

Bettie Lake: No. STRIKE THAT FROM THE RECORD! And get me some coffee.

Recording stopped for ten minutes to get interviewee coffee

Deputy Lloyd: Miss Lake, I'd like to talk a little bit more about-

Coughing, choking, spitting

Bettie Lake: Alright. I confess. I know who the killer is. IT'S THIS CRAP YOU CALL COFFEE AND WHOEVER MADE IT. YOU SHOULD ARREST THEM IMMEDIATELY!

Deputy Lloyd: Miss Lake, I need you to be serious about this.

Bettie Lake: I am ALWAYS serious about coffee. Do I need a lawyer?

CHAPTER 3

Instant human. Just add coffee.

—Coffee Mug

"**H**OLY SHIT!" I shout, jerking awake with a start and jumping up ungracefully from my chair when I feel something touch my shoulder.

With my arms flailing to stop myself from face planting to the ground, they smack into something in the dimly lit room and warm liquid splashes against the front of me.

"Son of a bitch," I mutter, looking down at my wrinkled, and now soaked, silk blouse, then glancing quickly over my shoulder to make sure all the commotion didn't wake the person in the hospital bed. When I see her eyes are still closed and her chest is moving up and down in the deep, steady rhythm of sleep, I wish I could say it calms me down, but it just makes me think about the phone call I got from the hospital yesterday.

"Your friend Emma Jo Jackson has you listed as her emergency contact and we need you to come to the hospital as soon as possible. She has a black eye, a shattered cheekbone, and a cracked rib."

Rubbing the sleep and the memory of that phone call from my eyes with my fists, I try not to cringe when lifting my arms makes the wet blouse slide against my stomach and chest.

"Sorry, didn't mean to startle you."

At the sound of a deep, masculine voice speaking in a low whisper, I jump with a squeak of fear and remember that someone touching my shoulder is what woke me up in the first place. Turning my head away from the hospital bed, I come face-to-face with a chest. A very broad, muscular chest covered in a light blue t-shirt clinging to the muscles. It takes me a second to remember I'm in Kentucky and not Chicago, and a strange man waltzing into a hospital room before dawn and touching you doesn't require you to pull a shiv out of your purse or scream for help.

"I hope I didn't ruin your shirt."

When he speaks again, the southern twang in his voice gives me another reminder that I'm indeed in Kentucky and I didn't dream everything that happened since yesterday afternoon when I got that phone call.

Before my eyes can move up beyond the wall of chest and get a better look at who's talking to me, my nose takes over. I catch a whiff of what spilled all down the front of my shirt and notice the chest also has arms and is holding a cup of coffee between us. It smells so delicious that I'm not sure if I should pull my shirt up and start sucking the liquid off the silk, or grab the cup out of the chest's hand and guzzle it.

"Coffee," I mumble in a daze, staring as the chest with arms brings the cup up to his mouth and takes a sip.

I lick my lips, not entirely sure if it's because of the coffee tease happening a few inches in front of me or the freshly-shaven chiseled jaw, full lips, and dimples that are attached to the chest with arms. He's got dark blonde hair, cut close on the sides with a messy spike on top, and my eyes lock onto the bluest set of eyes I've ever seen as they stare down at me in amusement when he pulls the cup away from those perfect lips that I'm sure now taste like coffee.

"Hey, how are you?"

The raspy, baritone question pulls my head out of my coffee daze and I stare up at him in confusion for a few seconds. If I was still in Chicago, this question would make me think I know this guy, but that's not possible. He's too hot and manly and...muscly. I'm pretty sure I'd remember a guy like this if I'd met him before. Thankfully, even with my lack of coffee for what feels like ten thousand hours, I remember again that I'm in Kentucky and people are actually nice here. They say hello to strangers and make polite conversation.

Either I've forgotten how to make polite conversation after living away for so long, or I've become one of those women who gets all weird and giggly around a good-looking guy.

"I'm great! I haven't showered in twenty-four-hours or looked in a mirror since I got here, and I'm thinking about licking my shirt because I need coffee to live," I ramble.

With a giggle.

So, option two it is.

Even without a mirror I can feel a trail of dried drool on my cheek from sleeping while sitting up in a hospital chair for the last four hours. Glancing down at my hands I see my knuckles are now covered in black smudges of mascara from rubbing my eyes, which means there's even more of that shit smeared on my face. My twenty-four-hour lip stain is only covering my top lip since I worriedly nibbled it off the bottom one during my travels, and the long, blonde beach waves of my hair now resemble something in the Medusa family going by the frizzy, fly-away strands I can see out of the corner of my eye. The tailored black dress pants and sleeveless pink silk blouse I wore to work yesterday were wrinkled and stained long before he spilled coffee on me, so I can't even blame *him* for that part of my appearance. The only good thing about any of this right now is that Emma Jo decided to check herself into Baptist Health Hospital in Louisville, an hour away from Bald Knob. It's bad enough I'm so close to my hometown, running into someone I might actually know when I look like road kill would be worse.

"You look like you've had a long night," he tells me with a soft smile.

Okay, so having my horrible appearance confirmed by the

hottest guy I've ever been in the same room with is right up there with running into someone I know.

"Still the prettiest girl I've ever seen, though."

I giggle. AGAIN. Not only do I giggle, I reach up and smack his chest playfully.

"Oh, stop!"

The girly giggling continues as my palm flattens against his pectoral muscles and the lack of caffeine in my system is evident when I have to stop myself from asking him if he's some sort of super hero or something.

I mean, Jesus, it's like he's carved from stone.

"So, um, are you here visiting someone? I mean, um, you're not wearing a hospital gown? So I guess you're not a patient? Do you live around here?" I ask stupidly with another giggle, my voice rising a few octaves with each question like one of those idiot DePaul college girls I hate.

The smile on his face quickly falls and the dimples in his cheeks disappear, probably because I'm still standing here with my hand pressed to his chest like some sort of touchy stalker, giggling and sputtering like a twelve-year old.

Honestly, what is wrong with me? I just broke up with my boyfriend of five years and one of my oldest friends I haven't seen since high school is lying a few feet away in a hospital bed after getting the shit kicked out of her. Am I seriously getting googly-eyed over a stranger in the middle of this chaos? It's the lack of coffee, that's got to be it. I now have blood running through my

veins instead of the usual Kona beans, and I've clearly lost my
mind.

"I'm a friend of Emma Jo's. Just wanted to check on her before I went to work," he tells me, his eyes searching my face for a few seconds before he lets out a sigh and moves away from me.

Thankfully, his movement forces my hand to drop from his chest and I don't have to suffer through any further mortification by him asking me to remove it and stop touching him. What he says finally catches up to my slow-working brain, but before I can ask him how he knows Emma Jo, he steps a few feet away, grabs something from a side table, and holds it out to me.

"I brought an extra coffee. You could probably use some liquid crack right about now."

My laughter comes out in a high-pitch, nervous twitter when he uses my favorite words for coffee and the reason why I chose them as the name of my shop. I snatch the travel mug out of his hands as fast as I can and bring it to my lips before I start rambling about my shop like an idiot.

As soon as the warm liquid hits my tongue, I moan against the plastic lid and the pounding headache I've had since my plane touched down in Kentucky quickly fades away.

"See you around," he mutters with a nod, looking back over his shoulder at Emma Jo one last time before moving around me.

With the mug still attached to my lips, my eyes follow him as he walks toward the door, and I'm thankful he doesn't look back at *me* as he goes. Otherwise, he'd see that I can't stop looking at his great ass in those faded and tattered jeans he's wearing, or how coffee dribbles out of my mouth and down my chin while I continue ass-gawking until he disappears around the corner.

"Farewell, Hot Guy. Sorry for molesting your chest muscles. Here's to hoping we don't meet again, because I can never come back from *that* pathetic display," I whisper into the room as I hug the travel mug of coffee to me and go back to my chair next to Emma Jo's bed, flopping down to finish my liquid crack and wait for her to wake up.

"OH, MY GOD, I look like an extra on a horror movie!" I complain, closing the small-mirrored compact in disgust and shoving it back into my bag on the floor. "I can't believe I stood here talking to Hot Guy looking like this. And you didn't even have the decency to wake up and save me."

Emma Jo laughs softly and shakes her head at me.

"You look beautiful, Payton, stop it now. I still think you were dreaming and none of that actually happened. I don't have any male friends, and certainly none I'd refer to as Hot Guy," she informs me with a smile.

"I'm telling you, he was here a few hours ago, scared the hell out of me, spilled coffee all down my shirt, said he was a friend of yours, and then left," I explain to her again, having gone through all of this with her when she first woke up a little bit ago. "I don't know when they started making men like that in Kentucky. He must be a transplant from somewhere else. Like heaven. Hot guy heaven."

Emma Jo laughs again and seeing the smile on her face just makes my eyes move around to the mess that it is right now. The bruising around her eye that is more black than purple, the popped blood vessels in that eye from the force of the punch she took, and the red, angry mark on her cheek where that same fist shattered her bones.

Our eyes meet and I see hers fill up with tears, mine quickly doing the same. When Emma Jo woke up and saw me sitting next to her bed, she turned her face away from me quickly in embarrassment and softly cried. Instead of starting right in on her with a hundred questions and kicking her when she was down, I diffused the tense situation by yammering on and on about Hot Guy until she pressed a button on her bed to lift herself upright. Sharing my humiliating morning got her to smile and laugh and that made me feel good. But fun time is over and we both know she needs to start explaining things.

"I just can't believe you're really here. I can't believe you came," Emma Jo whispers, swiping away at a tear on her cheek and wincing when her fingers brush over a bruise.

"Honestly, I can't believe I did either. I realize that makes me sound like a shitty person, but I haven't talked to you in years, Emma Jo. What in the world made you put *me* down as your emergency contact?"

She looks away from me and stares down at her hands folded together in her lap. Even with a battered face and twelve years of time that has passed since I've seen it last, she still looks just like she did the last time I saw her, on her wedding day, a week after we graduated. Even looking like she went ten rounds with Mike Tyson, I can see she still has a flawless completion. No wrinkles or crow's feet around her eyes and her long, thick auburn hair doesn't have one strand of gray in it. She's still just as slim as she was back then, and though we've only been sitting here talking for a few minutes, her voice is the same quiet, timid one it was when we were eighteen.

"Who else would I put?" she whispers, still staring down at her hands as she clasps and unclasps them nervously. "It doesn't matter how long it's been since we've talked, Payton. You'll always be my best friend no matter where you are or how much distance separates us. I knew you were the only person I could trust about this."

When you live in a small town, your best friend options are pretty limited, but I always knew I'd lucked out with Emma Jo. Our mothers were friends, and when we were born a few days apart from each other, there was no question that we'd be joined at the hip as soon as we could talk and walk. Everyone in Bald Knob liked to joke that we cancelled each other out because of how different we were. When Emma Jo was too shy or scared to try something new, I gave her confidence and dragged her into whatever crazy idea I got in my head. When we would inevitably get caught for that crazy idea, Emma Jo would sweetly talk our way out of it so neither of us got in trouble. She was the calm to my storm and I was the push in the ass she needed to break out of her shell every once in a while.

I never realized how much I missed her and her friendship until right this minute, sitting here next to her in the hospital. I can't help the guilt that over-whelms me, wondering if I'd been a better friend, then maybe this wouldn't have happened to her.

"So, Jed did this?" I ask her quietly.

She nods without saying a word, and I watch as another tear falls down her bruised cheek.

I didn't really need to ask her to confirm my suspi-cions, but I needed something to say before I broke down in tears right along with her. Emma Jo admitting that I was the only person she could trust with this was all the confirmation I needed. All those pushes in the ass I gave her growing up, pushed her right into the arms of Jed Jackson our sophomore year of high school. Jed was two years older than us, a senior at the time, and I never liked him. He was a popular jock and a bully, but for some reason, he made Emma Jo happy. When your best friend tells you she's getting married the week after high school, you keep your mouth shut and wish her the best, because you just want her to always be as happy as she is right in that moment.

My mother keeps me up-to-date with all the latest Bald Knob gossip whenever we talk on the phone, so I already knew Jed Jackson ran the town and everyone who lived there was halfway in love with him. Because of his good looks, fake charming personality, and how he's the seventh generation of Jacksons to rule over Bald Knob, I understood why Emma Jo thought I was the only person she could trust. I'm not under Jed Jackson's spell now, nor have I ever been.

"It started a month after we got married," she admits quietly, sniffling through her tears and still refusing to look up at me. "You know he's the mayor of Bald Knob, right?"

I nod, not saying anything as she takes a deep breath and continues.

"I know it's a small town, but he's still under a lot of pressure all the time. It's hard being the wife of the most popular man in town, and you know I like to keep to myself. All those functions we have to attend and parties we have to throw at our house, and then there's voting year when things get even more stressful and hectic…"

She's making excuses for the rat bastard and I can't stand it. I want to scream at her, I want to shake some sense into her, and I want to stand her in front of a mirror and remind her that plenty of husbands have stress, but they don't leave their wives looking like she does right now. But I don't do any of that. I know it's not what she needs. What she needs is my confidence and one more swift push in the ass for old time's sake.

Leaning forward, I hit the red call button on the bed railing.

"What are you doing?" Emma Jo asks when the static voice of a nurse comes through the speaker next to the button asking what we need.

"Could we get a doctor in here immediately? Ms. Jackson is ready to leave, and we need to get the discharge paperwork started," I talk toward the speaker.

The nurse confirms that she'll send someone in right away and I push up from my chair, pulling the blanket off of Emma Jo's legs as I go.

"I'm busting you out of here," I state, answering her question as I bend down and wrap my arms around her waist to help her out of bed, careful to move her slowly and not hurt her ribs.

"Payton, I can't go home. He's out of town today, but he'll be back tomorrow night."

Her voice is even more quiet and timid than normal, and now it's shaking with fear.

"Good. We have time to change the locks and file a restraining order. And when he shows up tomorrow, I'll be nice and rested and full of enough coffee to tell him to go fuck himself," I reassure her, trying my best to keep the rage out of my voice as I leave her leaning against the edge of the bed and go to the small closet to grab her clothes.

"But people will see me. They'll *know*," she whispers uneasily.

When I pull out a white Bald Knob Wildcats t-shirt and see splatters of blood on the neck, chest and arms, I forget all about keeping the anger out of my voice so I don't freak her out. Tossing the shirt into the garbage can next to the closet, I walk back over to Emma Jo and squat down to my rolling suitcase, pulling out a pair of black dress pants similar to the ones I'm wearing and a peach sleeveless sweater, handing them to her as I stand back up.

"So, let them see you. Let them know that the man they elected to run that town is nothing but a dickless pussy with shit for brains," I speak through clenched teeth when she gently takes the clothes from my hands. "Maybe if we're lucky, the whole town will turn on him and burn him at the stake in the middle of the town square. If not, I'm just gonna need a hell of a lot more coffee so I can be in the right frame of mind to plot his death."

Exhaling loudly, I give Emma Jo a reassuring smile. When she returns it and asks me to help her get changed in the bathroom, I know I definitely made the right decision getting on that plane. Everyone in Bald Knob might like Jed, but if he comes anywhere near my friend, Jed is dead.

CHAPTER 4

Recorded Interview
June 2, 2016
Bald Knob, KY Police Department

Deputy Lloyd: I know this is a difficult
time for you right now, Mrs. Godfrey, but
I need you to answer the question.

Starla Godfrey: I just don't know if my
heart can take this right now, Buddy.

Deputy Lloyd: Mrs. Godfrey, this is an
official sheriff's office investigation on
record. Could you please not use my first
name?

Starla Godfrey: I am eighty-years-old and
I've earned the right to call anyone
whatever I please. I think we should
discuss the fact that you've been living
here for three months and I have yet to
see you attend a service at Bald Knob
Presbyterian.

<u>Deputy Lloyd:</u> Mrs. Godfrey, please try and focus. We brought you in today because you are a witness to one of our suspects threatening the victim. I need for you to tell me exactly what you heard Miss Lambert shout the night of the murder.

<u>Starla Godfrey:</u> That girl got herself all citified and does a lot of yelling now. She yelled at my poor Bo Jangles when he took a tinkle on her foot. He was so terrified I couldn't get him to go outside the whole next day.

<u>Deputy Lloyd:</u> Weren't you the one who placed a call to Mrs. Jackson's home right before the body was discovered and told her that Bo Jangles was outside barking at something in her backyard? So, you must have been able to get him out at some point, which would make your statement false. I need to remind you that this is a sworn testimony you're giving here today, Mrs. Godfrey.

<u>Starla Godfrey:</u> Don't try to trip me up with your fancy detective words, Buddy Lloyd. I've seen every episode of Cagney and Lacey, and I know what you're trying to do here.

<u>Deputy Lloyd:</u> I'm not trying to trip you

up, ma'am, I just need you to answer the question. What did you hear Payton Lambert shout at the victim on the night he was murdered?

Starla Godfrey: I'm a good Christian woman, young man, and I could never repeat what she said. Let's just say it had something to do with removing a man's body part and killing him with it.

Deputy Lloyd: Can you tell me exactly what body part Miss Lambert referred to?

Starla Godfrey: I can tell you the only ones I've ever seen were Mr. Godfrey's, God rest his soul, and they weren't all that nice to look at. Is that what happened? Did he really choke on them? I just can't imagine that's a good way to go. He was such a nice young man, too. Well, I'll say a prayer for him on Sunday that it was quick and painless. You'll be there to join me, won't you, Buddy?

Deputy Lloyd: Mrs. Godfrey, please sit back down, I'm not finished with the interview.

Starla Godfrey: Bo Jangles has been locked up in the house all morning and I need to take my back pills. You come to church on Sunday and we can finish our talk then.

There's a potluck after the morning service so bring something nice. And don't be going down to Knob Grocery and just picking up a bag of cookies. What you need is a woman in your life. Someone who can make these things for you. I hear Emma Jo is single now. I always thought you two would make a lovely couple.

<u>Deputy Lloyd:</u> Mrs. Godfrey, we're investigating the murder of her husband. The one that happened just a few days ago. I don't think that's appropriate at this point in time.

<u>Starla Godfrey:</u> She kept staring over at you when you were at her house the other morning. Every time you turned your back, she had her eyes on you. And those were eyes of interest.

<u>Deputy Lloyd:</u> They were? She was? Like, every time I turned around or just-

Recording stopped abruptly

CHAPTER 5

Coffee keeps me going until it's acceptable to drink wine.
—Coffee Mug

"I DON'T THINK this is a very good idea," Emma Jo warns me, glancing around her living room nervously like someone is going to jump out from behind a piece of furniture and yell at her.

Which makes this idea all the better and will help calm her nerves, hopefully keeping me from taking Emma Jo's car and driving around town until I find the asshole responsible for making her jump every time she hears a noise.

"When have I ever had a bad idea? It's just wine, Emma Jo, not crack. You're thirty-years-old and you're allowed to have a glass of wine. Or ten. I'm leaning more toward the double-digit area, just so you know. And since you don't own a coffee pot, the wine is what's going to keep me from killing anyone," I explain, pushing the glass of Moscato into her hand and raising one eyebrow until she brings it up to her mouth.

"Oh my. This is delicious. And did you really just

ask me when you've ever had a bad idea? What about that time you made me go skinny dipping in Fligner's Pond? Or when you stuffed my bra with your dad's rolled-up gym socks?"

I laugh when she takes another huge gulp, lifting my legs up onto the couch next to her, and then taking a drink from my own glass.

After the doctor finally showed up and discharged her, I got Emma Jo's car out of the parking garage, picked her up at the front door, and off we went. With a stop at a hardware store in Louisville and another at a liquor store, I drove her home and spent the rest of the afternoon changing her locks while she took a shower and got comfortable. No matter how hard I tried, I couldn't get Emma Jo to let me take her to the sheriff's office to file a complaint and a restraining order against Jed.

While she was in the shower, I called and left a message and told them to send someone over as soon as they could. I'm hoping if I can get her to drink enough of this wine, she won't be mad at me by the time they show up. *If* they show up. It's now after six o'clock, and if someone doesn't get here soon, I'll march down there and raise hell. I guess there's no better way to let Bald Knob know I'm home than by making a scene in the middle of the sheriff's office.

"I think I'll have some more, please," Emma Jo says softly. "And then we can talk about all the bad ideas you came up with over the years."

I shake myself out of my thoughts to see her holding her empty wine glass out toward me with a smile. Grabbing the bottle, I refill her glass and top off my own, setting it back down on the coffee table.

"First of all, I had no idea Fligner's Pond was infested with leaches and that a stray dog would come up and shit on our clothes while we were swimming," I explain. "If I recall correctly, when Sheriff Cooper caught us running naked in between houses, you did quite well telling him we were hiding behind the bushes of Mr. Landry's house and refused to come out because we'd started a Neighborhood Watch and we weren't allowed to leave our post."

Emma Jo rolls her eyes, taking another drink of her wine, and I continue.

"Second, how was I supposed to know that when you changed into your white t-shirt at gym everyone would be able to see the red stripes of my dad's socks through the material? You brought *that* one on yourself."

It doesn't take long before we've finished two bottles of wine while laughing and reminiscing about all the stupid stuff I convinced her to do growing up. She asks about the shop and about Benjamin, already knowing almost everything about both because my mother calls her mother two seconds after we hang up the phone. I want to ask her more about Jed and why she's put up with his abuse for twelve years instead of talking about Benjamin, but I'd rather see the smile on her face right now than the sadness from earlier in the hospital. I open another bottle of wine and I tell her all about Liquid Crack's franchising and Benjamin's refusal to take no for an answer.

"Your mom showed me a picture of him one time. He's really good looking," Emma Jo states, swaying to the side and sloshing some wine on her yoga pants.

"Not as good looking as Hot Guy in the hospital. You should have touched his chest. It was all chesty and muscly and pretty."

She giggles, clinking her glass to mine.

"I'm so proud of you, Payton. You got out of this town and you made something of yourself. You got out, and I just sat here and did nothing. I sat here, and I didn't go skinny dipping, and I didn't stuff my bra, and I didn't drink wine, and I just let him order me around and I let him hit me. Over and over, I let him do it. Why did I let him do it?" she whispers, sniffling and bringing the wine glass up to her mouth and drinking quickly to stop herself from crying.

"Rule numero uno of wine drinking – there is no crying in wine drinking. Rule number B...I don't know, just drink more wine and don't cry. I'm not going anywhere until I know you're okay so drink more wine and don't cry," I demand, the wine buzz strong with this one.

Setting my glass down on the coffee table, I decide it might be time for me to stop drinking if I want to make good on my promise to Emma Jo. I won't be able to make sure either one of us is okay if I pass out on the couch. We sit in silence for a few minutes as I look around the living room. After I made the phone call to the sheriff's office, I took the rest of the time Emma Jo was in the shower to wander the house. To an outsider, it's the perfect home for a happily married mayor and his wife. It's an older home, just like all the houses in Bald Knob, but every room in the house has been updated and upgraded, filled with nothing but the best carpet, furniture, appliances, and home entertainment systems. On every table, across the fireplace mantle, and hung on every wall are pictures of Emma Jo and Jed, documenting everything from when they were dating, to their wedding, to buying their first home, and each one of Jed's mayoral induction ceremonies.

If I was a stranger walking into this house, looking at all of those pictures, I would believe the fairytale. I would believe that the mayor of Bald Knob is a good man and a loving husband. I would believe that the smile on Emma Jo's face in every photo is a real one. Looking at the handful of framed photos scattered around this room with the eye of a friend, even if I haven't been here for all of those events, I can see that the smile never reaches her eyes. I can see that she always stands a few inches away from Jed like she's afraid of touching him, and I can see the tight clench of his fingers wrapped around her hip, or her shoulder, or her side, letting her know with the pinch of his hold that he's never going to let her go. And not in a devoted, caring way either.

A knock on the front door makes both of us jump and Emma Jo stares at me with wide, frightened eyes.

"It's okay, it's fine," I reassure her with a pat on her thigh as I get up from the couch.

Even though I know it's probably someone from the sheriff's department, because I have a feeling when Jed comes home and finds the locks changed, he'll be doing a lot more screaming than knocking, the look on Emma Jo's face as her eyes dart back and forth between me and the front door makes my heart pound in my chest.

"Just in case," I tell her with a reassuring smile as I grab a heavy glass object in the shape of a triangle from the side table, glancing at it as I move to the door.

"Number One Mayor and Number One in Our Hearts," I read under my breath, rolling my eyes and raising my arm, bringing the stupid thing up above my head as I get to the door.

"Who is it?" I shout, looking back over my shoulder and giving Emma Jo a cheerful smile.

"Sheriff's department," a muffled voice calls back through the door.

With a relieved sigh, I unlock the new deadbolt and fling the door open.

"YOU!" I yell in shock, my eyes widening when I see who's standing on the front porch.

"Me," Hot Guy from the hospital replies, glancing

up at the award I'm still wielding like a weapon over my head. "Can you put that thing down? I don't know if you've had your coffee yet, and I don't trust you."

My arm drops from over my head, but I don't put the heavy glass down. Instead, I aim the pointy end right at his uniform covered chest.

"Did you follow me here? What kind of creeper are you?" I ask, thrusting the award closer to him.

"Payton?" Emma Jo calls from the living room worriedly.

I lean back around the open door so she can see me, my eyes locked on Hot Guy, who I will now refer to as Hot Guy Creepy Stalker, as I answer her.

"Emma Jo, call the police. That guy from the hospital followed us here and stole a sheriff's uniform," I explain, bringing my weapon up higher and pointing it at his face.

The face, while still incredibly good-looking, wears a smirk and isn't the least bit scared that I could shove this thing through his heart if I so choose. You know, if his chest wasn't all muscly and made of steel. And he didn't have at least five inches on me and a hundred pounds.

"You mean Hot Guy? The one with the super hero chest and cute dimples?" Emma Jo yells to me.

Hot Guy Creepy Stalker actually has the nerve to laugh.

"Super hero chest?" he asks with another damn smirk.

"You shut your mouth. You're not allowed to laugh when you're a stalker and I'm the one holding a weapon."

With a raise of one eyebrow, he points to the gun on his holster by his hip and the Taser on his other hip, and then pulls a can of mace out of a front compartment of the holster, holding it up for me to see before quietly sliding it back in place.

"Ha! And that's how I know you're not really with the sheriff's department. The worst crime that's ever happened here in a hundred years was when Billy Snyder got drunk on homemade moonshine and accidentally shot his foot. Nice try there, slick," I state smugly.

"Actually, I had to use the Taser three days ago when Mr. Snell wouldn't stop kicking his cows," Hot Guy Creepy Stalker informs me.

Damn, that chest looks even better in uniform than it did in a tight t-shirt. And those arms…they could crack a watermelon in half. He looks more like a stripper cop than an actual man in law enforcement.

"Mr. Snell was kicking his cows? PRINCIPAL Snell?" I ask distractedly, forcing myself to look away from how his uniform sleeves tighten around the thickness of his biceps when he crosses his arms in front of him.

Jethro Snell was the principal when Emma Jo and I were in school. He was always nice and I have a hard time picturing him doing something like this out on his farm at the edge of town, even if it has been twelve years since I saw him last.

"He retired six years ago. And he said the cows wouldn't stop looking at him funny. I'm assuming this was a result of the same homemade moonshine," Hot Guy who is hotter than earlier, but still falling under creepy stalker territory no matter how much the low rumble of his voice makes my low parts feel rumbly. "Can you put the weapon down now?"

He looks over my shoulder and the amusement on his face drops like a lead balloon. His eyes narrow and his arms slowly uncross and drop to his sides, his hands clenching into fists.

"Jesus Christ," he mumbles through clenched teeth. "You were on your side facing away when I stopped in earlier and I didn't see...that son of a bitch..."

I'm confused for a minute when he speaks until I hear Emma Jo sigh softly from behind me and realize she must have walked up when we were discussing Principal Mayford kicking his cattle and Hot Guy Creepy Stalker got a look at her face.

"See? It wasn't a dream. He really *was* in your hospital room this morning," I tell Emma Jo triumphantly. "Wait, that means you *are* friends with a Ho-,"

I stop myself from finishing that statement, but Emma Jo kindly does it for me with no regard whatsoever to my well-being.

"Hot Guy? Yes, if I thought of him like that, I guess you could say I'm friends with a hot guy. Or actually, *your* Hot Guy." She smiles, reaching around me and taking the award from my hands to set it on a small table next to the door. "I can't believe this is who you wouldn't shut up about all morning. And in the car on the way home. And all night tonight."

She laughs again and shakes her head at me.

"She's exaggerating," I explain to him, not at all jealous that Emma Jo is friends with him and the smile he gives her is soft and sweet, when the one he gave me was cocky, bordering on irritating.

"You called him chesty and muscly," Emma Jo reminds me with another laugh, wrapping her arm around my shoulder and giving me a squeeze when I shoot her a dirty look.

"Don't forget cute dimples," Hot Creepy Stalker Guy, who shall now be referred to as Rude and Annoying Hot Guy, adds with a wink at me.

"There is still a pointy weapon within my reach and I've had a lot of wine tonight, buddy. There's no telling where I might shove that thing if you keep provoking me," I threaten him, giving him the sweetest smile I can manage as I glance down between his legs so he knows exactly what part of his body I'm threatening right now.

"My eyes are up here, honey. First, you won't stop touching my chest at the hospital, and now, you're picturing me naked. I don't remember you being this flirty."

My mouth drops open with a gasp and I stomp my

foot like a toddler.

"I was NOT picturing you naked! I was threatening your manhood, get it right. And how would you remember anything about me? You don't even know me!" I fire at him, trying to sound indignant and not like I was absolutely wondering what other kind of weapon he was packing behind the zipper of his pants.

"Wait a minute, you really don't know who this is? I thought you guys were just messing around," Emma Jo says in confusion, looking back and forth between the scowl on my face and the stupid cocky smirk on Rude and Annoying Hot Guy.

"It's okay, Emma Jo. I look a little different, and Payton here is, what? Forty, forty-one now? I'm sure her mind isn't what it used to be."

"Oh, that's it! You're definitely getting stabbed in the crotch with a glass triangle!" I shout, lunging for the side table as Emma Jo tightens her hold on me and keeps me from being able to reach it.

"Alright, that's enough you two," Emma Jo scolds. "Payton, this is Leo. Leo Hudson, from school. Remember? He was two years ahead of us. He graduated with…"

She stops before she can say Jed's name and my anger over the age comment quickly fades when I see her eyes fill with tears.

"Anyway, you remember Leo, right? Didn't you used to tutor her in math?" she asks quickly, blinking away the tears as when she looks away from me and at…

LEO HUDSON?! Nope. No way. Not buying it.

"You…you're…you…" I stammer, unable to spit any other words out as I look him up and down from head-to-toe.

Leo Hudson was scrawny and a Dungeons and Dragons nerd. He had long hair and acne, and while it's true he gave up a lot of his free time after he graduated to come back and tutor (me being his most trying student since Geometry and I hated each other with a fiery burning passion), there is no way I can believe the guy standing in front of me right now is the same person.

"I believe the words you're looking for are *Hot Guy* and *muscly*," Leo says with a satisfied smile, "but you can call me Sheriff Hudson."

Emma Jo shifts me out of the doorway and pushes the door open wider, inviting Leo to come inside. I remain mute as he gives her a nod and moves into the house, going right into the kitchen opposite the living room. I watch as he walks to the fridge and pulls it open, grabbing a bottle of water like he owns the place.

"Why don't you go take a shower and relax and I'll talk to Leo?" Emma Jo suggests.

I move my angry glare away from Leo, who casually leans against the kitchen counter drinking his water, and glance down at myself.

Shit. Of COURSE I'm still wearing the same clothes I've been in for a day and a half and God only knows what I smell like right now. That's twice Leo has seen me looking like ass and dammit, why do I care? So what if he's no longer the scraggly nerd from high school and looks like he just stepped off a calendar for hot men in uniform? He called me old and he's an arrogant jerk.

Emma Jo gives me a pat on the back and walks over to the kitchen, stopping when she gets close to Leo. I watch quietly as he sets his water on the counter and brings his hand up to her chin, gently turning her face from one side to the other as he examines the damage. He leans in to her and they start talking quietly and easily, with a familiarity that absolutely does NOT make me jealous.

Dammit.

Instead of heading upstairs to take a shower, I walk right out through the still-open front door and down the steps of the porch to get some fresh air. Standing in the middle of the yard, I close my eyes and tilt my head back, taking a few deep breaths.

Right when I finally start to feel calm and like I don't want to march back inside and smack the smirk off of Leo Hudson's face, I feel something warm and wet splash against my bare foot. My eyes fly open and I look down, screaming and cursing at the tiny little dog that just pissed on me as I shake my foot in disgust. All of a sudden, he starts barking his fool head off, his whole body trembling in rage with each yap that comes out of his mouth. I'm not afraid of dogs; in fact, I love dogs and if I didn't live in the city and I had a yard for one to run in, I would have bought one a long time ago. But this thing, it's not a dog. It's an overgrown rat with a Donald Trump comb-over and crazy eyes that are popping out of its head with the exertion of his barks. I'm afraid to move in case he decides to lift his leg and pee on me again or use his tiny, razor sharp teeth to eat my toes.

"Bo Jangles! That's enough now. You go on home to Starla," Leo scolds from behind me.

The dog immediately stops barking, tucks his tail between his legs and takes off running.

"THAT'S RIGHT, YOU UGLY LITTLE RAT DOG! RUN AWAY BEFORE I PUNT YOUR SCRAWNY, FOOT-PISSING ASS INTO A TREE!" I shout, throwing my middle finger up at the scurrying dog just for good measure.

Turning around, I stomp back toward the house and ignore Leo standing on the porch, leaning against the railing with a smile on his face. I pound my urine-soaked bare feet up the steps and don't bother looking in his direction as I walk past him.

"You're not even going to say thank you?"

"Screw you," I mutter, walking back into the house.

"Don't you mean, 'Screw you, *Hot Guy*?'" Leo shouts with amusement in his voice.

I make a detour into the living room when I hear his booted feet clomp inside behind me, snatch the bottle of wine from the coffee table, and point the same finger at him that I did Bo Jangles before heading up the stairs, stomping my feet extra loudly as I go.

CHAPTER 6

Recorded Interview
June 2, 2016
Bald Knob, KY Police Department

Deputy Lloyd: Sorry to bring you back in here. I just needed to ask you a few more questions.

Bettie Lake: Wow, Payton was right. Sheriff Hudson is pretty hot. Why isn't he interviewing me?

Deputy Lloyd: He's lived here all of his life and it was decided that it's best if someone impartial did these interviews. I just moved here a few months ago. So, let's get started, okay?

Bettie Lake: Okay fine, shoot! Sorry, I didn't mean to say shoot. Is that a bad thing to say when we're talking about a man that was murdered? Shit. Was he shot? Am I in trouble?

Deputy Lloyd: No, he wasn't shot. Just try to relax, okay? I'm only trying to put some pieces together so you have nothing to be nervous about. On the night of the murder, the phone records we received show that you and Miss. Lambert spoke to each other a few hours earlier. Did the two of you speak about the victim?

Bettie Lake: We mostly talked about how hot Sheriff Hudson is. She compared him to Thor.

Deputy Lloyd: *Muffled coughing and laughing*

Bettie Lake: Seriously, it's uncanny. Same color hair, same color eyes, same uber-muscles. No wonder she never shuts up about him. I mean, you're no slouch yourself, Deputy, you're just not my type.

Deputy Lloyd: Ma'am, please answer the question.

Bettie Lake: What was the question again? Sorry, I was distracted by Thor…I mean Sheriff Hudson's muscles. I asked him if I could touch them. Is that the real reason why he didn't want to interview me?

Deputy Lloyd: Miss Lake, I just need to

know if you and Miss Lambert spoke about the victim during the phone call you two had right before he was murdered.

Bettie Lake: Well, she told me about what he'd been doing to his wife all these years. And about how Sheriff Hudson was being all sweet and making googly eyes with the wife that night when he stopped over to have her fill out the restraining order. Payton was *really* jealous about that. She wouldn't admit it, but I could tell. I know my friend. I told her to apologize to him for being a snob. Did you know he was a total dork in high school? I'm talking Dungeons and Dragons meetings every Wednesday night.

Deputy Lloyd: Miss Lake, I can't discuss personal things during an official interview. So Miss Lambert told you about the alleged abuse?

Bettie Lake: Alleged? Really? Does everyone in this town smoke crack? I'm pretty sure Emma Jo didn't punch herself in the face, dislocate her own shoulder, or crack two of her ribs.

Deputy Lloyd: According to her medical records, Mrs. Jackson was prone to accidents.

Bettie Lake: Yes, sure, accidents. She *accidentally* fell into her husband's fist. Five times.

Deputy Lloyd: Miss Lake, I'm not here to make any judgments about what happened before the murder. I'm just trying to get the facts straight so we can solve this and let the people of Bald Knob sleep a little easier at night.

Bettie Lake: I hope all you morons stay awake for the rest of your lives. Honestly, you elected a wife abuser as your mayor for how many years in a row? It's a good thing my family doesn't live here. They're in the sanitation business, if you catch my drift. They would have killed that guy years ago if he was my husband.

Deputy Lloyd: Ma'am, I'm going to need you to make me a list of all your relatives and their contact information.

Bettie Lake: That was a joke! I swear, I'm just kidding. I mean, Uncle Stewart is technically the manager of Chicago Streets and Sanitation, and there was that one time he accidentally threw a cat into the back of his garbage truck, but he didn't know the thing was still alive and he bought the family a new kitten to make up for it. He wouldn't kill anyone, even if I asked.

Deputy Lloyd: When we went through your phone records, we found a text from you to your Uncle Stewart, asking him how easy it would be to dispose of a body.

Bettie Lake: Why isn't there a sarcasm font for text messages? Honesty, how has no one invented this? Do I need a lawyer yet?

CHAPTER 7

I'm not really a bitch without coffee. Just kidding! Go
fuck yourself.

—Coffee Mug

"TELL ME AGAIN about his muscles."

I hear Bettie sigh through the speaker of my phone and roll my eyes as I unwind the towel from my head and toss it onto the bed.

"Did you hear anything I said? I'm in a crisis here," I complain in irritation, scooping up the phone from next to my discarded towel and pacing at the foot of the bed.

"Sorry, I stopped listening after you said this guy has a chest carved from marble."

"One of my oldest friends has been abused by her husband pretty much since the day they got married, and you can't stop thinking about Leo the jerk," I mutter.

"You know your voice gets all breathy when you say his name? You kind of sound like a phone sex operator. Does he have dimples? What about his hair? Tell me he has a man-bun..." Bettie trails off with another lustful sigh.

I came upstairs to take a shower and hide in the spare bedroom until Leo left and I *still* can't escape him. It's bad enough Emma Jo has knocked on the door to check on me twice, having her own fun at my expense by telling me through the closed door that it was so cute how flustered I got around the man. I don't need this shit from Bettie, too.

"You're annoying. I called to check on the shop and get some advice, and now I'm regretting it. You suck at this," I scold, stopping in front of the mirror hanging above the dresser to stare at my reflection.

Even make-up free with wet hair draping over my shoulders, it's a much better improvement than earlier. I no longer look like a hooker in a gang bang with mascara smudged halfway down my cheeks, my stained and dirty clothes have been thrown in the trash and replaced with a tank top and shorts, and I don't smell like the piss of Bo Jangles, the dog from hell. Why couldn't Leo show up *now* when I actually look halfway decent?

"You didn't call for advice. You called so I'd agree with you about how annoying Hot Guy was and make you feel like less of an asshole because it was totally fine for you to drool over some random Chesty McChesterson, but now that you know he's the nerd you knew from high school, you think it's appalling to be hot for him," Bettie informs me.

"That's not it at all!" I argue. "I don't care if he was

a complete weirdo in high school. I care that he's a now cocky jerk of an adult who most likely has the hots for my best friend. You should have seen the way he looked at her and spoke to her, all sweet and gentle. I mean, she's a married woman! Sure, she's married to an abusive tool, but still."

Bettie laughs through the line.

"And you should hear the way you're talking right now. You're jealous!"

"I am NOT jealous! I just think it's indecent for the town sheriff to be mooning over a married woman," I reply indignantly, wishing I would have Facetimed her so she'd see the stink-eye I'm currently aiming at my phone.

"You're totally jealous, nice try. From what you told me, it sounds like he was all sweet and gentle with you too, until you didn't recognize him. Talk about a blow to a man's ego. You're lucky Bo Jangles is the only one who pissed on your leg. If I was a dude and some woman I had a crush on in high school came back to town, I would have lifted my leg and pissed all over you myself for not knowing who I was," Bettie says with another laugh.

Okay, so I may or may not have known back in school that Leo had a big crush on me, and I may or may not have completely ignored it and did my best not to hurt his feelings back then. I even stuck up for him when Jed and his jock friends would pick on him, and this is the thanks I get?

"Fine, so I didn't recognize him when I saw him in the hospital, but can you blame me? The guy went from looking like Anthony Michael Hall in *The Breakfast Club* to Chris Hemsworth, all Thor-like and…pretty," I complain, annoyed all over again that he knew I thought he was hot and didn't hesitate to keep rubbing it in my face.

"Listen, as far as the whole Emma Jo thing goes, all you can do is what you're doing right now, which is be there for her, and you know that," Bettie tells me softly. "You don't need my help with *that* situation. And regarding Sheriff Hudson? Might I suggest apologizing for not recognizing him and then laughing in his face when you found out who he was? It might stop him from arresting you for being a menace to society and use those handcuffs of his for good instead of evil."

She continues talking about Leo and his weapons but I don't hear a word she says. All I can picture is myself naked and chained to Leo's headboard with a pair of his cuffs, while he looms over me with that stupid smirk on his face and his bare, muscular chest rubbing against mine.

"Alright, that's enough," I scold Bettie, stopping her mid-*I wonder if he carries rope in his trunk for S&M dates*. "I need to get back downstairs to Emma Jo now that he left."

The last time Emma Jo checked on me, she told me she filled out the restraining order and that Leo left to go back to the station to file it and notify Jed. I'm sure she's down there freaking out that *he's* going to freak out and come back to finish the job he did on her.

"Remember, next time you see Hot Guy, say you're sorry. You're much cuter when you're being all apologetic instead of standing there with a stick up your ass," Bettie reminds me.

"You always say the sweetest things," I reply sarcastically. "Don't run my business to the ground. And if Benjamin comes in, make up something about me joining Habitat for Humanity or something. Maybe he'll get the hint if he thinks I left the country."

I've already ignored three voicemails from him since my plane landed. I know I need to have yet another conversation with him about how we are not getting married and things are over between us, but there's only so many serious conversations a woman can handle at one time.

"He already stopped in right at closing tonight looking for you. I sent a text to my Uncle Stewart to see how hard it would be to hide a body in the city dump, but he hasn't gotten back to me yet. In the meantime, I told Benjamin you reconnected with the love of your life from childhood and flew back home to marry him. Who knew I was psychic?!"

"Tell me you didn't…"

"Soooooooo, I guess we'll talk soon," Bettie says quickly. "Make nice with the sheriff and maybe he'll let you touch his weapon. Too-da-loo!"

Bettie disconnects the call before I can scream at her. I stare at the screen of my phone for a few seconds and then toss it back on top of the bed. I can hear Emma Jo moving around downstairs and I know I can't keep hiding up here in her spare bedroom forever.

Hopefully there's still enough wine left in this house for me to forget about Leo for the time being and not do something stupid like accuse my best friend of sleeping with him. I mean, who cares if that's true anyway? It's not like *I* want the guy.

"ARE YOU SLEEPING with Leo? I mean, it's totally fine if you are. It's not like *I* care or anything. You two make a cute couple. He's all tall and hot and cocky, and you're all short and cute and quiet. Opposites attract and all that. I won't tell anyone if you've been cheating on Jed and you've been planning to leave him, if that's what you're worried about. I mean, after what that asshole has been doing to you all these years, it's completely justified. Your secret is safe with me!" I ramble, grabbing a newly opened bottle of wine from the kitchen counter.

Emma Jo stares at me with wide, shocked eyes while I drink from the bottle like some sort of animal. You know, if that animal felt like an idiot and had diarrhea of the mouth.

"It's none of my business what you do with your

personal life, as long as it makes you happy. But as your oldest friend, I've got to say, I don't know if Leo Hudson is the best boyfriend material. I mean, secret lover – sure! But as a boyfriend, he kind of sucks. He obviously knew about what Jed was doing to you, otherwise he wouldn't have shown up at the hospital, and he definitely didn't look shocked when he saw your face tonight. Pissed off, yes, but not shocked. What kind of a boyfriend wouldn't kick Jed's ass or throw him in jail for that shit years ago?"

I finally stop talking and take a breath. And then chug some more wine from the bottle just so I'm not tempted to open my mouth again and spew more crazy at Emma Jo. Bettie is right, I totally sound jealous. I hate when Bettie's right. She never lets me forget it.

"Okay, first of all, I think you've had enough wine," Emma Jo informs me, taking the bottle out of my hand and setting it on the counter next to us with a *clunk*. "Secondly, I am not, nor have I ever, slept with Leo Hudson. I wouldn't know the first thing about having an affair and even if I did, Leo wouldn't be my first choice. I already told you he's like a brother to me."

I cross my arms over my chest and lean my hip against the counter, pretending like I'm not completely thrilled by this information, because that would make me a hypocrite and Bettie would be right about yet another thing.

"So, Leo just showed up at the hospital because

you two are friends?" I ask.

"Yes, he showed up at the hospital because we're friends. And you're right, he had some suspicions about Jed and the abuse, but he never had any proof because I always covered for him," she explains quietly, picking at the label on the wine bottle nervously. "Leo was nice enough to never come right out and ask me about it because he didn't want to embarrass me, but he'd always ask me if everything was okay. I knew that he knew, but just like I've been doing with everyone else, I lied and I pretended, and I covered it up because I *was* embarrassed."

Reaching up between us, I grab a clean wine glass out of the cabinet above our heads, not wanting to stop Emma Jo from talking just to go into the living room and grab the one she was using earlier. I pour her a full glass and hand it to her.

"So, how did he know you were in the hospital? Did you call him?"

I do my best to keep more jealousy out of my voice when I ask this question. It was kind of nice knowing I was the only person in the world Emma Jo trusted with this situation, and all of that will be for nothing if I find out she trusts Leo just as much. Maybe even more since he's been here, living in Bald Knob with her, and she can go to him with her problems so much easier than she could with me.

Emma Jo shakes her head when she grabs the wine glass from my hand and takes a sip.

"He told me he has a friend who's a nurse and was working in the Baptist Health emergency room when I came in. I guess she works as a temp nurse and travels all around Kentucky. She recognized my name from when I went to a different hospital she was working at about six months ago and I put down Bald Knob as my hometown instead of making up a different one like I usually do."

Tears fill my eyes when she tells me this and I grab the wine bottle from the counter and take another big gulp to try and stop myself from dwelling on the fact that Emma Jo has been bouncing around to different hospitals all over the state for years, lying about where she's from so no one would find out what was going on.

"The nurse remembered me and knew I was from Bald Knob, even though I wrote down Louisville. I was so out of it when I went in there and I don't remember what I said to her, but it was enough for her to call Leo since she knew he was the sheriff," Emma Jo finishes.

"That was kind of awesome of her. I mean, she could have lost her job by doing that without your permission."

Emma Jo nods. "I know. I told Leo to make sure she knew I wasn't mad or anything. If it wasn't for her, and you coming out here for me, and Leo promising me that he would do everything he could to keep this quiet for as long as he can, I don't think I would have been strong enough to file that restraining order tonight, Payton. I would have left the hospital, hid away here at home until I healed, and then went back to pretending like everything was fine. I owe you and Leo so much."

Well, the jury is still out on how much she owes Leo. I mean, he had his suspicions for years but he never did anything about it? What kind of friend does something like that? What kind of *sheriff* does something like that? Maybe Leo forgot about how much of a dick Jed Jackson was to him in high school, and now *he's* under the same Jed-spell everyone else in this town has been under. Just because he's nice to look at doesn't mean everything on the inside is nice. Jed is a prime example of *that*.

Not wanting to make Emma Jo feel worse by bringing up this point, I quietly give her a smile and rub my hand up and down her arm soothingly.

"I know I already said this once, but I promise everything will be okay. I talked to my manager and the shop is fine without me right now. I'm here for as long as you need me," I reassure her.

Emma Jo gives me a small smile and takes a deep breath before sipping some more of her wine. I quickly decide to continue doing whatever I can to keep her happy and calm like this by suggesting we watch a few mindless chick flicks. Emma Jo agrees and heads down the hall to the office to grab a few DVDs from the shelf where she keeps them stored. My feeling of contentment as I head into the living room to turn the

TV on is short-lived when I hear a loud pounding on the front door as soon as I walk by. I pause in the entryway and a chill races over my skin when the pounding is replaced by someone trying to turn the handle from the outside.

"EMMA JO! WHY IN THE HELL DOESN'T MY KEY WORK?"

I look back over my shoulder, wondering if Emma Jo can hear the shout from the other side of the door. This house is pretty big and the office is clear on the other side, facing the backyard. I don't see her come around the corner and she doesn't say anything, which means she thankfully isn't hearing what I am right now – an angry man trying to get into his home and wondering why he can't, making him more pissed-off by the second.

A fist pounds against the front door again, so hard that it rattles the doorframe, making my heart beat wildly in my chest wondering what the hell I'll do if he kicks the damn thing down and storms in here.

"Open up the fucking door, Emma Jo! I don't know what kind of shit you're trying to pull here, but enough is enough. I cut this business trip short a day early so we could spend some quiet, alone-time together. I left my meeting with a potential campaign investor early for you, and this is how you thank me? Do you have any idea how much money I could lose out on now?"

Jed's voice through the door and the shit he's spilling from his mouth immediately put an end to my fear and replace it with anger. I made a promise to my friend that everything would be okay, and there's no way I'm going to stand here like a coward and not do anything about it. Jed Jackson might have been able to push his wife around all these years, and he might have been able to cast his spell over all of Bald Knob, but that shit doesn't fly with me. If I can handle a bunch of hipster college kids making a mockery of coffee, I can handle a pencil dick asshole who makes himself feel powerful by picking on someone smaller and weaker than him. I am neither small, nor weak, and Jed Jackson just pissed off the wrong woman.

Before he continues yelling and Emma Jo hears him, I move quickly to the front door and unlock the deadbolt. With the resting bitch face I've perfected over the years firmly planted on my face, I fling open the door so hard that it bangs against the opposite wall.

With his black hair, sweet-looking baby face, slim build, and the few inches of height he has on me, throw a football jersey and a pompous smile on his face and Jed Jackson would look just as he did in high school. Even with his slicked-back hair and three-piece suit, he still looks like he hasn't aged a day, which I'm sure helps him charm the brains out of everyone in this town.

He quickly takes a few surprised steps back when I come stomping out of the front door, clearly confused that I'm the one who answered the door instead of his wife. I take full advantage of his momentary lapse of shouting and cursing to charge right up to him and jab my finger into his chest.

"I don't know what kind of shit *you're* trying to pull here, Jed, but Emma Jo doesn't answer to you anymore. You put your hands on her for the last time, asshole. Do yourself a favor and get off this porch before I rip off your balls, shove them down your throat, and choke you with them," I seethe through clenched teeth.

His eyes narrow as he looks down at me, and then he has the nerve to smile and let out a small, mocking laugh to go along with his stupid smile.

"It's nice you can laugh about this situation. You won't be laughing when you get a copy of the restraining order Emma Jo filed on your ass tonight, or when your worthless self is locked up behind bars," I inform him, my whole body shaking with rage while he continues to stare down at me like I'm nothing more than a nuisance. "Pretty sure you should have checked your voicemails before you cut that important business trip short. You'll find one from the sheriff explaining how far away you're supposed to be from Emma Jo, and I do believe you're in violation of the restraining order just by pulling into the driveway, you piece of shit."

The smile on Jed's face falls and he moves so quickly that I don't have any time to duck or run back into the house. He advances on me like a hunter stalking his prey, his hand coming up and wrapping around my neck tightly as he shoves me backward. My feet move automatically to keep up with him so I don't trip until I slam into the side of the house next to the open front door with a gasp when pain radiates up my spine.

"Payton Lambert, still just as much of a trouble-maker as you were in high school," Jed speaks lowly, moving his face down until his nose is almost touching mine.

He squeezes my neck harder until I see spots at the edge of my vision. My heart is back to beating double-time as I struggle to take in air and bring my hands up between us to claw at the back of his hand.

"It's been so nice and peaceful without you here the last twelve years. Too bad you weren't smart enough to stay gone. You have no idea what kind of trouble you just brought on yourself by sticking your nose in something that doesn't concern you," he threatens with a sick and twisted smile, tightening his hold on my neck to yank me forward.

I'm too busy trying not to pass out from lack of oxygen that my body moves like a ragdoll, flopping bonelessly when he pulls me toward him, and again when he shoves me back. My head slams against the vinyl siding with a *thump* that jars my teeth and brings tears to my eyes.

I definitely underestimated Jed. My overconfidence and anger about what he's done to my friend made me act without thinking. I should have known better than to come charging out here. I've seen what he did to Emma Jo, and she never mouthed off to him or fought back. God only knows what he'll do to someone who tried to stand up to him.

I can't scream for help because he's clutching my neck so tightly that I'm pretty sure he's two seconds away from collapsing my vocal chords. Or killing me. And if I could scream, would any of the people in this town come help? Starla Godfrey, who was older than dirt when *I* lived here, is within shouting distance, but she probably heard me curse at her damn dog earlier and wouldn't help me if she *wasn't* a thousand years old. Mr. and Mrs. Pickerson still live on the other side of Emma Jo's house, but Mrs. Pickerson once caught me squatting in her backyard after drinking seven wine coolers and not being able to hold it until I got home. I'm sure she's still pissed at me and would pull down her shades if she heard me screaming. And then there's Frank and Teresa Jefferson who live across the street. I used to babysit for their son when he was around three-years-old, but I let him watch *Mean Girls* with me when it first came out and he took to yelling at his mother, "Boo, you whore!" after that, so I'm pretty sure *they* would turn their backs on me as well.

"Now, we're going to go inside MY house, you're going to pack your things, and you're going to get the fuck away from my wife. Are we clear?"

My sweaty palms slip up and down Jed's wrists as I

continue to struggle and try to pull his hand off of my neck, but it's no use. I do the only thing I can and nod my head jerkily.

Jed gives me a satisfied smile and finally loosens his hold on me. His arm drops down to his side and he slides both of his hands casually into the front pocket of his suit pants, like we're standing here on the front porch discussing the weather and not like he didn't just threaten me and try to kill me. My eyes water as I immediately bend at the waist and start gasping and coughing, drawing in as much air as I can while wrapping both of my hands gently around the aching skin of my neck.

Instead of doing what he ordered, instead of trying to find my voice so I can scream at the top of my lungs, I once again act with my heart instead of my head. While Jed is distracted watching me clutch at my neck, bent over and hacking up a lung, I make my move. Flying back upright, I grab onto his shoulders for leverage and bring my knee up as hard as I can between his legs.

"YOU BITCH!" Jed shouts, his voice thundering around the yard and the quiet street as his hands fly out of his pockets to cover his crotch and give his junk the same loving care I tried to give my tender neck.

This time, I'm ready for him and see him coming. I don't have time or any room to move around him and get the hell away, but at least I have time to wrap my arms around my head and protect myself from his fist when he pulls it back.

"You lay your hands on her one more time, and I won't hesitate to put a bullet in your skull."

When I hear a familiar, and for the first time since I got here, *welcome* voice, followed by the *click* and *slide* of a gun being cocked, I slowly lower my arms to see Jed still standing in front of me with his fist raised, but not moving a muscle, aside from the one ticking in his jaw as he clenches his teeth.

"Put your hands up and step away from Miss Lambert. NOW!" Leo orders, shouting the last word when Jed stupidly starts to lean in my direction instead of away, like he was told.

"He has a gun pointed at your head, you might want to listen to him," I warn Jed with a scratchy voice.

Jed finally lowers his arm with a sigh, the rage on his face quickly replaced with a sickeningly sweet smile when he turns away from me and addresses Leo, who is still standing at the base of the porch steps with his weapon pointed right at Jed's face.

"Good evening, Sheriff Hudson, it's always a pleasure. We're just having a little misunderstanding, but it's all cleared up now. Isn't that right, Payton?" Jed asks, turning his gross, fake smile at me when he glances back over his shoulder.

"The only thing cleared up is any tiny inkling I might have had that you AREN'T a complete piece of shit," I rasp, each word making my throat scream in pain.

"Payton, go back inside the house," Leo orders in a low voice, moving up to the bottom step while still aiming his gun at Jed.

"Screw that! Give me your gun so I can shoot him myself," I fire back angrily with my hoarse voice, holding my hand out in Leo's direction without taking my eyes off of Jed. "Better yet, you shoot him in the head, then let me shoot him in the dick. Everyone wins!"

My throat hurts, and my pride is a tad wounded that I thought I could put this idiot in his place all by myself, but at least now I'm much more inclined to listen to Bettie and I actually *want* to apologize to Leo. He deserves a whole shit ton of apologies for showing up here like my knight in shining armor, and I'm not ashamed to admit that the few glances I've shot in his direction have done amazing things for my ego. The way he keeps looking back and forth between what I'm sure is an angry red mark on my neck and Jed, it isn't hard to see the barely concealed rage going on within him. The muscles in his arms bulge and ripple while he holds tightly to his gun, forcing himself to remain professional while at the same time, wanting to rip Jed's limbs from his body and beat him with the bloody stumps.

Jed wisely lifts both his hands in the air and takes a few steps back and away from both of us when Leo makes it up the steps to stand next to me.

"Sheriff elections are coming up again soon, aren't

they, Leo? How about you and I head down to Picker-son's bar and discuss your plans for reelection?" Jed asks Leo with a grin, actually having the nerve to try and blackmail him right in front of me and get him to forget about what happened here tonight.

As *if* my knight in shining armor would do some-thing so stupid! Also, I just remembered another reason why Mrs. Pickerson wouldn't have come to my aid tonight. I'm pretty sure those six wine coolers were stolen from Mr. Pickerson's bar the night I peed on her lawn. It really is a good thing Leo showed up when he did.

"That sounds like a fine idea," Leo replies, lowering his arm and sliding his gun back into his holster.

"You have GOT to be fucking kidding me!" I shout angrily.

Well, it's more of a croak of anger, but still. My feelings are made known when I shoot an angry glare at Leo and let a whole slew of more curse words fly until he wraps his hand around my arm and pulls me across the porch until we're out of hearing distance from Jed the Jackhole.

"Let me handle this, Payton. Go inside and check on Emma Jo," Leo whispers, his warm, minty breath skating across my lips from his close proximity, but his eyes aimed over my shoulder, keeping an eye on Jed.

"Let you handle this by kissing that piece-of-shit's ass? Like you've been doing for twelve years? Hell no! I don't give a rat's ass what kind of strings he pulls for you or what kind of money he slips the sheriff's department under the table for you to turn a blind-eye on all of his horse shit. He just threatened me and tried to kill me. You're seriously going to go down to Pickerson's, toss back a few brewskies, measure your dicks, and call it even?" I fire back. "I can't believe I was actually going to apologize for not recognizing you!"

Leo finally takes his eyes off of Jed long enough to glance down at me.

"Trust me, Payton, this isn't what it looks like," he confides softly. The serious look on his face softens when he smiles down at me. "Get in the house, check on Emma Jo, stop picturing me naked, and I'll let you apologize to me later. I'll make a list of ways you can show me you really mean it."

With those parting words and a wink, Leo steps out from around me. His boots thump against the porch as he walks across it toward Jed, holding his arm out for Jed to lead the way.

With an angry growl under my breath, I storm into the house and slam the door behind me, securing the deadbolt and making up a bunch of new nicknames for Sheriff Stupid-Face Hudson.

CHAPTER 8

Recorded Interview
June 2, 2016
Bald Knob, KY Police Department

Deputy Lloyd: Mrs. Pickerson, can you tell
me what you remember about the night of
May 31st?

Justine Pickerson: Well, I was heading out
to my car to drive into town and help my
husband, Roy, close up the bar. I heard
some shouting coming from across the
street at the Jackson's. I try not to pay
too much attention to gossip, mind you,
but I heard from Starla Godfrey, who heard
from Teresa Jefferson, who heard from
Andrea Maynard down at the Hungry Bear
that Payton Lambert was back in town. I
figured her first stop would be to go see
her mamma and daddy, but obviously she
felt the need to cause trouble for Emma Jo
and poor, poor Jed. Is he really gone? I
just can't believe it. He was such a nice
man and took such good care of the people

of Bald Knob.

Deputy Lloyd: Why do you think Miss Lambert would cause trouble for Emma Jo and Jed?

Justine Pickerson: I caught that girl squatting in my yard, doing her business in the wee hours of the morning. No pun intended. She also stole alcohol from our bar.

Deputy Lloyd: You saw Miss Lambert going to the bathroom in your yard and stealing alcohol on the night of the murder?

Justine Pickerson: Well, no. It was back when she was seventeen, but that girl has always had bad news written all over her. If there's trouble in Bald Knob, you can bet Payton Lambert had something to do with it.

Deputy Lloyd: So, you're referring to an incident that happened thirteen years ago, when she was in high school?

Justine Pickerson: Don't you look at me like that, Deputy Lloyd. A girl freely drops her drawers in front of God and all creation when she's a teenager, Lord only knows what she'll do now that she's an adult.

Deputy Lloyd: Ma'am, can we please get back to the night of May 31st. You said you were walking to your car and heard shouting. Do you remember what you heard?

Justine Pickerson: A lot of cursing and bad words, I can tell you that. I mean, I'm not one to eavesdrop, mind you, but our houses are close together and Payton was yelling loudly. I heard her threaten to shoot Jed Jackson. Was he shot? I heard from Andrea Maynard, who heard from Teresa Jefferson who heard from Starla Godfrey that he was shot. Starla lives right next door to Emma Jo and Jed, you know, and I heard she discovered the body so it must be true.

Deputy Lloyd: Actually, Mrs. Godfrey didn't discover the body, and no, Jed Jackson wasn't shot.

Justine Pickerson: Was he stabbed? I heard from Teresa Jefferson who—

Deputy Lloyd: He wasn't stabbed. That's all I can really tell you about this since it's an ongoing investigation, and I'd appreciate it if you kept what we're discussing in this room to yourself until we can finish questioning everyone.

<u>Justine Pickerson:</u> I told you, I'm not one for gossip, so you have my word that nothing we talk about will leave this room.

<u>Deputy Lloyd:</u> Thank you for your cooperation. Now, can you remember what Jed Jackson was doing when Miss Lambert was shouting at him? Did you see a weapon in his hand or hear any shouting from him?

<u>Justine Pickerson:</u> Jed Jackson has never raised his voice at anyone, he was a wonderful and kind man. Whatever he might have said to Payton, I'm sure it was warranted considering, all the nasty things she said to him. Are you going to arrest her?

<u>Deputy Lloyd:</u> I can't disclose any of that information with you, Mrs. Pickerson. We aren't making any arrests until we finish with the interviews and gather as much information as we can.

<u>Justine Pickerson:</u> Well, you *should* arrest her for indecent exposure and theft. Those wine coolers cost us $1.75 a piece.

<u>Deputy Lloyd:</u> We can't arrest someone for something they allegedly did thirteen years ago.

<u>Justine Pickerson:</u> First it's stealing wine coolers, then it's selling your body for the marijuana, and next thing you know, you're murdering someone in cold blood. I've seen *Cops*, I know how fast people spiral out of control. Payton has been living in Chicago since she left town. I heard from Mo Wesley who owns the Gas n Sip who heard from his son Roger who had a friend that visited Chicago once and told them it's a seedy place full of good-for-nothing criminals. I heard Payton owns a coffee shop called Liquid Crack. You know crack is a fancy word for drugs, right? She probably sells drugs and hangs out with a bunch of rabble-rousers.

<u>Deputy Lloyd:</u> Mrs. Pickerson, do you remember anything else from the night of May 31st?

<u>Justine Pickerson:</u> I don't think so. But I'm having lunch with Starla after this, so I'll ask her and get back to you.

CHAPTER 9

Coffee: Do stupid things faster with more energy.

—Coffee Mug

"**B**ETTIE, SHUT OFF the music."

I wince at the sound of my own voice, even though it's muffled and raspy. The combination of my voice and the song blasting through the room makes my head pound so hard that I want to cry.

"Bettie, seriously, turn off the damn music!" I complain again, opening my eyes and immediately regretting that decision when bright sunlight hits them and it feels like a million knives are stabbing into my skull. I roll over on the couch in the back room of Liquid Crack with a groan, quickly sitting up when I realize I'm not on the couch at Liquid Crack, I'm on a floor.

With my hand over my eyes to shield them from the sunlight streaming into the room, I glance around and it all comes back to me. Well, some things come back to me, but most of it is a blur because of the wine hangover sloshing around in my brain and curdling in my stomach. Shoving an empty wine bottle away, I roll over on my hands and knees on the living room floor of Emma Jo's house, reaching under the coffee table for my phone, A.K.A., the source of the music I had been sleepily arguing with Bettie to turn off.

I grab it and flop over onto my butt, leaning my back against the couch as I finally cut off the ringtone – "Coffee Song" by Frank Sinatra. Normally, this is one of my favorite songs, hence the reason for it being my ringtone, but right now, every noise hurts and makes me want to puke.

" 'Yep," I speak into the phone, unable to form any other words at the moment.

"I can't believe you've been in town for more than a day and I have to hear it from Starla Godfrey! You are the worst daughter in the entire world. I bet you wouldn't care if I died. I could have been lying here in my own bed, dead from a broken heart, and you wouldn't care," my mother complains in my ear.

"Mama, can you do me a favor and not talk too loudly?"

"DON'T YOU SASS ME, YOUNG LADY!" she shouts, jamming more knives into my aching head.

"I'm not sassing you, I had a rough night, and I just woke up. I was going to call you today, I swear."

She huffs loudly. "I heard you did plenty of swearing last night. It's all over town that you threatened Jed Jackson right on his own front porch. Honestly, Payton, what has gotten into you? Have you been hanging out with hoodlums in Chicago doing drugs? Is that why you never come home to visit? Thirty hours of labor with you, and you're still making me suffer."

I've tried to explain to my mother over the years why I never come back home to visit, and instead buy plane tickets for my parents to come out and see me whenever they can, but she doesn't listen. She doesn't understand that I love Chicago and outgrew Bald Knob and everyone being in your business a long time ago. Clearly nothing has changed since I've barely been here for twenty-four hours and I'm already the main source of gossip in this town.

"Jed Jackson isn't the nice guy everyone thinks he is, Mama. I've been telling you that for years, and now I finally have proof," I inform her.

"Payton Lambert, I still have to apologize to Justine Pickerson every time I see her in church for that time you robbed her bar and urinated in her yard. Whatever you did, you better fix it before they kick me out of the knitting club."

I sigh, closing my eyes and letting my head drop back to the couch cushions.

"Mama, I'll come out to the house to see you and Daddy later on today, and I'll explain everything, okay? Right now, I need to find some coffee before I go on a murderous rampage," I tell her.

With a quick "I love you," I end the call before she can yell at me some more and sit perfectly still while I try to will my stomach to calm down before I have to get up, run to the bathroom and throw up ten gallons of wine.

"What is happening to me right now? Why does everything hurt? Even my hair hurts."

Cracking open one eye, I watch Emma Jo shuffle into the room, holding her hand against her forehead and looking as miserable as I feel.

"It's called a hangover. Welcome to Hell."

She slowly ambles over to me and gently lowers her body onto the couch, moaning in pain until she gets seated and rests her elbows on her knees and her head in her hands.

"Did we make pie last night? Why do I remember making pie?" Emma Jo asks.

Leaning forward, I glance into the kitchen and see a mess of flour all over the counter, dirty dishes piled in the sink, and a broken egg splattered on the tile.

"I vaguely remember baking something. And it was pink. Wait, no, blue. It was blue. What the hell did we make that was blue?"

Emma Jo laughs softly, cutting herself off when my cell phone rings in my hand. Glancing down and seeing that it's my mother again, I quickly hit the button on the side to silence the call, waving Emma Jo off when she gives me a questioning look.

"I remember now," Emma Jo says brightly. "After Leo left with Jed, we drank the rest of the wine, and I told you that I was supposed to make Jed a blueberry pie for when he got home from his business trip."

I scrunch up my face in concentration until some

more memories from last night come fluttering back. I remember stomping back into the house all pissed off about what Leo said and did, hoping Emma Jo was still busy looking for DVDs and had no idea what happened on her front porch so she wouldn't get upset. Keeping my lips sealed about it would have worked, if I hadn't forgotten all about the angry red marks on my neck from where Jed tried to choke the life out of me. She came down the hall from the back of the house a few minutes later, her arms full of chick flicks and her face bright with a smile until she stopped in her tracks and dropped all of them to the floor when she saw my neck. I had no choice but to tell her what had happened and instead of breaking down in a puddle of tears, Emma Jo lifted her head high, walked into the kitchen, and grabbed every bottle of wine that was left. We drank, we bitched about Jed, argued about Leo's decision to go to the bar with him, and then we came up with a brilliant idea when we polished off the last of the wine.

"Did we really make that douchebag husband of yours a poisoned blueberry pie?" I ask, even though I already know the answer to that since I'm still staring into the kitchen and can see an empty white bottle of Lysol Toilet Bowl Cleaner tipped onto its side next to the stove.

My cell phone rings again and I cut it off once more when I see my mother's name on the display, rolling my eyes when I tell Emma Jo who it is and why she's calling.

"Anyway, yes, yes we did make a poisoned blueberry pie," Emma Jo confirms when my phone beeps with an incoming voice message from my mother. "It was actually a great idea since the pie was blue and Lysol Toilet Bowl Cleaner is also blue. Sadly, we didn't think that plan through very much, considering Jed isn't supposed to come within a hundred yards of me and we'd have no way of feeding him the pie."

I nod with a sigh. "Maybe once our hangovers pass, we'll be able to come up with a new plan."

Emma Jo's home phone starts ringing from the side table, and I hold up my hand to Emma Jo when she starts to reach for it.

"I guarantee you it's my mother. You don't need to listen to her scream about what a horrible child I am because I won't answer my phone. I'll get it," I lament, pushing up from the floor and moving over to the table to answer the call.

"Mama, I told you, I'll stop by and talk to you later."

"Emma Jo, there's something in your back yard," a woman on the other end of the line whispers, sounding nothing like my mother.

"This isn't Emma Jo. Can I tell her who's calling?" I ask nicely, remembering my manners so word doesn't get back to my mother that I'm a horrible phone conversationalist and someone kicks her out of her Sunday afternoon Bridge club for it.

"Payton Lambert, is that you? I heard you were back in town. Bo Jangles has been fit to be tied ever since you yelled at him last night, and now he won't stop barking at something in Emma Jo's yard. I think he's traumatized and he thinks it's you. Are you outside in the back?"

I try not to sigh too loudly when I realize it's Mrs. Godfrey on the other end of the line, Emma Jo's neighbor and the owner of dog who pissed on my leg.

"Hello, Mrs. Godfrey, and yes, this is Payton. And your dog almost attacked me and then peed on my leg," I tell her in the nicest voice possible and without any swearing.

I should get a medal.

"Bo Jangles wouldn't attack anyone! I'm sure he only lifted his leg on you because you frightened my poor baby. He's been outside all morning sitting at the fence and barking over at Emma Jo's yard. My eyesight isn't what it used to be, but I can see something out there in the grass," she informs me.

With my pounding headache, the phone call from my mother, and taking a trip down drunk memory lane with Emma Jo, I didn't notice the barking coming from outside. Now that I do, it's all I can hear and it's worse than knives to the brain. Much worse. It's high-pitched and yappy, and even from outside in the next yard, it's loud and annoying.

Pulling the phone away from my mouth when Emma Jo asks me in a whisper what's going on, I quickly explain to her in a hushed voice about the psychotic dog and Mrs. Godfrey's claim that he's barking at something in her backyard. Emma Jo shakes her head and leaves the room, heading down the hall to one of the rooms that face the backyard.

"I already called Sheriff Hudson about it because Bo Jangles is so upset, and I need to get him to calm down and come inside to take a nap. It looks like a deer or some other kind of large animal back there. I saw Mayor Jackson's car in the driveway last night so I know he's home early from that meeting of his. Tell him to go outside and see what it is. He's always so nice and helpful, and Bo Jangles loves him. Bo Jangles would never lift his leg on *him*," Starla retorts in a snotty voice.

"Mayor Jackson actually isn't home right now, but don't worry Mrs. Godfrey, I'll go outside and see what it is that Bo Jangles is barking at. You can call Sheriff Hudson back and tell him we don't need him," I snap angrily, counting to ten in my head before I let a whole string of curse words loose. "Thanks for calling and have a wonderful day!"

I quickly hang up the phone, cutting Starla off mid-sentence, knowing that it will only be a matter of minutes before my mother hears about how rude I was to her.

"That woman is just as annoying as she was when we were in high school. I don't know how you can handle living next door to her," I complain to Emma

Jo when I hear her walk back into the room.

"Payton, it's…" Emma Jo whispers, her voice cracking with emotion as she trails off.

I turn around to see her eyes wide and unblinking and her mouth dropped open in shock. As I start to walk toward her, there's a knock at the door.

"Don't move, I'll get it. I'm sure it's Mrs. Godfrey, coming over here to sick her dog on me for hanging up on her," I try to joke as I move toward the door, getting a little bit worried about how pale Emma Jo's face is right now.

Turning the deadbolt, I open the door to find Leo standing on the front porch. I want to slam the door in his face, but my eyes zero in on the coffee cup in his hand and my mouth starts to water.

"I left to go get some coffee for you since I know Emma Jo doesn't drink it, when I got a call from the station that Mrs. Godfrey phoned in with a complaint. I can't leave you alone for ten hours without you causing problems," he sighs, handing me the cup of coffee.

I take a sip to get my brain in working order before I reply, but sadly, it tastes like the bottom of someone's shoe and does nothing for my brain activity.

"Sorry, I know it's not Liquid Crack, but it's the best I could do without driving into Louisville," Leo adds with a smile.

He's trying to make a peace offering and butter me up after what went down last night, but I'm not falling for that shit. I don't care if he DID come back here after he had a laughing good time with Jed, probably yucking it up about silly little women, parking his car across the street to keep an eye on the house. I don't care if he called Emma Jo when he came back to tell her he planned on staying there all night, just to make sure Jed didn't come back to the house and that he'd explain everything in the morning. He's a lying liar-face, and I am not about to let how good he looks in a uniform mess with my head. Or his dimples. Or his bright blue eyes. Or how nice it was that he went out and got me coffee even though it tastes like what Bo Jangles pee smelled like.

"Um, Sheriff, you're gonna want to come to the backyard…."

I lean to the side to look around Leo and find another man in uniform standing at the bottom of the steps with a worried look on his face. He's about the same height as Leo and looks around the same age, with a cute face, short brown hair and a lean build, unlike Leo's in-your-face-I-can-squash-you-like-a-bug-muscular one.

"Payton Lambert, this is one of my deputies, Buddy Lloyd. He just moved to Bald Knob a few months ago. I thought it would be a good idea to bring him out here with me this morning since he'll probably be coming here quite a bit when more neighbors start complaining about you," Leo says with a soft chuckle.

"It's nice to meet you, Deputy Lloyd. Pay no attention to Sheriff Hudson, he was dropped on his head a lot as a baby," I inform the man, still standing at the bottom of the steps, wringing his hands together nervously.

"It's nice to meet you too, ma'am," he says, his eyes darting behind me and his hands quickly coming up to smooth down his hair. "G-good morning, Mrs. Jackson. H-how have you been?"

I look back and forth between Emma Jo, who came up behind me, and Deputy Lloyd, who is suddenly nervous for a whole new reason and I can't hide my smile when he trips over his words and keeps trying to make sure his hair looks good as she moves up next to me in the doorway.

"Payton…" Emma Jo whispers, completely ignoring poor lovesick Buddy Lloyd and saying my name in the same, worried voice as before when she came back into the living room.

"What's going on?" Leo asks, suddenly noticing the look on Emma Jo's face and remembering what Buddy said when he first walked up to the porch, turning away from Emma Jo to look back at him. "What's in the backyard?"

Buddy looks at me and Emma Jo, then motions for Leo to come down off the porch with his hand. As soon as Leo walks down the steps and he and Buddy start speaking in hushed voices, Emma Jo's hand wraps around my arm and she squeezes so tightly that I let out a little yelp of pain.

"We killed him!" Emma Jo whispers frantically, her eyes wider than they were before in the living room.

"What the hell are you talking about? Killed who?" I ask in a soft voice, glancing down at the two men to see that they're still deep in conversation and not paying any attention to us.

"I went to the laundry room at the back of the house and looked out the window to see what Bo Jangles was barking at, and…oh, my God, we killed him," Emma Jo whimpers.

I can still hear the damn dog barking up a storm at the back of Starla's house, and I take another sip of the shitty coffee Leo brought me. I need the caffeine right now more than something that tastes good if I want to be able to make sense of anything that is coming out of Emma Jo's mouth right now.

"Sheriff, did you get a look at what's in the backyard? Is it a deer?"

Emma Jo whimpers again when Starla comes waltzing over from her house, walking much faster with her cane than I thought humanly possible.

"Hey, Mrs. Godfrey! Hello Sheriff, Deputy Lloyd," a teenage boy shouts in greeting, walking across the street and into Emma Jo's yard to join the party. "My mom sent me over to see if everything is okay with Bo Jangles. We've been hearing him barking all morning."

I squint to get a good look at the kid and smile when I recognize who it is.

"Caden Jefferson? I used to babysit you! Holy shit,

you're all grown up now. It's me, Payton Lambert. Do you remember me?" I yell to him with a smile and a wave of my coffee cup, even though Emma Jo is now clutching onto my other arm with both of her hands now.

Caden's happy-go-lucky smile dies when he sees me, and he stops in the middle of the yard before quickly starting to take a few steps back toward the street.

"Sorry, Miss Lambert!" he shouts. "My mom heard you were back in town, and she said I'm not allowed to talk to you because you're a bad influence."

"Oh, for the love of God," I mutter as I watch him turn and flee, running across the street and into his house like the devil is on his heels.

I realize Leo and Buddy have stopped talking and are both staring at me.

"Honestly, it's not my fault that kid was a parrot and wouldn't stop calling his mother a whore after I watched a movie with him one night. It was years ago. Don't people ever forget anything around here?" I complain.

"Plenty of people around here forget things. Like the guy who helped you pass Geometry and gave you the name for your coffee shop," Leo informs me with a cocky smile.

Son of a bitch. SON OF A BITCH! Leo used to always call coffee Liquid Crack and teased me about how I couldn't survive without it back when he was tutoring me. I can't believe I forgot about that. When it came time for me to pick a name for the shop, it was the first thing that popped into my head. I can't believe I forgot that it came from Leo. No wonder he's taking such great pleasure in torturing me since I got back here. Great, now I owe the guy TWO apologies. This is officially the worst week ever.

"Seriously, I need you to come into the backyard, Sheriff. Right now," Buddy reminds him, his eyes darting up to me and Emma Jo.

"Just spit it out, Buddy. You've been standing here stammering and stuttering for two minutes, and I don't have time for this right now. I need to make sure the town doesn't start protesting in the square, demanding I lock up Miss Lambert for pissing everyone off," Leo tells him, aiming another smirk in my direction.

"Ha, ha, you're hilarious. Go do something useful and shut that damn dog up," I complain as Bo Jangles' barks get louder and more yappy.

"What the hell is he barking at?" Leo mutters.

"He's barking at *him*!" Emma Jo whispers in my ear, yanking me out of the doorway and back into the foyer. "Oh, my God, we're gonna go to prison!"

She's back to freaking out again, and I suddenly regret my decision of introducing her to copious amounts of wine last night. It clearly ate away all her brain cells and her hangover has made her crazy.

"Did you find another stash of wine I don't know about? What is wrong with you?" I ask as she paces back and forth in front of me, stopping suddenly to look out into the yard at Leo and Buddy as they walk to the side yard to get to the back.

"The pie. It's not on the windowsill. I checked when you answered the door, and OH MY GOD, THE PIE IS GONE!" she screeches, her voice louder now that the two men aren't within hearing distance.

I step around Emma Jo and look into the kitchen to the window above the sink and sure enough, the pie we left there to cool last night is gone. Under normal circumstances, we probably shouldn't have left a window to the house wide open all night when there was a lunatic out there somewhere probably waiting for the right opportunity to come back and make good on his threats, but we knew Leo was parked outside all night and he'd make sure nothing would happen. And also, wine…wine had a lot to do with us leaving the window open all night.

Turning back around to face Emma Jo, I shrug. "So, the pie isn't there. It's not like everything we did last night is exactly clear. Maybe we only *thought* we put it there. I'm sure it's in the fridge.

Emma Jo shakes her head frantically. "No. It's not in the fridge, it's not in the oven, and it didn't fall out of the window. I checked. WE KILLED HIM!"

"For the love of all that is holy, will you stop talking crazy? Take a deep breath, slow down, and tell me what the hell you're talking about."

Emma Jo grabs my hand and pulls me down the

hallway instead of replying. I let her drag me to the back of the house and into the laundry room, glancing out the window when she pulls the curtain aside and points to the backyard.

All I see is Leo and Buddy standing next to each other, staring down at something, until Buddy suddenly races away toward the side of the yard, bends over, and throws up all over a pink rose bush.

My eyes go back to Leo and I finally get a good look at what they were looking at, and the source of Bo Jangles' incessant barking all morning.

"WE KILLED HIM!" Emma Jo screams again.

I clamp my hand over my mouth as I stare out of Emma Jo's laundry room window, at Jed Jackson lying face-up in the grass, still wearing the same three-piece suit he had on when I saw him last night, unmoving with his eyes wide open in death.

"Never mind. *Now,* it's officially the worst week ever," I mumble, before turning around and racing back down the hall to the guest bathroom, making it to the toilet just in time to throw up all of last night's wine and bad decisions.

CHAPTER 10

Recorded Interview
June 2, 2016
Bald Knob, KY Police Department

Deputy Lloyd: You spoke to your daughter on
the phone right before the body was
discovered, is that correct?

Ruby Lambert: Yes. I called to tell her
what a horrible child she was for not
letting me know she was home. Can you
believe I had to hear it from Starla
Godfrey that my own daughter was in town?
Thirty-seven hours of labor and she
doesn't even care about her own mama. Not
to mention the apologies I had to make
around town all the time when she was
growing up and causing trouble. I still
have to make Pastor John twenty pumpkin
rolls every year for the church bake sale
so he won't kick Payton's father and I out
for what she did Christmas of 2001.

Deputy Lloyd: What happened during

Christmas of 2001?

Ruby Lambert: She rearranged the Three Wise men in front of Bald Knob Presbyterian into vulgar poses. It probably wasn't the best idea for the church to use old department store mannequins with bendable joints, but that's neither here nor there.

Deputy Lloyd: So your daughter regularly did things to rile people up and often times broke the law?

Ruby Lambert: Well, only when people did something that put a bee in her bonnet and she wanted to get back at them. Pastor John's sermon that previous weekend was about making amends to people we've wronged, and he singled Payton out, asking her if she'd like the opportunity to apologize to Mo Wesley for hanging a sign on his Gas n Sip coffee machine that said "Don't drink this coffee. It tastes like farts smell."

Deputy Lloyd: Does she still exhibit this type of behavior as an adult? If someone were to do something to upset her or make her angry now, do you think she's capable of doing them harm to, as you said, get back at them?

<u>Ruby Lambert:</u> Well, I guess it depends how bad it upset her or made her angry. And then you have to think about whether or not she's got any coffee in her system. That child is hell on wheels without her coffee, let me tell you. During our phone call the other morning, you know, when I called to tell her what a horrible child she was for not calling her mama first, she told me she would go on a murderous rampage if she didn't get her coffee.

Light chuckling

<u>Deputy Lloyd:</u> Ma'am, you do know your daughter is a suspect for the murder of Jed Jackson, correct?

<u>Rudy Lambert:</u> Lord Almighty…How many pumpkin rolls do you think it takes to fix something like that?

<u>Deputy Lloyd:</u> Mrs. Lambert, we're talking about the murder of one of our most prominent citizens and the mayor of Bald Knob. I don't think pumpkin rolls are going to fix anything.

<u>Rudy Lambert:</u> Have you tasted one of my pumpkin rolls, young man? I don't need an exact number, just a ballpark figure. What do you think, forty? Forty-five? You know

what, I'll just make fifty to be on the safe side and drop one off to you tomorrow morning. How does nine o'clock sound?

<u>Deputy Lloyd:</u> Ma'am, I think right now you should be more concerned with getting your daughter a lawyer.

<u>Rudy Lambert:</u> Don't worry, I already called Billy Ray Lewis.

<u>Deputy Lloyd:</u> Ma'am, I think Payton will need someone with a little more experience in criminal law. Billy Ray Lewis has never even stepped foot in a courtroom and only handles divorces and the occasional traffic violation.

<u>Rudy Lambert:</u> And he did a wonderful job for Andrea Maynard when that good-for-nothing husband of hers left town a few years back and got himself a new family over in Lexington. Plus, Billy Ray loves my pumpkin rolls.

CHAPTER 11

I haven't had my coffee yet. Don't make me kill you.
—Coffee Mug

"I 'M JUST SAYING, is it too much to ask for a little compassion? It's not like I need him to fawn all over me, but how about asking if I'm okay or checking to see if I need anything?" I complain to Emma Jo as we sit huddled next to each other on the hanging swing on her front porch.

After I threw up the contents of my stomach and finally got Emma Jo to stop screaming about how we killed her husband, we'd spent the last hour sitting on the front porch with our arms linked, watching Leo, Buddy, and Billy Ray Lewis go back and forth between their cars parked in the street and the backyard. The only reason I was able to get Emma Jo to stop freaking out and announcing to the entire town that we were murderers, was the appearance of Billy Ray. Sure, he's the coroner for Bald Knob and that would make some people nervous who may or may not have baked a pie filled with toilet bowl cleaner for the man who is currently lying dead in the yard, but it didn't make *us* nervous. Billy Ray is also the town lawyer, a bagger at Knob Grocery, runs the feed store at the edge of town, and dumber than a box of rocks. How on earth he ever got a law degree and was appointed as Bald Knob's coroner is beyond me. Billy Ray was the guy in high school who ate his own boogers and drew penises on everything he could get his hands on – textbook spines, lockers, desks, chalkboards, and every piece of home-work or test he turned in. Billy Ray Lewis being the one in charge of determining how Jed Jackson died makes me feel a lot better about my chances of wearing prison jump suit orange for the rest of my life.

"You doing okay, Emma Jo?"

I try not to huff when Leo pauses at the base of the porch steps and directs his question at Emma Jo, just like he's done every time he's passed by us. Emma Jo gives him a tight smile and a nod, and he returns both before going on his way to the side of the house.

"Seriously? Am I invisible? I could be having a nervous breakdown right now, and he wouldn't care," I complain when he's out of earshot, getting more and more annoyed every time I see him smile sympatheti-cally at Emma Jo, give Emma Jo a hug, or check on her wellbeing.

Sure, he's closer friends with Emma Jo since they've lived in the same town together all this time, and sure, he's still irritated I didn't recognize him and probably still has a bug up his ass about how I ignored his crush on me back in high school, but give me a break. I just saw my first dead body too, you know. I wouldn't turn down a hug or a reassuring pat on the back. Hell, I'd even take one of his stupid winks or smirks at this point.

"You look perfectly calm. I'm sure that's the only reason he hasn't said anything to you."

"I could be crying on the inside. He has no idea, the jerk," I grumble.

When Emma Jo doesn't respond, I turn my head and look at her profile. Her face is still pale, her eyes are red-rimmed and puffy from crying, and now *I'M* the jerk in this situation and it doesn't feel good.

"God, I'm such a bitch. Your husband is dead in your backyard and here I am complaining about some guy not paying me enough attention. And a guy I don't give two shits about, at that," I mutter softly.

Whatever. I'm not lying, YOU'RE lying.

"You definitely don't give two shits about him. I think you're probably up to about twenty shits, by my last count," she jokes, bumping her shoulder into mine.

"Can you keep your voice down? Next thing you know, it will be all over town I take twenty shits a day," I complain, nodding in the direction of Starla and half the people who live on this street, huddled over in Starla's front yard, whispering and pointing in this direction.

Even if Leo is too selfish to spread his comfort and kindness to me, at least I can appreciate him doing it for Emma Jo by ordering everyone off her lawn and telling them they needed to stay out front where he could see them for the time being. It kept the gossipers from hounding us with questions about what was going on or waltzing right into Emma Jo's backyard to find out for themselves.

"I've been sitting here this whole time assuming you're fine because Jed was an abusive asshole who probably never would have let you go, but he was still your husband. You loved the guy and you spent twelve years of your life with him. I'm sorry, Emma Jo," I whisper, swallowing back the tears of guilt and sadness for my friend and what she must be feeling right now.

"You have nothing to apologize for, Payton. Honestly, I don't know why I'm crying. I'm sitting here saying to myself over and over, '*Jed is dead, Jed is dead, Jed is dead,*' and I saw his body and I know he's really gone, but I still can't believe it. I can't believe I'll never be afraid of waiting for him to walk through the front door, worried about what kind of mood he's in. I can't believe I'll never have to lie or make up excuses or hide what he did to me. I can go anywhere, do anything, say anything, and not be scared. I'm not sad, I'm…relieved."

She finally turns her face toward mine and lowers her voice.

"Does that make me a bad person? I've wished that he was dead every day for twelve years, but I never thought it would actually happen."

Leaning forward, I press my forehead against hers,

just like we used to do when we were younger and one of us needed a little extra love or support. Her eyes stare questioningly into mine, and I do my best to make her feel better.

"Jed is dead, baby. Wishing for it is not what made it happen, therefore it does not make you a bad person," I reassure her. "Baking him a pie laced with bleach, ammonia, and artificial coloring, however…"

Emma Jo laughs at my attempt to make a joke, pulling her head back from mine as we both silently watch Billy Ray come around from the side of the house and make another trip out to his car parked by the curb.

When Buddy finally stopped puking in the rose bushes earlier, Leo sent him out to his car to phone in a report to the station and call Billy Ray, coming inside alone to break the news to us. He had no idea we'd already seen Jed's body through the laundry room window, and Emma Jo put on a great show of shock and the required sadness when he told her he suspected Jed most likely got to her backyard without Leo seeing him by sneaking through other backyards on the street, and then probably suffered a heart attack. Watching Billy Ray grab another bag of medical equipment from his trunk to go with the one he already took to the backyard when he first got here, doesn't do anything to help keep me calm about the bumbling lawyer/bagger/feed store operator/coroner.

"What if Billy Ray finds out it wasn't a heart attack?

What if he tests the contents of Jed's stomach? We're in big, big trouble, Payton. He'll know Jed ate a poisoned blueberry pie and my kitchen is a blueberry pie disaster," Emma Jo speculates quietly.

"Don't worry about the kitchen, I cleaned everything up as fast as I could after I finished puking and you were still losing your shit in the laundry room. Everything's in a garbage bag in the coat closet in the hallway until we're alone and can burn it or something," I update her quickly out of the corner of my mouth as Billy Ray comes up to the porch steps.

"Hey, Emma Jo, by any chance do you have one of those do-hickey's that you use on people when they're sick and have a fever?" he asks.

"Um, do you mean a thermometer?"

Billy Ray snaps his fingers, smiles widely, and points at her. "THAT'S what it's called! Yeah, I need one of them thermometer things. I just Googled what I'm supposed to do in a situation like this and I guess I need to check the temperature of the body to see when he died. I tried using *my* thermometer thing, but it's telling me Jed died at 87.5 degrees. I think mine's broken."

It takes a lot of effort for me not to giggle like a little girl and give Emma Jo a fist-bump when she looks down at me with her own barely concealed smile of joy as she pushes up from the swing to get Billy Jo a "thermometer thing." I'm pretty sure we're both a little more confident knowing that Billy Jo couldn't find his own ass, yet alone the cause for someone's death.

Emma Jo disappears into the house and Billy Ray climbs up the steps to follow her. The front door barely clicks shut behind them when a 1986 silver Buick Regal pulls into Emma Jo's driveway. I let out a low groan of annoyance seeing the car my parents have owned since the year I was born, and another one to go with it when my mother gets out of the driver's seat, slams the door closed, and stomps across the yard.

"Payton Marie Lambert, what have you done?" she fires at me, clumping up the steps in a pair of yellow slippers that match the yellow robe she threw on over her yellow and white plaid nightgown. The only thing clashing with her ensemble right now are the five giant blue curlers on top of her head.

She stops right in front of me on the swing with her hands on her hips to glare down at me.

"My phone has been ringing off the hook all morning. First, Starla called to let me know you assaulted Bo Jangles, then she called to tell me you killed a deer in Emma Jo's backyard, then Teresa Jefferson called to say you tried to corrupt poor Caden again. I had to take my phone off the hook after Roy Pickerson called and said he saw a car from the sheriff's department here and wanted to know if you had robbed another bar. Honestly, Payton. Forty hours of labor with you, and you're still making me suffer," she complains in one breath.

"How come every time you think I'm in trouble,

the number of hours you were in labor with me gets higher?" I ask, pushing up from the swing when she opens her arms and taps her slipper-covered foot.

"Don't sass me, young lady," she scolds when I lean into her and she wraps her arms around me. "You might be thirty-years-old and a big, fancy business owner, but I can still tan your hide."

She tightens her hold on me and starts swaying us from side to side, letting me know that even if she's irritated, she still loves me more than anything. I wrap my arms around her waist and take a deep breath of the Jovan Musk perfume she's worn since before I was born, the smell reminding me of being a little girl, safe and loved and happy. My eyes get blurry with tears when I rest my head on her shoulder. Even though my parents just flew out to Chicago two months ago for my dad's birthday, after everything that's happened in the last few days, it seems like much longer, and I didn't realize how much I needed a hug from my mom until right this minute. Standing in her arms while she rocks me gently and runs one of her hands down the back of my head, I forget about all the reasons why I never wanted to come home to visit and wish I'd done it much sooner.

"RUBY! DID YOU ASK HER IF IT WAS TRUE THAT SHE CAME BACK HERE BECAUSE SHE REALIZED SHE'D ALWAYS BEEN IN LOVE WITH SHERIFF HUDSON?" Starla shouts from her front yard.

"YEAH! I RAN INTO MAUREEN AT THE HUNGRY BEAR THIS MORNING AND SHE SAID SHE SAW THE TWO OF THEM STANDING REAL CLOSE TO EACH OTHER RIGHT THERE ON THE PORCH WHEN SHE DROVE BY EARLIER!" Another front-yard gawker shouts over to my mother.

"I hope he doesn't plan on marrying her. You should have heard the way she spoke to Bo Jangles. Can you imagine how she'd treat a husband?" Starla says to no one in particular. She's no longer yelling for the entire town to hear, but due to the close proximity of the houses, her voice carries just fine, unfortunately.

I hear a muffled laugh and pull out of my mother's arms just in time to see Leo come around to the front yard, giving the group of gossiping idiots a wave before coming up the steps to greet my mother.

"Ruby, you're looking beautiful as always," he tells her, leaning down to give her a kiss on the cheek.

My mother, one who has never been at a loss for words in all of her sixty-five years, blushes, giggles, pats the curlers on her head self-consciously, and needs three attempts before she can remember how to speak without stuttering.

"Oh, Leo, stop it!" she admonishes him with a wave of her hand. "Has my daughter been giving you trouble this morning? What on earth is going on?"

Leo's eyes flash to mine, then quickly down to my neck before he shields whatever I just saw on his face and smiles at my mother. I immediately bring my hand up and place it against my neck, forgetting about the red mark on my throat and knowing the only reason my mother didn't see it as soon as I pulled away from her was because she was distracted by the annoying hot guy standing next to us. That's just what I need is for her to see it, start shouting, and give the neighbors something else to blather about. I caught Leo looking at my neck several times this morning, and I waited for him to ask me if I was okay or how I was feeling, and each time he quickly looked away like he did just now, not saying a word.

Again, is it too much to ask for a little compassion? I was almost choked to death last night, and now a guy I threatened to choke with his own balls not more than twelve hours ago is dead a few hundred yards away.

"Payton has been giving me trouble for a lot longer than just this morning, Mrs. Lambert," Leo confides with a wink, which makes my mother go all aflutter once again, giggling and blushing and acting like a fool.

"Don't you have something else you should be doing instead of flirting with my mother?" I ask him irritably, realizing as soon as the words leave my mouth that the *something else* is figuring out why there's a dead man in Emma Jo's backyard. That we probably poisoned. With toilet bowl cleaner pie.

Leo leans in closer to me and I suddenly get a faint whiff of the cologne he's wearing – something light and woodsy and so delicious that I lick my lips and hold my breath when he drops his head close to mine. He veers his face to the side of mine, so close that I can feel his warm breath against my cheek until he stops right by my ear. My heart starts beating faster and I smile to myself, realizing that he's *finally* going to ask me if I'm okay. I don't care if my mother is standing right here, I don't care if half the town is watching from the next yard over, I'm so happy he's finally realized I could use a little of the concern he's been showing Emma Jo that I don't think I'll be able to stop myself from throwing my arms around him.

You know, to thank him for being nice to me and maybe butter him up a little so he doesn't arrest me for murder, not to sniff him again or anything.

"Don't tell your mom anything right now, at least not until Billy Ray is finished and I have a little more information. Oh, and don't leave town. I'm gonna need you to come down to the station later and answer a few questions," Leo whispers in my ear.

He pulls back, gives me a terse nod then gives my mother another kiss on the cheek before excusing himself to return to the backyard.

"He is such a nice young man," my mother muses as she blatantly stares at Leo's ass when he walks down the porch steps, giving another wave to the crowd of people and reassuring them that everything is fine and he'd come back and talk to them as soon as he could.

"Stop scowling, you look like you want to murder someone. Have you had your coffee yet this morning?"

my mother asks when she finally turns away from Leo's backside. "How about we grab Emma Jo and go down to the Hungry Bear? We can have a nice long chat about what Billy Ray and Sheriff Hudson are doing here, and you can tell me why I'm the last one to know you've been in love with him all these years."

She takes my hand and pulls me toward the front door, pausing right in front of it to look back over her shoulder and address the crowd.

"DON'T WORRY! I'LL FIND OUT ALL THE JUICY DETAILS AND GET BACK TO YOU! PAYTON NEEDS HER COFFEE FIRST. THIS CHILD WILL MURDER EVERYONE IF SHE DOESN'T HAVE HER MORNING COFFEE!"

Just like that, I remember why I haven't been home in twelve years. And hope my mother doesn't mind visiting me in prison instead of Chicago for the rest of my life since she just announced to the entire street that I'd kill someone over a cup of coffee. God only knows what they'd do if they knew about Jed, the ball choking comment I made, or the pie.

Boy, it sure is nice being back home...

CHAPTER 12

Recorded Interview
June 3, 2016
Bald Knob, KY Police Department

Deputy Lloyd: Ma'am, I know this is difficult, but I'm going to need you to stop crying for just a few minutes so I can ask you some questions.

Teresa Jefferson: HE'S DEAD! OH, MY GOD! JED JACKSON IS DEAD!

Crying, sniffling, nose-blowing

Deputy Lloyd: I'm sorry for your loss, Mrs. Jefferson. Were you close to Mayor Jackson?

Teresa Jefferson: Of course we were close! He lived across the street and he's been our mayor since he graduated from college. He used to always wave to me when I was outside getting the mail and he was coming home from work. Who's going to wave to me now when I go get my mail?

Deputy Lloyd: Can I get you another box of tissues? You're almost finished with the first one. Maybe we should take a five-minute break, and then we can continue with the questions about the night of the murder.

Teresa Jefferson: *Crying, sniffling, nose-blowing* HE'S DEAD! SOMEONE MURDERED HIM! OH MY GOD! JED JACKSON IS DEAD!

Deputy Lloyd: You know what, let's just take that break now. I'll go get you some water. Do you want me to call your husband?

Teresa Jefferson: *Nose-blowing, sniffling* I can't believe he's really dead. Are you sure? I mean, did you double check? Maybe there was a mistake.

Deputy Lloyd: Ma'am, he's been in the morgue for three days now, and Billy Ray is in the middle of assisting a medical examiner from Louisville with the autopsy.

Teresa Jefferson: Billy Ray used his fork to get a piece of bread unstuck from his toaster last week and electrocuted himself. Then there was that time a few

months ago when he was submitting the
paperwork for Marge and Rusty Calhoun's
divorce and filed adoption paperwork
instead. Now Marge is Steve's mother and
she's had to pay him child support for the
last two months because Rusty says if the
court of law says she's his mother, then
that's how it is and there ain't no take-
backs until Billy Ray figures out how to
fix things. Are you really going to trust
Billy Ray to make the judgment call on
whether or not our mayor is dead?

Deputy Lloyd: Ma'am, he's definitely
deceased. I've seen the body and believe
me, there wasn't any mistake made.

Teresa Jefferson: HE'S DEAD! OH, MY GOD!
JED JACKSON IS DEAD! WHY, GOD,
WHYYYYYYYYY?!

Deputy Lloyd: You know what, I have someone
else I need to interview, so how about I
give you a call sometime tomorrow to come
back in?

Teresa Jefferson: *Crying, sniffling, nose-
blowing* That's probably a good idea. I'm
just so upset over this whole thing and I
can't possibly think about anything else
at a time like this.

<u>Deputy Lloyd:</u> I understand, Mrs. Jefferson. You take care now, and I'll be in touch with you tomorrow.

<u>Teresa Jefferson:</u> *Crying, sniffling, nose-blowing* My heart is broken. I don't know if I'll ever get over this or be able to live a normal life or do anything normal ever again. Oh, before I forget, is it true that Payton Lambert and the sheriff are getting married? And if she's the one who killed Mayor Jackson, which I'm sure she did considering the things she taught my son when she used to babysit him, what kind of marriage are they going to have if she's in prison? It's not right I tell you, not right. There are plenty of eligible women in Bald Knob who would jump at the chance to become Mrs. Sheriff Leo Hudson. My sister is single and has always had a thing for the sheriff. You've met Chrissy Lou, right? She's fifty-three and runs the Bald Knob library. She wears a wig on account of that nervous tick she has where she pulls out all her hair, but it's a lovely red wig and she's real sweet. Not a murderer and child-corrupter like Payton. How about I leave Chrissy Lou's number here and you can give it to the sheriff?

<u>Deputy Lloyd:</u> I don't… that's not… Ma'am, you seem to be doing a little better, how about I ask you those questions now so we can get them over with?

<u>Teresa Jackson:</u> HE'S DEAD! OH, MY GOD! JED JACKSON IS DEAD! WHY, GOD, WHYYYYYYYYY?!

CHAPTER 13

A good man can make you feel strong, full of energy, and ready to take on the world. No, sorry...that's coffee. Coffee does that.

—Coffee Mug

I 'M WATCHING YOU, you little rat bastard. Don't you dare take a dump on this front lawn," I mutter under my breath while kneeling on the couch, my arms resting on the back of it while staring out of Emma Jo's window at Bo Jangles as he sniffs his way from Starla's yard to this one.

The ugly little mongrel's head jerks up and looks right at me, almost as if he could hear me and I give him a middle finger salute.

After the chaos of today and now that there are no longer people milling around the house, Emma Jo went upstairs to take a nap as soon as Jed's body was taken away. Jerk-face Leo came inside and held Emma Jo's face in his hands when he told her all soft and sweet that they would wait until it got dark outside and people went back inside their homes before taking him away. I want to feel bad about calling him a jerk-face considering he knew Emma Jo would freak out if the neighbors saw Jed's body being wheeled out from the backyard. He knew it and he solved the problem before it even became one, leaving Emma Jo with nothing to do but smile and thank him for being so thoughtful and good to her.

And really, if I wasn't so annoyed with him, I'd probably be halfway in love with him for the way he handled Emma Jo all day. He kept her updated on everything they were doing; he spoke to her in a calm, soothing voice; he made sure she ate something by calling one of his other deputies and having him bring over a whole kitchen full of groceries; he kept the nosey neighbors at bay; he answered the house phone whenever it rang when he was inside; and his eyes always went to her when he was too far away to speak, silently checking to make sure she wasn't two seconds away from a completely meltdown. Oh, and he made up a lie to tell my mother about how the sheriff's department was using Emma Jo's backyard for some kind of law enforcement training, explaining to her we couldn't join her at the Hungry Bear because we'd volunteered to help them if they needed it.

Okay, so that kind of helped me out too since I didn't have to sit through breakfast with my mother where she would have grilled me about pining away for Leo all these years. I don't think I would have been very good at squashing those rumors, while at the same time not letting it slip that Emma Jo's husband was dead and I helped make the poisoned toilet pie that killed him and, "Oh, by the way, his rotting corpse was in Emma Jo's backyard when you stopped by. Who wants dessert? I'd avoid the blueberry pie if I were you." Since my mother quickly realized she wouldn't be getting any dirt from me anytime soon, she told me if I didn't come to the house tomorrow she'd take me out of her will, and then she left and all was quiet and peaceful again.

Whatever. Just because Leo did one little thing that helped me out does not mean I'm going to stop thinking he's a jerk-face. He literally went out of his way to ignore me all day. It was almost like he knew I was guilty…

Holy shit. HOLY SHIT! He knows I'm guilty!

Was he looking through the kitchen window when I cleaned up our pie mess and stashed it in the hall closet? Did he see remnants of blueberry pie around Jed's mouth when he was looking at the body? He was there last night when Jed attacked me, but who knows how long he'd been there before he cocked his gun and told Jed to get away from me. Did he hear me tell Jed I'd rip off his balls and make him choke on them? If he didn't, he sure as hell heard me when I ordered him to give me his gun so I could shoot Jed in the junk. The sheriff of Bald Knob heard me threaten one of its citizens, who just so happened to wind up dead in his own backyard, where I'm currently staying. And the only thing he said to me all day today was not to leave town and that he needed me to come down to the station to answer some questions.

Oh, my God. He definitely knows I'm guilty!

Before I can start screaming and lose my shit all over Emma Jo's living room, the streetlamps outside illuminate Bo Jangle's scrawny little ass as he squats right in the middle of the side yard, looking back over his shoulder at me.

"You psychotic little maggot, are you seriously taking a dump and giving me the side-eye while you're doing it? I will punt you like a football right through Starla's bedroom window, asshole," I threaten him through the glass, pointing two fingers at my eyes and then at him.

"It's been a long day, can you please try and avoid killing the neighbor's dog? I can't deal with another phone call from Starla Godfrey complaining about you."

My head whips around when I hear Leo's voice to find him lounging against the doorframe between the front hallway and the living room. He's no longer in his sheriff's uniform, but sweet mother of God, he's wearing those same worn jeans he had on at the hospital. The ones that hug his ass and thighs and look like he's spent a lot of hours doing manual labor in them while getting all hot and sweaty and...hot. He's got his hands in the front pockets, pulling them down so they ride low on his hips, and he's wearing a dark blue t-shirt that clings to his chest and biceps, the cut of his muscles highlighted through the soft cotton material like he just got finished with a wet t-shirt contest. His forearms are lightly tanned just like his face, and I wonder if his parents still own the sweet corn farm out on the edge of town and that's where he got some sun. I also wonder what kind of exercise one does in order to get that kind of muscle definition in the forearms I'm currently staring at while they flex as he pulls his hands out of his pockets.

"How the hell did you get in here?"

High-five to me for managing to spit *that* out instead of "Can I lick your forearms and let you bench-press my body above your head?"

Leo pushes away from the wall and walks across the room, not answering the question until he sits down next to me on the couch, leaving only a few inches between us. The warm weather outside that heated his skin radiates off him and brings with it the faint woodsy smell of his cologne that rendered me stupid and speechless earlier today.

"You smell like outside," I mumble under my breath.

Great, so the speechless part has decided to fuck me over, and oh, hey! Hello there, stupidity!

One corner of his mouth tips up but thankfully, he doesn't say anything about my moronic comment. With the way he's got me all jumbled up in the head right now, there's no telling what would have happened if he said something cocky. I did just kill a man, after all. Leo should probably fear me.

"I got in here by turning the handle and opening the front door," he informs me, answering my previous question. "The owner of this house was just murdered in the backyard. You and Emma Jo should probably keep the doors locked."

He's still giving me that cocky little smirk, and I start wondering if he's doing it because he knows it annoys me, or as some sort of inside joke between us because he knows we murdered Jed and he's all *Ha ha, get it? It's funny because the murders are actually IN the house!* Then I start thinking Leo should get some new material because he's not funny AT ALL, and *then* what he said finally sinks in.

Seriously, why does he have to be so hot and smell so good? My brain has the dumb and it's all his fault.

"M-murdered? You s-said murdered," I stutter. "So, it definitely wasn't a heart-attack?"

Leo sighs and leans forward, resting his elbows on his knees and stares down at his hands clasped between them.

"I can't say much because there needs to be an of-ficial investigation now, but yes. Jed Jackson was definitely murdered," Leo confirms, lowering his voice and glancing toward the stairs that lead up to the bedrooms.

"She's asleep. She passed out a few hours ago. Don't worry, I'm pretty sure after the day she's had, not even a dump truck crashing through the front door would wake her," I reassure him, knowing immediately that he's concerned about Emma Jo overhearing what he said.

Leo nods and since he's still busy looking down at his hands, I can stare at his profile as much as I want without it being creepy or him making some stupid comment about picturing him naked. Which, I mean, I am, but it's not like he needs to know that. I realize as I sit here looking at him just how hard all of this must be on him as well, and I feel a tiny bit guilty about how many times I called him a jerk and also for that song I made up when I took another shower after Emma Jo went to bed.

It was to the tune of Wind Beneath My Wings and went a little something like, "Did you ever know that you're a jeeeee-eeeerk? You're everything I wish I could punch..." It was a lovely little ditty with stellar lyrics, but now I think I'll keep it to myself instead of serenading him.

Sitting this close to Leo and studying his face, I immediately see how exhausted he is. His short hair is all messed up on top of his head and I can picture him running his hands through it in frustration and worry. Not only did someone in the town Leo has sworn to protect die, and that someone was the mayor, he was murdered. Something like that has never happened in Bald Knob as far as I know. On top of dealing with the murder of one of his citizens, Leo also has Emma Jo to worry about, as well as figuring out how to break it to this town that their leader was killed and that killer is still out there somewhere.

Or, you know, sitting right next to him.

"You've had a long day too, huh?" I ask softly, turning away from the window to sit facing him, crisscrossing my legs in front of me.

I decide to suck it up, stop feeling sorry for myself, and play nice. If anything, this is the guy who could potentially keep me from being Big Bertha's bitch in the clink and fighting for packs of smokes in the yard. I'm not a fighter, or a smoker, so it really wouldn't end well for me.

"You have no idea…" Leo trails off, finally lifting his head up to gaze at me.

His blue eyes stare right into mine, and even though they look tired and like they've seen way too much for one day, they're still mesmerizing and I have a hard time looking away.

"How about you? How are you doing?" he asks gently, his voice filled with the honesty of his worry as he cocks his head to the side waiting for my answer.

Just like that, the spell is broken and I forget all about what kind of stress he's under because he drives me insane and something about him triggers the part of my brain that does all my rational thinking for me and renders it useless.

"Oh, so NOW want to know how I'm doing? You spent all day ignoring me and never once showed any kind of concern for my wellbeing, but by all means, go ahead and act like you care now, when the most traumatic day of my life is almost over," I tell him with a roll of my eyes as I push up from the couch to get away from him.

He doesn't say a word, just sits there and watches me pace back and forth when I get to the other side of the room where I can't smell him or get another urge to lick his arm.

"I've never seen a dead body before, but I've especially never seen the dead body of someone I know, who was married to my best friend. But don't worry, I'm fine. I'm totally fine!" I shout through my manic pacing. "I left my life and my business and everything I know and love to fly back home for the first time in twelve years to find out my best friend has been getting the shit kicked out of her since I left. But it's okay, I'm fine!"

I don't glance over at Leo while I rant because I know if I take one look at him my brain will shut down and my ovaries will take over, so I keep right on walking in a circle and bitching out loud.

"I can't cry, I can't scream, and I can't lose my shit because my best friend needs me to be the strong one, but hey, I'm fine. And really, it's not like I'd actually cry over that asshole, but I'd at least like to have that option and maybe have someone checking to make sure *I'm* doing okay. But noooooooooooo, you just looked the other way all day and made sure everyone else was okay and didn't say one word to me because I didn't fucking recognize you when I first saw you and I didn't apologize right away for that or for using the name Liquid Crack or for whatever the hell else I did to make you act like I don't exist and DIDN'T JUST SEE MY FIRST DEAD BODY!" I rant in one long, run-on sentence without taking a breath.

I finally stop pacing when I see Leo get up from the couch and move toward me. Scratch that, he's not just moving in my direction, he's *stalking* across the carpet with his hands fisted tightly at his sides and a muscle ticking in his jaw. I take a step back when he gets right up in front of me, a little freaked out by the serious look in his eyes, but he quickly leans down and wraps one of his arms around me, yanking my body to his.

"What are you doing?" I whisper in a garbled voice while I stare up at his face and his arm tightens around me, pulling me up on my tip-toes and as close to him as possible until my breasts are pressed against the rock-hard wall of his chest.

He doesn't answer me as his eyes trail slowly down over my face and his free hand comes up between us. I swallow thickly and let out a shaky breath when the tips of his fingers ever-so-lightly feather across the skin of my throat, right where the red mark Jed's choking hold left behind last night.

"Do you have any idea how hard it was to remember I'm an officer of the law and I couldn't just shoot that fucker when I saw him put his hands on you?" Leo asks in a rough, low voice. "I've never had to shoot my gun in the line of duty, and I've never wanted to as badly as I did last night."

I can't speak, I can't think, and I can't move. I don't know what's happening right now. All I know is that there is nothing hotter than Leo Hudson holding me against him, saying all the things I needed to hear from him and then some.

"I've spent years sitting on the sidelines, knowing what that asshole was doing to Emma Jo and not being able to do anything about it because she refused to admit it. All of those years feeling helpless, but it was *nothing* compared to walking up to that porch and seeing him hurting you," he admits as he continues to stare down at my neck and graze his fingertips over the still-tender skin.

He flattens his palm lightly against my throat, then slides his hand up to my jaw, holding my face while he brushes the pad of his thumb back and forth across my cheek.

"I'm sorry I didn't make sure you were okay today. You were always the strongest person I've ever known, and I made the mistake of assuming you didn't need or want anyone to take care of you."

I finally remember how to speak, swallowing a few times before I open my mouth to make sure my words don't come out with on a high-pitched squeak to echo my nerves.

"So, you avoided me today just because you thought I could take care of myself?" I ask, meeting his eyes when he finally looks away from my throat to look at my face.

"No, not just because of that. Mostly, because twelve years is a really fucking long time to have the same fantasy playing in your head over and over again."

My eyes narrow in confusion and he brings his face closer, pausing when his lips are hovering right over mine, almost touching but not quite.

"I didn't talk to you today and I didn't come near you today because I was in uniform and I was working, and I knew if I saw the slightest hint that you were going to crumble or I got close enough to touch you, I'd never be able to stop myself from doing what I've been dreaming about for twelve fucking years," he says softly, his breath skating across my lips.

"And what's that?" I whisper, thinking I know the answer, but wanting to hear him say it after making me feel like a bitchy, jealous shrew all day. And also, because at this point, I only have the ability to use about five percent of my brain and I'd like verbal confirmation from him before I say or do something else stupid in front of this man.

I have a few fleeting seconds before he answers me to remind myself that this is Leo Hudson. The same Leo Hudson who was the biggest nerd in the history of Bald Knob, weighed eighty pounds soaking wet, snorted at his own jokes, and was a member of Future Farmers of America. You know, one of the kids who walked around all the time in those short navy blue, velvet jackets and would talk about how to inseminate a cow over lunch. I feel a hysterical giggle bubbling up in my throat at the idea that I'm standing here in Leo Hudson's arms and he may or may not be getting ready to kiss me. Something about this entire situation feels hilarious to me, and I know now isn't the best time to laugh, but I honestly don't know if I can help it.

"Kiss you until you forget about any other man who ever kissed you before, and ruin you for any man that comes after me," Leo mutters, answering my question and putting an end to any desire I might have had to laugh when he tips his head to the side and crashes his lips against mine.

CHAPTER 14

Recorded Interview
June 3, 2016
Bald Knob, KY Police Department

Deputy Lloyd: So, how's it going?

Emma Jo Jackson: Um, fine, I guess.

Deputy Lloyd: Good, good. That's good.

Emma Jo Jackson: Uh, and you? How's everything with you?

Deputy Lloyd: Oh, you know, the usual. Keeping Bald Knob safe and all that.

3 minutes of silence

Emma Jo Jackson: Did you…I mean, I thought you had some questions for me or something.

Deputy Lloyd: Oh, ha ha yes! Yes, some questions. That's right. I need to ask you some questions.

Papers rustling, muffled cursing, chair legs scraping across floor, more muffled cursing

<u>Emma Jo Jackson:</u> Do you need me to help you pick that up?

<u>Deputy Lloyd:</u> NOPE! I got it, it's fine. Just give me a second.

Papers rustling, muffled cursing

Okay, where were we? Questions… let's see…

Papers rustling, muffled cursing

<u>Emma Jo Jackson:</u> Do you need a few minutes? I can go get something to eat and come back if you want.

<u>Deputy Lloyd:</u> No, no, you're fine, it's fine, I'm fine. Everything is fine! Let's just start with an easy question. Do you know anyone who would have wanted to kill your husband?

<u>Emma Jo Jackson:</u> That's your easy question? I can't wait for the hard ones…

<u>Deputy Lloyd:</u> I'm sorry! Shit! I mean shoot, not shit. Dammit. SHIT! You know what, maybe we should take a break. This isn't starting off very well.

Emma Jo Jackson: Um, okay, sounds good. So, you'll just call me then?

Deputy Lloyd: Call you? Like, on the phone? You want me to call you?

Emma Jo Jackson: To tell me when you're ready to get back to the questions. You know, give me a call when you're ready to do that since we're taking a break.

Deputy Lloyd: Oh, ha ha, yeah! Call you about this interview and the questions I need to ask and the… interview. Yep. Sure, no problem. So, I'll just call you about… that.

Emma Jo Jackson: Okay, well, I'll talk to you soon.

Deputy Lloyd: Yes, on the phone. Where I'll call you to talk about the interview. Excellent.

   Chair scraping, door opens and closes

Deputy Lloyd: Shit, shit, shit, shit, shit!

CHAPTER 15

Coffee: You can sleep when you're dead.

—Coffee Mug

L EO HUDON'S TONGUE *is in my mouth.*
I repeat, LEO HUDSON'S TONGUE IS IN MY MOUTH!

Sweet mother of God this man can kiss. Just the right amount of pressure from his lips, just the right speed of his tongue swirling around mine and the nibbling of my bottom lip, and how his hand moved from my cheek to slide around to the back of my neck, clutching a handful of my hair in his fist...

A moan floats from up from my throat and he angles his head to the other side, deepening the kiss until I want nothing more than to hop up into his arms and wrap my legs around his waist. As it is, I'm already fisting handfuls of his shirt up by his chest and if this kiss lasts any longer, I might just rip the thing right from his body.

Leo's hand at the small of my back that holds me firmly against him suddenly starts moving south and before I know it, his hand is on my ass, pulling me right up against the hardest erection I've ever felt.

LEO HUDSON'S HAND IS ON MY ASS.

I CAN FEEL LEO HUDSON'S PENIS.

My brain starts malfunctioning and instead of thinking about how this is the best kiss I've ever had in my life, I start hearing his teenage snort in my head and his squeaky puberty voice explaining to me how the Pythagorean Theorem works in between fun facts about a goat's scrotum. It happens before I can stop it.

I laugh.

Right into Leo's mouth.

"I'm sorry, I'm sorry!" I apologize in between giggles when he pulls his head back and looks down at me with one eyebrow raised questioningly at me.

"Not to brag or anything, but I've never had a woman laugh when I was kissing her before," he deadpans, giving my ass a little squeeze.

I giggle again, removing my clutching hold of his shirt with one hand to clamp it over my mouth.

"Mer muffing my muff," I mumble from behind my hand while my shoulders shake with even more laughter when I hear my own voice and how the words came out.

Leo lets go of the hold he has on my hair, brings his hand around between us, and removes my hand from my mouth.

"Try that again. In English," he requests, still looking down at my face in confusion and probably a little regret that his twelve-year fantasy isn't really living up to his expectations.

"I said, you're touching my butt," I repeat, a weird choking sound coming from my mouth when I try to stifle another laugh.

"Yes, you have a very nice butt. Is there a problem?"

I shake my head back and forth, but I'm still smiling like a loon and trying not to laugh out loud. This went from hotter-than-standing-in-the-middle-of-a-forest-fire to wondering if I'm on an episode of *Candid Camera* and someone is going to jump out from behind me and shout, "How does it feel to be kissing Leo Hudson, the nerdy guy in high school who knew just how far you could stick your arm up a cow's ass before it would become uncomfortable for them?!"

When I don't answer Leo's question and just continue to shake my head back and forth, trying my best to shake the funny out of my system until it falls out of my brain forever, his eyes suddenly narrow and he shuffles his feet forward, moving me backward as he goes.

He keeps staring down at me with a serious expression on his face and when my back slams into the wall behind me, I forget everything that was funny just two seconds ago. Leo bends his knees and uses his hips to push me up the wall until I have no choice but to wrap my arms around his shoulders and hold on tight. His hand slides from the ass of my pajama shorts and his warm, rough palm glides down the back of my thigh, pulling it up and hitching it over his hip.

"Still feel like laughing?" he asks in a low, rough voice.

Laughing? What's laughing? Who's laughing?

I can't remember how to speak, and when I don't answer him, he bends his knees again and pushes up, his erection hitting me right between the legs now that he's got me spread open for him and still holds my thigh tightly in place on his hip.

"How about now?" he questions in a quieter voice, dipping his head down and pressing his lips to the skin of my neck right under my ear.

Even if I could figure out what words mean and how to use them, I wouldn't open my mouth to answer him if you paid me all the money in the world. My silence just makes him keep going, and there's no way in hell I'm stopping anything right now.

His lips make a trail of kisses across the edge of my jaw until he gets to my mouth and pauses before putting those masterful things back where I want them.

"Just to give you a head's up, I'm gonna touch your ass again. Then I'm gonna kiss you *while* touching your ass because I really like how it feels in the palm of my hand. Just for the hell of it, I might even touch your tits because they feel really fucking good pressed against my chest right now. Any objections or laughter you need to get out of your system before then?" he asks in total seriousness.

I shake my head frantically back and forth, the tingling between my legs while he spoke growing into a damn inferno while I thought about and anticipated everything he said he would do to me, wanting it more than I want air to breathe right now.

"Excellent. Brace yourself."

Leo's mouth crashes to mine again and he swallows my groan of pleasure at the same time his hand slides back up to palm my ass and he pushes his hips harder between my legs.

I see stars, I hear choirs of angels singing, and I most definitely am not thinking about the workings of a pig's urinary tract. When he pushes his tongue past my lips and kisses me deeper, all I can think about is that tongue pushing into another place on my body and his hands touching more than my ass.

My hips move up to meet him, wanting to feel more of that hardness between my thighs, wondering how in the hell I've gone thirty years without ever experiencing this kind of heat and need for another person and the crazy, insane notion that the person I'm feeling it with is someone I've known practically my whole life.

Leo lets out a groan from the back of his throat when my thigh tightens around his hip to pull him into me harder. My hands move from his shoulders to grab onto fistfuls of his hair at the back of his head, clutching and tugging on it to make sure he keeps his mouth on mine and never stops kissing me. My back slides up and down the wall with each slide of his hips between my legs and when my toes leave the floor, I take the opportunity to wrap my other thigh around his waist to join the first one. I'm so lost in the moment, clinging to him like he's a tree I want to climb, that I don't hear the creak of the stairs until it's too late.

"OHMYGOD, OHMYGOD, OHMYGOD!" Emma Jo shouts in surprise.

Leo throws his arms up in the air like he's being held at gunpoint and moves away from me so quickly that I slide down the wall and land in a heap on the floor.

"Heeeeey!" I complain, scrambling back up to my feet and rubbing my sore ass that slammed against the hard ground.

"I'm sorry! Oh, my God, I'm sorry! I didn't know you were still awake, and I didn't know Leo was here, and I'm sorry! Oh, my God!" Emma Jo rambles, throwing a hand over her eyes.

"You don't have to cover your eyes now, the show is clearly over," I deadpan, shooting Leo a glare for dropping me on my ass. The same ass he just told me he really liked and I can't believe he would let that kind of harm come to it.

"Sorry," he mouths to me with a sheepish grin and a shrug of his shoulders before turning to face Emma Jo. "Sorry about that, Emma Jo. Did we wake you?"

"Nope, no, not at all. I just got up to get something to drink. Don't mind me, feel free to carry on with…whatever," she tells us with one hand still covering her eyes and the other one making some sort of circular motion in our direction before she turns around and runs face-first into the wall behind her. "I'm fine, it's okay, I'm fine!"

Walking around Leo, I rush over to Emma Jo. Grabbing her by the shoulders, I turn her to face me, reaching up and pulling her hand away from her eyes.

"Seriously, we're done here," I inform her.

"We're nowhere close to being done here," Leo says from behind me.

Emma Jo laughs and I roll my eyes, shooting him another glare over my shoulder since my bruised ass is a little pissed off at him right now.

There's a light knock at the front door and when I move to answer it, Leo holds up his hand to stop me, stalking over to it and asking who it is.

"It's Buddy, I saw your car out front. You got a few minutes?" we hear through the door.

Leo pulls it open and steps back, motioning for Buddy to come inside. Buddy lifts his foot to move, glances up and sees Emma Jo standing behind me, and immediately puts his foot back down and shuffles backward out onto the porch.

"You know what, I'll just wait out here. It's fine. Don't want to impose or anything. How are you doing this evening, Mrs. Jackson?" Buddy shouts from out on the porch.

"Um, I'm fine. Uh, and you?" Emma Jo yells back.

"Fine! Just fine. Everything's good," he replies

loudly.

"Buddy, you want to tell me what you came over here for, or are you just going to shout it from outside there for the whole neighborhood to hear?" Leo asks with a sigh, still holding the door open while he shakes his head in annoyance.

"Um, well, it's about *Mayor Jackson's autopsy*," Buddy says to Leo in a quieter voice, whispering the last part in an effort to keep anyone else from hearing, and I suddenly remember about the whole *not a heart attack* thing and how Emma Jo doesn't know yet.

"Autopsy? Do you normally do an autopsy on someone who died from a heart attack?" Emma Jo asks, hearing everything Buddy said just as clearly as I did.

To the normal observer, it would sound like Emma Jo was just casually asking a question, but to me, I can hear the slight quiver of panic in her voice and see her eyes dart to mine, all wide and freaked out before she quickly masks them when Leo turns around to face us.

"Emma Jo-" Leo starts in a soft voice, but I quickly cut him off and turn to face her, grabbing onto her shoulders again and blocking her face from the guys with my head.

"Emma Jo, it looks like Jed didn't have a heart attack. He was *murdered*," I inform her, stressing that last word even though I don't know why the fuck I felt the need to stress it. Saying the word *murder* is stressful enough without that added emphasis, especially when the ones who murdered him are standing right here next to two officers of the law, one of which I was just dry humping against the wall.

"WHAT?! HE WAS MURDERED! OH, MY GOD, NO!" Emma Jo screams, her bottom lip quivering while her shoulders start to shake with the worst fake crying I've ever seen in my life.

I quickly pull her into my arms and pat her back, shushing her with a fake soothing voice and speaking loud enough for the guys to hear, telling her I'm sorry and that everything will be okay. She wails louder and throws her head down on my shoulder, her whole body shaking as I hold her and rock her back and forth.

"Overkill! Bring it down a notch, crazy!" I whisper in her ear before looking back over my shoulder and giving Leo and Buddy sad smiles while they stare at us uncomfortably, like any good men do when faced with a hysterical woman.

"I'm so sorry, Emma Jo. I wanted to tell you earlier today when I first found out, but we needed to run some preliminary testing on the cause of death first before I could say anything," Leo explains gently.

Emma Jo whips her head up from my shoulder and stares at me with wide eyes.

"It's fine. Be cool. They have no idea about the pie or they'd be arresting us right now," I whisper out of the corner of my mouth while Emma Jo sniffles loudly a few times to cover my whispering.

Buddy finally chooses to step inside the house,

moving to stand next to Leo in the open doorway, nodding his head.

"I'm sorry too, ma'am. Hey, is that blueberry I smell? Did you make a blueberry pie?" he asks, lifting his chin and sniffing the air a few more times.

"What? What blueberry pie? There's no blueberry pie here. We don't know how to make pie," I ramble, turning around and moving next to Emma Jo to fling my arm around her shoulder and give her a tight squeeze of warning and a little *Please God help me!*

"Nope, no pie baking here. I don't like blueberry pie. The smell makes me gag. Blech," Emma Jo adds with a scrunch of her face in disgust.

"You make blueberry pies every year for the church bake sale. The whole town raves about them and is always saying you should open your own pie making business," Leo reminds her with a confused look on his face.

"Really? REALLY?" I ask with a wide fake smile, my head whipping to the side to stare at her.

"Oh, yeah. I guess I forgot. You know, on account of how my husband was murdered and all? OH, MY GOD, I CAN'T BELIEVE HE'S GONE!" she wails, turning into me and burying her face in the side of my neck.

I give the two confused men standing in the doorway another sad smile while I pat Emma Jo's back soothingly as she continues to moan and cry like a dying pig against my throat.

"It's been a long day. I think I need to get Emma Jo back up to bed," I tell them.

Buddy nods his head in understanding, turns and walks out the front door as fast as he can, obviously beyond uncomfortable with the scene happening right now and how much Emma Jo is carrying on. Her cries get louder and louder until I'm pretty sure I can hear dogs howling in response down the street.

Unfortunately, Leo doesn't move as fast as Buddy. He stands by the door for several minutes, looking back and forth between me and Emma Jo in my arms. I can't tell if that's a knowing look on his face or one of complete and utter confusion, but I hope to God it's the second one. I really don't want to go to jail, and with my ass still stinging from him unceremoniously dumping me onto the ground, I'd really like a repeat performance of what happened tonight, preferably not from behind bars or during conjugal visits, thank you very much.

"We'll talk tomorrow. First thing in the morning. Don't go anywhere," Leo says, pointing his finger at me all caveman-like. He takes one last look between me and Emma Jo, shakes his head with a sigh, turns and walks out the door.

As soon as it clicks closed and I hear Leo's footsteps thump down the porch steps, I pull Emma Jo out of my arms and throw my hands up in the air.

"*I don't like blueberry pie. The smell makes me gag. Blech!*" I mock in my best Emma Jo voice.

"I'm sorry! I panicked! Do you think they know?"

"That you gagged about the pies you make EVERY YEAR FOR THE CHURCH BAKE SALE?! Yep, I'm pretty sure they caught that!" I shriek.

"It's fine, I'm sure it's fine. If they knew, they would have arrested us immediately, right? I mean, from what I saw when I came down here, Leo wasn't exactly getting ready to slap his cuffs on you," she says with a wag of her eyebrows. "Or was he?"

I smack her in the arm even though I'd really like to know the answer to that question myself.

I wonder if he brings his handcuffs with him when he's not in uniform? If Emma Jo hadn't interrupted us, would I be handcuffed to a headboard right now screaming Leo's name?

"Well, there's only one thing to do. You need to keep doing what you were doing when I walked in on you guys. There's no way Leo will arrest you if he's busy sticking his tongue down your throat," Emma Jo says with satisfied nod.

"And what about you? Are you going to stick your tongue down Buddy's throat to keep *yourself* out of jail?" I ask sweetly.

"What?! What are you talking about? Buddy Lloyd? Like he'd really want to kiss me," she scoffs, her cheeks reddening in embarrassment.

I laugh, moving over to the hall closet, opening the door, and pulling out the white garbage bag I stuffed in there this morning.

"What are you doing?" Emma Jo asks, following

behind me as I carry it through the house.

"Sneaking out of the laundry room window to burn the evidence in your backyard so no one sees. And then we're going to sit down and discuss Deputy Lloyd and how long exactly you've had a thing for him."

"You sound like your mother," Emma Jo complains when I flip the light switch in the laundry room.

"Eat me," I growl with a flip of my middle finger.

CHAPTER 16

Recorded Interview
June 3, 2016
Bald Knob, KY Police Department

Deputy Lloyd: Are you sure you don't want
your parents present for this interview,
Caden?

Caden Jefferson: You want to talk about the
night Mayor Jackson was murdered, right?

Deputy Lloyd: Yes.

Caden Jefferson: Then definitely not. My
parents thought I was in my room all
night, but I was really at a party down at
Bald Knob lake with a bunch of friends.
You're not going to tell them what I say
in here, right? Because, I'd be grounded
for life if they knew I lied.

Deputy Lloyd: No. Everything so you say is
confidential right now. Unless of course
this goes to trial and you're called in as

a witness.

Caden Jefferson: Oh, man. They're going to kill me if I have to testify against Payton and they find out where I was that night. Do I really have to get up on a stand and say she murdered Mayor Jackson? I mean, she was really nice when she used to babysit me. I don't want to be the one to send her to jail.

Deputy Lloyd: Right now, Payton isn't going to trial because she hasn't been charged with anything. We're just trying to piece together what happened that night. So, you were at a party down at the lake. What time was the party over?

Caden Jefferson: Well, it was supposed to go all night, but Brad Miller and Eric Friedman got into a fight over who could tip the most cows at Mr. Mayford's farm, and Brad said Eric cheated, although I don't really know how you'd cheat at tipping cows unless Eric's got some sort of friendship with the cows and they tipped over all on their own to help him out. Anyway, we broke up the fight and then there wasn't much else to do so we all went home. I'd say it was around 2:30 in the morning and I heard some yelling from the Jackson's backyard when I was sneaking in my window. You're not going to tell my parents that, right?

Deputy Lloyd: No, I won't tell your parents what you said. Do you remember what you heard being yelled from the Jackson's backyard?

Caden Jefferson: Nah, it was just some loud voices and then they just stopped all of a sudden and I didn't hear anything else. I saw Sheriff Hudson's car parked a few houses down, but he wasn't in his car when I walked by. Do you think he saw Payton killing Mayor Jackson and tried to stop her? His knuckles were all bruised when I saw him a few days later in town, but he said he was changing a flat tire and that's how he hurt them. Is he going to marry Payton? Is she moving back to Bald Knob? My mom will go even more crazy if that happens. She thinks Payton is a bad influence on me and the worst babysitter ever.

Deputy Lloyd: Caden, it's really important for you to try and remember what you heard that night. Male voices, female voices, both?

Caden Jefferson: I really don't remember. I had a lot of beers to drink down by the lake. I MEAN SODAS! I had a lot of sodas to drink and, whew, that caffeine went right to my head! Oh, my God, don't tell my mom I was drinking beer. She'll KILL me. I mean, not really kill me. My mom would never kill anyone, especially Mayor Jackson. She loved Mayor Jackson. She's been crying every day since we got the news. I heard my dad telling her she was just crying because she felt guilty, so I think she was so upset because she hadn't gone over to say hello to the mayor in a few days or something. Anyway, I think it would be great if Payton moved back to Bald Knob. She's like, really pretty. My friend Ryan said he wouldn't mind her being a bad influence on him, but I told him to shut his mouth and not talk about my babysitter like that. Even if she did teach me to call my mom a whore.

CHAPTER 17

I don't like morning people. Or mornings. Or people.
—Coffee Mug

"I DON'T WANT to say anything over the phone. Someone could be listening," I speak softly into my cell phone, glancing quickly at my surroundings in the parking lot of The Hungry Bear to make sure no one is close by.

"Oh, for the love of God, just spit it out. You had sex with the sheriff, didn't you? Tell me all the dirty details," Bettie demands from the other end of the line.

"No! I didn't have sex with the sheriff!" I shout, my eyes widening in horror when I look up and see Justine Pickerson pause and look back at me over her shoulder with her hand hovering by the handle of the door to the restaurant. "Hi, Justine, how are you today? Lovely weather we're having!"

She looks at me in disgust before quickly rushing inside the building and I let out a loud sigh.

"Justine Pickerson...is that the one who owns the bar you stole wine coolers from?" Bettie asks.

"Allegedly!" I argue. "They were sitting out behind

the bar in an open box, how was I supposed to know they weren't expired and getting thrown away? Anyway, can you focus, please? Something bad happened. Something *really* bad, and I need to know how you'd feel about running Liquid Crack for the rest of your life."

"What the hell are you talking about? Was the sex with Hot Guy that bad? It's always the pretty ones who are all talk and no action..." Bettie trails off.

A brief flash of Leo holding me up against the wall and pushing his hips between my thighs takes over my brain and I have to shake away the memory and work extra hard to focus on what I'm supposed to be telling Bettie.

Speaking of extra hard...dammit, focus!

"Bettie, listen to the words coming out of my mouth. Ed-jay as-way, urdered-may," I explain, cupping my hand over my mouth and the speaker of the phone.

"Are you high? Did someone give you a pot brownie again? I thought you learned your lesson the last time when you hid under the bed for four hours because you thought every time the ice machine on your fridge started clinking that the cops were breaking down your door," Bettie reminds me.

"I'm not high! I told you, someone might be listening to this phone call," I remind her in a panicked voice, looking around the parking lot nervously again.

"Right. Pig Latin. Must be serious if you're speaking in a language that all the brilliant scholars in the world haven't been able to decipher for millions of years," she replies sarcastically. "So, Jed is really dead, huh? Kind of crazy that happened right after you got to town."

"On a scale of one to ten, what do you think my chances are of surviving prison?" I ask her distractedly, waving to Mo Wesley across the street when he comes outside to flip over the *Open* sign on the door of Gas N Sip. He gives me the finger and walks back inside.

"Is there a number less than one? Like zero, but times infinity?" Bettie asks with a laugh.

"Hey, I'm scrappy. I could totally be a gang leader in Gen Pop. I've heard that's the only way to make it, by being the leader of your own gang."

"Sure," Bettie responds with another laugh. "You'd totally be the leader of the Whitest White Girl Wasp gang. You'd win every riot by boring people to death about a skirt you got on sale at Nordstrom's and the importance of starting every morning with a good cup of coffee."

Before I can try and convince her I could kick her tatted ass all over the streets of Chicago, you know, after coffee, she gets a call on the other line and puts me on hold. She's back a few seconds later and if I wasn't nervous already, this would have pushed me right over the edge.

"Weird. I just got a call from a Kentucky number. You're the only person I know in Kentucky. Did you meet another Hot Guy and give him my number?" she asks in confusion.

"Oh shit! OH SHIT, what did they say? Who was it?"

"I don't know. I didn't recognize the number and I let it go to voicemail, like any rational human being does," she replies easily.

"Holy shit, it's the cops. It has to be the cops. They must be calling everyone I know for like a character witness thing or some shit. Fuck. I'm dead. How quickly can you make up some really awesome things to say about me and my character?" I ask, waving to my mother when she pokes her head out of the door of The Hungry Bear and points at her watch angrily before disappearing back inside.

After tossing and turning all night, my thoughts too busy to let me sleep since they were filled with Leo kissing me and then Leo arresting me for murder, I succumbed easily to my mother's pressure when she called at seven this morning and told me to meet her and my father for breakfast instead of going out to their house. In bad need of coffee, regardless if it was shitty coffee, Emma Jo let me take her car and reassured me she'd be fine home alone until I got back. She wanted to start making funeral arrangements for Jed so they'd be ready to go when the sheriff's office finished with their investigation. It's probably a wise decision to make those plans now since I'm not exactly sure how easy it is to plan a funeral from behind bars. And it's obvious Leo didn't just think Emma Jo and I were crazy last night, and he legitimately things we had something to do with Jed's death if he's already calling people I know.

"A five percent raise, Liquid Crack stock when the company goes public, and I want full custody of Cecil since you'll be too busy dropping the soap to worry about taking care of him," Bettie replies immediately without giving what I asked any thought.

"You could have at least pretended that it would be a piece of cake to tell the cops a bunch of glowing things about me," I complain, pushing away from Emma Jo's car and slowly making my way to the door of the restaurant.

"But then I'd be lying, and what kind of precedence would that set for me when I have to testify on your behalf on the witness stand?"

Bettie ends the call by promising to give me a full report about the voice mail as soon as the morning rush at Liquid Crack dies down, and I walk into The Hungry Bear for the first time in twelve years, stupidly assuming no one would notice or care that I'm back home.

THIS WAS A bad idea, a really bad idea.

"Everyone is looking at me," I mumble under my breath, trying to hide behind the sticky plastic menu of The Hungry Bear that hasn't been cleaned or updated since before I was born.

"They're all looking at you because you haven't been home to see your parents in twelve years. They think they're witnessing a miracle right in front of their eyes," my mother deadpans with a glare at me over the top of her own sticky, plastic menu.

"Leave the girl alone, Ruby. They're all staring because they can't believe how pretty you are." My father gives me a wink and a smile, pushing his own menu to the side since he always orders the exact same thing for breakfast, no matter what the specials are.

"Ruby, Dwight, you folks having the usual this morning?" Andrea Maynard asks when she comes up to our table and collects the menus, tucking them under one arm as she pulls a pad and pen out of the front pocket of her dress.

Andrea has been a waitress at The Hungry Bear all of her fifty-seven years and looks like she stepped right off the set of a 1950's movie about a haggard waitress. Her salt-and-pepper hair is pulled back into a low, messy bun with a white paper hat on her head and her pink-and-white-plaid apron-style waitressing uniform is already stained with coffee, bacon grease, and ketchup.

"Sausage and cheese omelets, home fries extra crispy, and orange juice, Andrea, thank you," my mother tells her with a smile, giving her the order for both her and my father.

"Excuse me! I'd like to order something too, Andrea," I speak up when she moves to walk away from the table without looking at me.

"We don't have none of that snobby, fancy coffee here," she informs me with a huge, inconvenienced sigh, chomping the gum in her mouth with extra enthusiasm.

"I'll just have what my parents are having, that's fine," I say with a wider smile, pretending as if I don't feel like a bug under the microscope with everyone in this place turned around in their chairs, blatantly staring right at me and ignoring the food in front of them.

"Don't worry, Andrea, Payton won't kill anyone if she doesn't have her coffee, she's too tired for that this morning," my mother laughs in a lame attempt at a joke, which of course makes everyone in the room gasp at the same time like a choir of judgmental, gossiping hens.

"Nice work, mom. Way to keep the gossip down," I mutter out of the corner of my mouth, wishing I could slide right out from under our booth and hide under the table.

The phone lines must have been on fire all through the night in Bald Knob. So much for Leo trying to keep a lid on what happened for a little while longer. At least he sent me a text this morning to warn me and Emma Jo that news traveled fast. And to remind me to stop by the station first thing. Ignoring his text and meeting my parents for breakfast instead is probably karma coming back to punch me in the face.

"Mayor Jackson was a fine man. Some people

around these parts think it's a little strange that he goes off and gets himself killed right after you show up back in town after all these years," Andrea says, finally looking up from her pad of paper to meet my eyes.

"Andrea, you know better than to listen to gossip around town," my mother scolds with a *tsk* of her tongue.

"So, it's not true that Payton here got into an altercation with Starla's Bo Jangles the other night?" Andrea asks.

"He pissed on my leg!" I argue, immediately wishing I would have kept my mouth shut when everyone in the room starts whispering even louder and pointing in my direction.

"I heard Mayor Jackson had a black eye when they found his body. Did you have an altercation with *him* too?" Andrea questions, smacking her hands down on our table and leaning over it like she's playing bad cop. All she needs is a rickety light hanging down from the ceiling, swinging back and forth over my head and blinding me every time it hits my eyes.

Just then, the bell above the door dings, and when I literally think I've been saved by the bell, Leo walks in. The mood in the room suddenly changes from angry mob with pitch forks to family members welcoming their hero home from the war. People shout greetings, two men get up and shake his hand, and Andrea finally leaves our table, rushes over to the pick-up window to grab a Styrofoam box, and hands it to him with a huge smile on her wrinkled, judgy face. I watch as he takes his time greeting everyone in the room before he strolls over to our table.

"Mr. and Mrs. Lambert, Payton," Leo greets us with a nod, his eyes quickly moving away from mine while I stupidly sit here gawking at him, wondering why he looks hotter in his uniform now than he did the first time I saw him in it.

"Leo, my goodness, what happened to your hand?" my mother asks, pointing to his hand holding the breakfast container.

Leo quickly shifts the container to his other hand, sliding that one into the front pocket of his uniform pants, but not before I noticed a few dried cuts and some bruising on his knuckles.

"Oh, nothing to be concerned about. Just a little stupid accident changing a flat tire," Leo tells my mother with a self-deprecating laugh. "I need to get back to work, but I just wanted to stop by and remind Payton that we have an appointment to go over a few things at the station."

He finally looks right at me, his blue eyes boring a hole right in my head like he's trying to read my mind. If he is, I hope he can hear me screaming, *"LIAR, LIAR, PANTS ON FIRE!"*, Flat tire my ass! Jed Jackson had a black eye according to Andrea and now I'm kicking myself for being too preoccupied with Leo's mouth to notice his knuckles last night when he had me pinned up against the wall.

Maybe Emma Jo and I really *didn't* kill Jed, and maybe Leo still has no idea about the pie and the fact that it was missing from Emma Jo's kitchen was all just a coincidence. Even with all the whispers and points in my direction that have resumed, I'm starting to feel a little bit better about my future. I'm not feeling so good about the fact that I might have made out with a murderer last night, but I'll deal with that part of my conscience later.

"You folks have a good day. Make sure you get a piece of pie before you leave. I hear the blueberry is excellent. Not as good as Emma Jo's, but delicious all the same," Leo speaks to my parents, but keeps his eyes on me the entire time he talks. "Don't forget to stop by the station, Payton."

My mother giggles and waves at Leo like a lunatic when he winks at her before turning away from our table and walking back out the door.

"EVERYONE, GO BACK TO YOUR BREAK-FASTS, NOTHING TO SEE HERE!" my mother shouts to the room after he's gone. "Let's just all have a moment of silence and say a prayer for poor Mayor Jackson and Emma Jo."

The patrons of The Hungry Bear finally stop staring at me to do as my mother says, bowing their heads over their plates of eggs and toast.

"See? Everything will be fine. It's not like people *really* think you killed Mayor Jackson, they're just in shock and upset. I'm sure Sheriff Hudson will find the real killer in no time, everyone will forget all about this, and then you two can get busy making me a few beautiful grandchildren," my mother states in an attempt to make me feel better.

Andrea comes back to our table while our heads our still down, my mother praying for beautiful grand-children while I pray Leo is too busy remembering what happened between us last night to dig any deeper into Jed's death. She gently sets down my parents' plates and drops mine in front of me, the bowl of lumpy oatmeal in the middle of the plate that I didn't order, splashing out onto the table.

"Payton is pregnant with Sheriff Hudson's baby? Oh, lord, this town is never going to forget something like *this*," Andrea complains with a huff before walking to another table to bend down and whisper with them.

Super. I've been here all of two days and I've mur-dered someone, gotten married, and now knocked up by the sheriff, according to the town. There's no way things could get any worse.

CHAPTER 18

Recorded Interview
June 3, 2016
Bald Knob, KY Police Department

<u>Mo Wesley:</u> Am I in here 'cuz you need a witness to swear about Payton Lambert?

<u>Deputy Lloyd:</u> You mean as a character witness or someone who was with her at the time of the murder and can vouch for her whereabouts?

<u>Mo Wesley:</u> I don't know nothin' about this character thing or whatever the blazes vouch means. Is that how the Frenchies say couch? Never did understand why people don't just speak English from the good old U.S. of A.

<u>Deputy Lloyd:</u> You asked if we needed someone to swear about Payton Lambert and it would be nice if we could have someone corroborate the story she's told us.

<u>Mo Wesley:</u> What? No. I just wanted to swear some about her and have it on official police record and whatnot. Will she get a copy of this report and know I called her a good-for-nothing coffee snob? Why aren't you writing this down?

<u>Deputy Lloyd:</u> Mr. Wesley, I just need to know where you were on the night of May 31st, sometime after midnight.

<u>Mo Wesley:</u> I wasn't killing Jed Jackson, that's for damn sure. Can you also add that Payton Lambert is no longer allowed in the Gas N Sip unless she follows the rules like everyone else? You only get free coffee with gas, you don't get to steal it like some sort of hoodlum. Those mean streets of Chicago have turned that girl into a thug, I tell you.

<u>Deputy Lloyd:</u> You're saying Miss Lambert stole a cup of coffee from your establishment?

<u>Mo Wesley:</u> No, I'm saying she stole a cup of coffee from the Gas N Sip.

<u>Deputy Lloyd:</u> So, the business that you own. Right. Do you want to press charges?

<u>Mo Wesley:</u> Why would I want to do that when

you can't even understand it when I tell
you she stole a cup of coffee from my
business? How do you people expect to
solve a murder when you can't understand
simple English? I bet you're one of them
Frenchies, aren't ya? First a murder, then
a stolen cup of coffee, next thing you
know it will be the American Revolution
all over again. My forefathers fought on
this great land so you could-

Deputy Lloyd: Mr. Wesley, do you have
anything you'd like to add about the night
of May 31st, the night Jed Jackson was
murdered?

Mo Wesley: Wait, yes! I almost forgot
something really important. Payton Lambert
shouldn't be drinking coffee anyway on
account of her being in the family way
with Sheriff Hudson's child. Caffeine
isn't good for the youngins I'm told. Why
aren't you writing this down?

CHAPTER 19

Coffee keeps me busy until it's time to get drunk.

—Coffee Mug

"I SEND YOU into town for an hour and you're already breaking more laws," Emma Jo sighs as she holds the front door open for me and I smack the car keys into her outstretched hand.

"I had a lovely time at breakfast with my parents where the whole town almost dragged me out of The Hungry Bear by my hair and burned me at the stake in town. Oh, and I ran into Leo and he told us to try the blueberry pie, thanks for asking," I reply, closing the door behind me and crossing my arms in front of me when Emma Jo looks at me nervously. "He told me to TRY THE BLUEBERRY PIE, Emma Jo. And then he winked at me!"

"He winked at you?"

"Well, he winked at my mother, but I was sitting right next to her so it was kind of in my general direction, and he did look really cute when he did it and those uniform pants hug his ass quite…dammit!" I complain, throwing my hands up in frustration and letting them smack against my thighs. "PIE!"

I scream that last word just to bring my point home, though I kind of forgot what my point was since I was picturing Leo's ass in those khaki-colored dress pants. And now I'm hungry for pie since I didn't eat the shitty oatmeal Andrea gave me instead of what I ordered, and I'm wondering if pie would taste even better being licked off of Leo's chest and…

"I think we have more things to worry about than pie," Emma Jo reminds me, breaking into my thoughts.

"THERE IS NOTHING MORE WORRISOME THAN PIE, EMMA JO! Pie that Leo knows about since he was all winky and shit, and I came home instead of going to the station like he asked because I don't know how to answer questions about pie!" I tell her, freaking out more so than usual because I'm hot and sweaty and hungry and horny and just one hour in downtown Bald Knob was enough to remind me why I hate this place and everyone who lives here.

"I thought I heard your overly-loud voice, Payton."

My mouth drops open when I look over Emma Jo's shoulder and see Sally Plunkett walk around the corner from the living room.

"My mother is more worrisome than pie, in case you missed that memo," Emma Jo whispers under her breath before turning around to face her mother with a smile plastered on her face.

"Thanks for the warning, asshole," I whisper back before pasting my own fake smile on my face as Mrs.

Plunkett stares me down.

At least I had the good sense to pack all my nice clothes when I scrambled around my house in Chicago and threw everything into a suitcase. Wearing a white and peach skirt that hugs my hips and flows out around my thighs and pairing it with a peach short-sleeved cotton top with white beading around the scooped neckline, I look casually professional and not at all like the Whore of Babylon that Mrs. Plunkett always thought I was when Emma Jo and I were growing up. Widowed when Emma Jo's father died when Emma Jo and I were in fourth grade from complications with a ruptured appendix, Mrs. Plunkett spent her life grooming Emma Jo to find the perfect husband with the perfect job and the perfect medical records. She thought she hit the jackpot having the mayor of Bald Knob as her son-in-law and I hope to God the woman hasn't been so blinded by the notoriety all these years that she didn't see what was happening to her own daughter. She loves Emma Jo, don't get me wrong. She just loved that everyone kissed her ass every time she walked through town almost as much. Let's just hope she realizes I'm a grown adult now and I'm not always to blame for everything that happens to Emma Jo.

"I thought I'd stop by and help my poor baby girl during her time of need, especially when I heard you were back in town and all the trouble you've been causing since you've been back here. Starla Godfrey called me on my way over here to tell me you accosted her dog again this morning," Mrs. Plunkett informs me.

Okay, so I guess I'm still an unruly teenager in her eyes. Good to know.

"It's not my fault the coffee from Gas N Sip sucks. I took a sip and it came right back out. I didn't do it on purpose, my mouth just naturally rejects things that taste like vomit," I explain with a shrug.

Of *course* the entire town already heard about how I walked out of Gas N Sip after breakfast with my parents, hoping against hope that Mo Wesley's coffee had improved over the years, only to spit it right back out as soon as it touched my lips. All over Bo Jangles as Starla Godfrey walked him through town. It didn't help the situation when Mo came running out after me, claiming I stole a cup of coffee and screaming to everyone on the street that I was trying to rob him blind. He shouldn't put a sign that says "Free Coffee" on his machine and he really shouldn't write "With the purchase of gas" underneath it, so small that a house fly couldn't even read it.

"Honestly, Payton, you've done nothing but harass the town since you've been back. I'm so upset I haven't been able to stop crying about that sweet son-in-law of mine, and Emma Jo is incredibly distraught."

Mrs. Plunkett pauses and when Emma Jo doesn't say anything because she's become an expert at tuning her mother out, I elbow her in the side.

"Oh, yes, yes, very distraught. So distraught I can't think straight," Emma Jo quickly pipes up, adding in a few sniffles and a swipe under her eyes for good measure. "Don't worry, Payton has been taking very good care of me and she's just as upset as I am about Jed."

"PIE!" I shout, tuning everything out myself since all I can think about is what Leo said to me at The Hungry Bear earlier.

"You're lucky you're friends with Emma Jo and she has me for a mother. I've already spoken to Billy Ray about your case and he's agreed to take it on under one condition," Mrs. Plunkett informs me, ignoring my pie outburst as she pulls a tissue out of the purse draped over her elbow and dabs it under her eyes.

"Wait, case? What case? What are you talking about?" I ask, Mrs. Plunkett letting out an exasperated sigh.

"Soooooo, it looks like the entire town is blaming you for Jed's murder," Emma Jo mutters, quickly moving to head to the kitchen. "Are you hungry? You look hungry. How about I whip us up something-"

Grabbing her arm, I yank her back to me and cut off her words with a few of my own.

"PIE!" I shout again like an idiot, unable to come up with any more words to express just how mad I am right now.

"Pie sounds lovely. Emma Jo makes the best blue-berry pies. Sweetie, why don't you bake a few, you know baking always relaxes you, and I'm sure it will only be a matter of time before people stop by with casseroles and food during your time of need. Make sure you call me as soon as they start arriving and I'll be here to greet everyone," Mrs. Plunkett tells her, moving around me to give Emma Jo a kiss on the cheek.

"What's the condition of Billy Ray taking on my case?" I ask when she opens the front door, quite proud of myself that I managed to ask a complete sentence and not scream about baked goods.

"You just have to go on a date with him and promise not to sue him if he loses your case. Emma Jo, don't forget to call me."

With that, Mrs. Plunkett walks out the door with a wave and right over to Starla Godfrey's house, probably to let her know I only spit on her dog because I'm on drugs, which was evident by all the screaming about pie.

"The good news is, my mother still works as Billy Ray's administrative assistant, so there's that," Emma Jo reminds me with a shrug when I slam the front door closed.

"How is that good news? How is ANY of this good news? The entire town now thinks I'm guilty of killing your husband, and don't you say ONE WORD about pie!" I warn her, holding up my hand when she opens her mouth to interrupt me. "I'm the only one allowed to yell about pie here!"

Emma Jo slips her hand through the crook of my elbow and starts dragging me toward the kitchen.

"The good news is that since my mother works for

him, I know he finally got that chronic halitosis taken care of and she refills his prescription for Viagra every couple of months, so your date with him should be one to remember," Emma Jo informs me as we move into the kitchen.

"I don't like you very much right now," I mutter when she pushes me down into a chair at the table and starts pulling things out of the fridge.

"You'll like me a whole lot better when I tell you all the gossip my mother filled me in on while you were with your parents. It turns out, there might have been a few people in this town who didn't really care for my husband," she tells me with a smile over her shoulder while she grabs a cutting board out of one of the drawers.

"So, not everyone is as dumb as they look. Good for them," I reply sarcastically as she starts chopping vegetables and other assorted items.

"Payton, don't you understand what this means? It means you aren't the only suspect, even though that's all the town is talking about right now. Well, that and you're currently pregnant with Leo's love child. And here my mother was right all along when I was in high school – just kissing a boy really *does* lead to pregnancy," she muses.

"OKAY, WHAT DO we have so far?" I ask Emma Jo as I lean back into the couch and take a drink of my wine.

After Emma Jo tried to butter me up with a lunch of homemade stir fry, she pulled out the big guns when I held my ground and pouted like a toddler for the rest of the day, refusing to talk to her – she grabbed a bottle of wine out of the fridge and said the magical words, "There's more where that came from."

It turns out, Mrs. Plunkett isn't only good at making me feel like an asshole, she's also excellent as the head of the town's sympathy committee, stocking Emma Jo's fridge with ten bottles of wine when she stopped by earlier. I'm starting to like that woman more and more.

"I've kicked your ass seven times in Tic-Tac-Toe, but I think one of those was a wash because we both used X's instead of one of us using O's," Emma Jo tells me, lifting up the notebook paper from the coffee table and squinting at it while she holds it at arm's length from her face and begins singing. "Ex's and the oh, oh, oh's they haunt me!"

I snatch the paper out of her hand and give her a dirty look even though that's a catchy tune and I really want to sing it with her. We're supposed to be compiling a list of possible murder suspects and granted, the games of Tic-Tac-Toe were my idea when I drew a stick figure of Jed with X's for eyes and I got all excited about how we used to always play this game together when we were little, but we need to focus!

"There's no time for musical theater, Emma Jo! We need to catch a murderer!" I remind her, looking down at the paper in my hand and wondering why everything is all turned around and nothing makes sense. "Jesus, your handwriting is atrocious."

Emma Jo takes the paper back out of my hand, flips it around so it's no longer upside down and pushes it back into my hand, all while holding her wine glass to her mouth and never spilling a drop.

"Ahhhhh, that's much better."

She drains her glass and leans forward next to me on the couch to refill hers and top off my own, which she then hands to me as she pulls her knees up to her chest next to me.

"Okay, remind me again whoosh on the lish," she slurs. "I mean, whoosh on the lish. The lish. THE LIIIIIIIIIIIIISH. That paper thing in your hand."

Emma Jo points at the paper when I give her a look of confusion, having been distracted by her making a duck face and trying to look down at her lips when she spoke.

"Right, the list," I mutter, taking a drink and trying to get the names to stop being so blurry as Emma Jo leans toward me and looks down at the paper.

"Justine Picker-Noser-Son," she reads, including my awesome nickname for Justine Pickerson that I added in parentheses behind her name.

I snort and then clear my throat and attempt to be serious.

"You said your mom told you she heard Justine got into a huge fight about flowers with Jed a few days ago, the day he left for his business trip," I speak, patting myself on the back for being able to decipher my notes by her name that said, "Flower power face punch".

Emma Jo nods excitedly and repeats what she already told me.

"Correct! Justine wanted to plant new rose bushes in front of Pickerson's bar, and Jed denied the request form she turned in at his office."

"And your mother heard it at the tail end of the Bald Knob gossip line, so who knows who started that rumor or who we should question first, but it's a start," I say, putting a question mark next to Justine's name.

"Why did you draw a stick figure with no arms or legs, upside down? Ooooooh, is that supposed to be Jed again? I liked it when you gave him X's for eyes. Do it again, do it again!" Emma Jo shouts, clapping her hands together and forgetting all about the glass of wine she's still holding.

It sloshes all over her arms and she does something that immediately brings a tear to my eye – she brings one arm up to her mouth and licks the wine off of her skin, then proceeds to lean forward and put her face an inch away from the paper.

"Wait, never mind, I see it better now. It's a question mark. I should maybe stop drinking," Emma Jo mutters when she sits back up.

"If I'm drinking, there's less of a chance that I'll start crying because everyone in this town thinks I'm a murderer."

"PIE DEAD!" Emma Jo suddenly shouts.

"Yes, I know I baked a poison pie, and I know that *technically* I might be a murderer, but they don't know that," I reply, easily deciphering her drunk yelling.

"ME PIE DEAD TOO!" she shouts again, pointing at herself with her wine glass.

"Right, you made the pie too, but they're all blaming me and aren't giving *you* a second thought," I remind her, sounding like an owner talking to his dog every time it barks and they act like they understand what the dog is saying.

What? Jed is dead? Who's a good girl, Emma Jo, who's a good girl?!

Emma Jo gives me a sad look and I feel bad about making *her* feel bad about the town's opinion of me. After her mother left, she was hell-bent on marching down to the town square and announcing to everyone that Jed abused her to bring the focus off of me. Which would only put the bull's-eye right square in the center of her poisoned-pie-baking chest, and I'm not about to let that happen. I'd much rather deal with the consequences of my actions than let Emma Jo take any more shit from anyone after having to live through her marriage to Jed. After making her promise not to do something crazy like that for me when she'd spent half her life hiding this information from the town, we sat down and put our heads together.

Two drunk heads are better than one, or something like that.

"I know! Let's play a drinking game. I've always wanted to do that. Every time one of us says *muskrat*, we take a drink!" Emma Jo explains, pouring more wine into both of our glasses.

"You do know how drinking games work, right? You're supposed to pick a word someone will use a lot, which then gives you more chances to drink," I explain to her.

"Starla Godfrey, number two suspect because Jed filed a noise complaint about Bo Jangles and his barking. MUSKRAT!" Emma Jo yells, chugging half of her glass.

"And your mom told us she actually heard that argument outside of his office last week and Starla told him he'd regret the day he was born. MUSKRAT!" I scream, quickly understanding the genius of Emma Jo's drinking game rules.

"Bo Jangles, because Jed kicked him when Bo Jangles wouldn't stop going to the bathroom in our yard. MUSKRAT!" Emma Jo adds.

When I don't join her in another chug of wine, she eyes my glass.

"What?" I say with a shrug. "It doesn't feel right to put Bo Jangles on the suspect list. He's a tiny little rat dog incapable of killing anyone."

"He pissed on your leg," Emma Jo reminds me.

"Death penalty for the Defecating Dog! MUSK-RAT, MUSKRAT, MUSKRAT!" I shout, clinking my glass with hers.

JED HAD TO DIE   175

My phone *pings* with an incoming text, and I groan when I grab it from the coffee table and look down at the screen.

"Who is it? What does it say? Is it my mom with more wine? Tell her I changed my mind and I'll take her up on that Xanax prescription. I'm feeling frisky tonight," Emma Jo says, letting out a sigh when I turn the screen around for her to read.

"Oh, no. You forgot to go up to the station and talk to Leo. Do you think he's mad?" she asks.

I read the text again that only says, *"Dammit, Payton…"*

"I don't know, does Leo normally use the word *dammit* when expressing glee? Like, *'Dammit, Emma Jo, you look lovely tonight!'* And I didn't forget to go talk to him, I avoided him on purpose because PIE!" I shout.

"And because he's a suspect on our list," she reminds me, pointing to the stick figure I drew with a muscular chest, six-pack abs and flexing one of his arms above his head next to a talk bubble that said, *Payton has a great ass and could never be a murderer, pass it on!*

"Right? Like, how dare he come down on ME when he's probably the one who beat up Jed and killed him. And how come Andrea Maynard knew about Jed's black eye and we didn't? You want to know why? Because Leo is guilty and he's covering it up! I bet he only made out with me last night to distract me from the murderous rampage he went on when he beat the shit out of Jed right in this backyard when we were sleeping. You can kill a guy from punching him a bunch of times, right?" I ask, still staring down at the screen of my phone.

I swear I'm just pissed about the fact that Leo is keeping secrets that would keep him safe and throw me in the slammer, and not about how he may or may not have only kissed me to keep me from looking at his hands.

"You do realize you might have made out with a murderer last night, right? Doesn't that creep you out a little bit? Like, good for him and all that, but still. He might have killed Jed with his bare hands and then he had those bare hands on your butt," Emma Jo remarks with wide eyes.

"I mean, if we're getting technical here, he kind of maybe made out with a murderer too, so I think our combined maybe-I-murdered-someone statuses cancel each other out."

"MUSKRAT!" Emma Jo shouts and we both take a drink of wine.

"I'm just going to keep ignoring him until I can figure out what I'm going to say to him. What's he going to do, drive over here and drag me to the station for not coming in?" I ask with a laugh.

Emma Jo and I both scream when there's a knock at the door.

"Oh, no. Did you forget to end the text? Do you think he heard us?" she asks, scrambling up off the couch with me when I start slowly moving toward the front door.

"Who is it?" I shout to the door, reaching for the stupid triangle award on the side table for protection, because if Emma Jo and I aren't the ones who killed Jed, that means the killer is still out there and we are entirely too drunk to defend ourselves with just our hands.

I pause in confusion and stare at the table when my hand comes up empty, forgetting about it and letting out a sigh of relief right along with Emma Jo when we hear a reply out on the porch.

"It's Deputy Lloyd, ma'am," Buddy speaks in a low voice.

"Awwww, look. Your boyfriend stopped by to check on you," I tease, which earns me a smack in the arm from Emma Jo as I open the door with a smile.

"Sorry to stop by so late, I hope I'm not disturbing you. How are you doing, Emma Jo?" Buddy asks, quickly swiping his uniform hat from his head and smoothing back his hair.

"We were just talking about muskrats," Emma Jo giggles, bringing the wine glass she carried with her up to her lips.

"I like muskrats," Buddy says with a nod, which just makes Emma Jo giggle and drink some more. "Are there muskrats in Bald Knob?"

"Weeeeee, this is fun!" Emma Jo announces, holding up her wine glass. "I'm so glad you stopped by, Buddy. We should sit down and talk."

While Buddy starts stammering and his face turns an alarming shade of red, I shake my head at Emma Jo. "No, we should *not* sit down and talk with Buddy. Buddy knows things!"

My attempt at whispering under my breath at Emma Jo fails and Buddy immediately pipes up. "I know a lot of things about muskrats!"

Which just makes Emma Jo take another sloppy drink, this one spilling all down her chin while she laughs with her face in the glass. It takes a few minutes and a lot of side-eye glaring to get Emma Jo to stop laughing and she finally puts on a serious face.

"To what do I owe you pleasure in your company, Buddy? I mean, to what do I pleasure you in front of company. Oh, my God!" Emma Jo complains, clamping her hand over her mouth while I take a little bit of delight in watching her blush while Buddy stares at her with wide, unblinking eyes.

"I think what she's trying to say is, to what do we owe the pleasure of your company?" I say, deciphering Emma Jo's drunk-speak once again.

Buddy clears his throat and tugs nervously on his tie, his eyes moving away from Emma Jo to me. "I'm sorry to do this, Payton, but Sheriff Hudson asked that I come over here and bring you down to the station."

I choke on the mouthful of wine I attempted to swallow after asking Buddy what he's doing here and Emma Jo pats me on the back.

"You have got to be kidding me?!" I shout angrily

when I finally get the wine to go down the right pipe. "He sent you over here to collect me, like I'm some sort of criminal?!"

Buddy shrugs sheepishly, taking a step in my direction while moving his hand toward the utility belt around his waist, which just makes me laugh. I'm five-foot-seven and weigh all of a hundred-and-twenty-five pounds. Do I look like someone who would fight an officer of the law or resist arrest?

"Sorry, Payton. He told me you might give me some trouble and I'm to use whatever means necessary to get you in the car and down to the station."

The wine floating through my veins takes a detour from "I'm fine, everything's fine, and I'm not that drunk" to "LEO HUDSON IS A JERK AND I WILL FIGHT YOU!"

Buddy moves closer, I throw up my fists in a fighting stance, Emma Jo screams *MUSKRAT* again, and that's pretty much the story of the first time I got Tased...

CHAPTER 20

Recorded Interview
June 3, 2016
Bald Knob, KY Police Department

Sally Plunkett: Why do your cheeks get red
every time I mention my daughter's name?

Deputy Lloyd: I…it's…um, it's a rash.

Sally Plunkett: I hope it's not contagious.

Deputy Lloyd: NO! I mean, it's not really a
rash, I don't know why I said that. And I
don't have anything contagious. I'm in
perfect health, I swear.

Sally Plunkett: Can we hurry this along? I
need to get over to the funeral home and
make arrangements for my son-in-law's
funeral. You know, since he was murdered
and my daughter has just been beside
herself with grief and doesn't need the
added burden of planning his funeral. Do
you know when his body will be released?

It's been extremely hard on me to make all of these plans when we don't know what day the funeral will be. Why, I'm getting calls left and right from people wanting to pay their respects, and it's just not right that I can't tell them when Jed's funeral is.

Deputy Lloyd: I'm sorry, Mrs. Plunkett, but we can't release the body until we get the final report on his cause of death.

Sally Plunkett: I thought everyone already knew Payton killed him? Why haven't you arrested her? I think she got my daughter addicted to alcohol. And I've been hearing all over town that Payton was yelling and threatening Jed the night he was murdered. Did you know she sprained her wrist trying to kidnap Emma Jo?

Deputy Lloyd: Wait, what? Emma Jo was almost kidnapped? Is she okay? Why didn't she call me? I mean, the station. Why didn't she call the station?

Sally Plunkett: Well, it was back when they were teenagers and they were trying to sneak out of the house to go to a party, but still. It served Payton right for falling out of that tree and landing on her hand.

Deputy Lloyd: Mrs. Plunkett, do you know any reason why someone would want to kill your son-in-law?

Sally Plunkett: Do I know any reason why someone would want to kill my son-in-law?

Deputy Lloyd: Yes, that's what I asked.

Sally Plunkett: You want to know if I have any knowledge of why someone would want to kill Jed?

Deputy Lloyd: Uh, yes. That's…I believe that's what I asked.

Sally Plunkett: Like, you want to know if I know if Jed made anyone angry enough to kill him?

Deputy Lloyd: Ummmmmmmm, yes?

Sally Plunkett: Like, so angry they couldn't see straight and they might have gone temporarily insane and did something they regret, even though it might have been justified at the time, but now they're really sorry and feel bad about it?

Deputy Lloyd: Uh, yes?

Sally Plunkett: Nope. I haven't a clue. I

noticed you're the only one who hasn't dropped off a dish to Emma Jo. We're running low on lasagna and green bean casserole. And while you're at it, can you start spreading the word that we'll be letting off doves at Jed's service and everyone should take heed and bring an umbrella?

Deputy Lloyd: I…Mrs. Plunkett, if you know anything about who murdered your son-in-law, I need you tell me everything you know. It's imperative for this investigation.

Sally Plunkett: I know we're almost out of lasagna, Buddy. What are people going to think when they stop by Emma Jo's house to pay their respects and she doesn't have any lasagna or green bean casserole?

CHAPTER 21

I'm just waiting to see if my coffee chooses to use its
powers for good or evil today.

—Coffee Mug

"I T DOESN'T HURT that bad. I had to be Tased at the
academy during training."

Leo leans over and holds out his hand to help me
up from the floor of Emma Jo's hallway, where I've
been twitching, drooling and cursing for the last forty-
five minutes until Buddy finally had to call Leo for help
when I told Emma Jo to grab me a butter knife so I
could saw off his penis.

Although, since I was in the middle of a full-body
spasm from the aftereffects of being Tased, it came out
like "I-I-I-I-I C-C-C-C-C-U-T-T-T Y-Y-Y-Y-OU D-
D-D-I-CK!". And in Buddy's defense, he thought I was
calling him a dick since there's no punctuation in
Taser-stuttering, and luckily didn't relay to the stupid
jerk of a sheriff standing over me that I had threatened
him with a kitchen utensil. I've already threatened the
penis of a man who is now dead and God forbid
anything happens to Buddy in the next twenty-four

hours. Although staring up at Leo while he grins down at me makes me want to grab *his* appendage and choke the life out of it.

I smack Leo's hand away and roll over onto my stomach so I can push myself up from the floor. My knees give out as soon as I'm upright and Leo swoops in, wrapping his arms around me and pulling me against him before I can hit the floor again.

He smells like soap and outdoors and I close my eyes and breathe him in with my cheek pressed against his chest, until I feel the rumble of his chuckle against my face. I yank myself out of his arms and growl at him when I take a couple of steps back and out of smelling distance.

"Sorry, I swear I'm not laughing about the Tasing thing. I just remembered how I used to follow you around school all the time and try to smell your hair. You always smelled like fresh coffee beans, and you still do. Best smell in the world," he admits with a small smile.

Yep, it's official. Pretty sure he just got me pregnant.

"Oh, no! Nice try, buster! Don't you come in here after one of your deputies Tased me on *your* order and say all kinds of sweet things that will make me all mushy and forget I'm mad at you!" I yell, pointing my finger at him and refusing to let him get under my skin.

"I make you mushy?" he asks in a low, deep voice, closing the distance between us until we're standing toe-to-toe. "Funny. You do the exact opposite to me."

He brings his point home by grabbing my hip and pulling the lower half of my body against his and there is NOTHING mushy about what's poking into me right now.

"It's not going to work," I tell him indignantly, keeping my arms pinned to my sides before I do something stupid like pull his shirt out of the waistband of his jeans and run my palms up the skin of his stomach and chest.

"What's not going to work?" he whispers, dipping his head down next to mine to slide his lips around along the edge of my ear.

I clench my hands into fists when he tugs on my earlobe with his front teeth and then kisses his way down the side of my neck.

"This little seduction scene you've got going on. I'm immune to your charms," I inform him, even as I tilt my head to the side to give him better access.

"Twelve years of fantasies…You taste better than I ever imagined," he breathes against my collarbone after using one of his fingers to pull the collar of my shirt back just enough for him to place a kiss there.

"Oh, hell no!" I shout, finally pulling my head out of my ass and shoving him away from me. "I know what you're doing, Leo Hudson! You're saying all this shit about dreaming of me for twelve years just to distract me. You did it last night and it might have worked then, but I'm onto you now. There's no way in hell you've held a torch for me after all this time and have been pining away for the day I might come back to town. No. Freaking. Way. Who does that? Someone who's guilty of something and just wants to cover it up, that's who!"

My hands are on my hips and my chest rises and falls rapidly with the heat of my anger.

"Are you finished?" Leo asks casually, crossing his arms over his chest as he leans against the hallway wall, his eyes flickering down to my boobs that are straining against my shirt each time I try to take in a deep, calming breath.

"Am I finished? AM I FINISHED?" I shout, my anger boiling over that he can stand there all calm and laid-back when I just got knocked up with a few kisses to the neck from him. "ONE OF YOUR DEPUTIES TASED ME!"

Of course I scream something stupid instead of saying what I really want to say: That I know he's been lying and totally using me to keep his own ass out of jail, and it stings a hell of a lot worse than fifty thousand volts of electricity to the gut. All of this just makes me angrier because why in the hell do I care if he's been using me? It's not like I'm in the market for a man since I've sworn off men for the rest of my life after getting another voicemail from Benjamin today asking me how many people were on my side of the guest list so his parents could book their country club. And it's not like I didn't have the fleeting thought of doing the exact same thing to him and try to distract him with my feminine ways. The point is, I didn't do it. I mean, I've been avoiding him and too busy spitting on dogs, stealing coffee, and having the whole town accuse me of murder, and I haven't had time to dazzle him with my charm today, but still. I wouldn't have done it because I have morals!

Well, aside from that one time I baked a pie filled with toilet bowl cleaner...

"I'm sorry Buddy Tased you. I swear I didn't tell him to do that. I knew you'd be difficult, and he must have taken me literally when I told him to bring you in with force," Leo apologizes.

"You knew I'd be *difficult?* Oh, you haven't even SEEN difficult yet!" I argue.

"MUSKRAT!" Emma Jo yells from the laundry room down the hall where she made herself scarce after Leo got here.

Technically, I made her go and hide in another room as soon as Leo walked in the door and sent Buddy back to the station. And thankfully she understands stuttering just as well as I understand her drunk slurring since all I whispered in her ear was "P-P-P-P-IE!". Even drunk as hell, she was able to realize what I was saying and knew she needed to get away from Leo until she sobered up a little since she's reached a level of drunk I like to call "I have the inability to lie and it's going to be soooooooo funny when I tell you how we killed Jed!".

Going by her shout from the laundry room, followed by a loud giggle, she's not doing a very good job of sobering up in there.

"Pay no attention to the drunk chick. She's had a rough week," I explain to Leo when he leans around me to look in confusion down the hall where Emma Jo's voice is coming from. "How about you just focus on what's important here? You're a jerk and your lips have now been placed on my Do Not Call list."

Leo sighs and runs his hand through his hair, making it stick up all over the place in the most adorable way until my hands itch to reach out and smooth it down for him. Then I catch a glimpse of the cuts and bruises on the knuckles of his right hand when he slides his palm down the front of his face and I have no problem telling my ovaries to shut the hell up and stop trying to cause trouble.

He catches me staring at his knuckles and he curses softly under his breath, rubbing his left hand over the scrapes while he stares down at what he's doing and doesn't meet my eyes.

"There was a minor incident after I left here with Jed the other night and things got a little heated between us, but you already know that," Leo begins, his cheeks puffing out as he blows out a frustrated breath of air.

Actually, I didn't know that. Not exactly. I was just getting all fired up over Bald Knob gossip and letting it mess with my head and second-guessing what's going on between us, but now that he's talking, I'm not about to correct him. Especially if it gets Emma Jo and I off the hook. I mean, it's not like I want Leo to go down for murdering Jed, but he'd clearly be the better choice to lead a gang in prison. I'm a delicate flower, dammit! I'd never survive the first hour.

"I know you were pissed when I got Jed away from here by agreeing to go to the bar with him and talk about my reelection," Leo continues, pausing to glance up at me from under his dark eyelashes.

Son of a bitch if it isn't yet another adorable thing he does that makes me want to take back what I said about his lips and re-add him to my call list, STAT, because this strong, gorgeous hunk of a man that could crush me like a nut suddenly looks nervous and worried.

I stay strong, keeping my legs rooted in place a few feet away from him, lacing the fingers of my hands together down in front of me. Hopefully to Leo, it looks like I'm as calm as a cucumber when what I'm really doing is praying as close to my vagina as possible so she doesn't betray me and make me fall for whatever bullshit he's going to spew.

"Anyway, I know we haven't seen each other in over a decade, and everything you know about me is left over from when we were teenagers, but please believe me when I tell you that I would never, *ever* jeopardize my career or put anyone in this town at risk because some pompous asshole with a God complex thinks he can blackmail me," Leo says, his voice getting deeper and angrier as he speaks. "I told you I had an idea of what he'd been doing to Emma Jo, and I told you that it killed me I couldn't do anything about it. I wasn't lying to you when I said that, Payton. I swear to God."

I nod in understanding, losing the will to argue with him when I see the look of conviction in his eyes and hear the truth in his words when he talks about being helpless with Emma Jo for so long. I've only spent a few days with Emma Jo after finding out what Jed did to her, and I've wanted to scream and cry and bang my head against the wall with all the guilt I've been feeling and what-ifs I've been asking myself. I can't imagine how I would feel right now if I'd kept in touch with her all these years and knew what was going on, but couldn't stop it. I don't want to think about how horrible Leo must have felt, being the sheriff of Bald Knob, sworn to protect everyone in this town and not being able to do a damn thing to save one of his friends.

Suddenly, the idea that I made out with a maybe-murderer last night doesn't seem like a bad thing at all. And not just because it would let me and Emma Jo off the hook, but because I've tasted a small bite of that anger and frustration and it only took a few hours for me to start plotting Jed's death, threaten to choke him with his own balls and then bake him a poisoned blueberry pie.

For twelve years Leo has stood on the sidelines feeling like this every single time he got a tip that

Emma Jo was in the hospital, or ran into her on the street in her dark sunglasses and caked on make-up, or listened to her give some sort of excuse about the bruises on her arms or the split in her lip. I suddenly don't care if he turned up the charm to stop me from asking any questions. I don't care if he kissed me so I'd forget about being pissed at him for acting like he was Jed's pal and shooting the shit with him over beers after he'd assaulted me. The only thing I care about now is making sure Leo and I are on the same page: No matter what happened that night, we will make sure Emma Jo stays as far away from accusations as possible and can finally have the happy, peaceful life she's always deserved.

"Stop. You don't have to say anything else," I whisper, moving quickly to stand in front of him, placing my hand over top of his to stop him from nervously rubbing the battered skin of his knuckles. "I don't care what you did with Jed when you left here, and I don't care what happened later that night. No matter what happens, I just want Emma Jo safe and left completely out of this. I promise I won't say anything to anyone."

He finally lifts his head to look at me, shaking it slowly with a low chuckle.

"And you honestly thought it wasn't possible for me to have a thing for you after all this time?" he asks softly, sliding his hands around my waist to rest against my lower back, pulling me closer until I can smell him again and feel the heat from. "This is why, Payton. Because you put your life on hold to fly home and help out a friend you hadn't seen since high school after one phone call. Because you'd do anything to protect her, including let this town rip you to shreds. Because you were always nice to me in school and stuck up for me when most of the guys thought it would be fun to pick on the dorky FFA kid who knew too much about cows. But mostly, because you didn't hesitate to offer your help to me, too. The nerdy guy from high school who followed you around like a pathetic puppy dog, just trying to get a whiff of your hair or a smile in my direction, and who acted like a nerd all over again when I let it slip that I haven't been able to get you off my mind for twelve years, no matter how hard I tried."

I swallow over the lump in my throat and silently tell my ovaries to stop blowing noise makers and throwing confetti.

"I know you don't believe it, Payton, but there hasn't been one day that's gone by that I haven't thought about you since you moved to Chicago. I joined the police force because I wanted to be bigger and better and not so much of a loser if you ever came back to town," he admits, clenching the material of my shirt at my lower back into his fists as he pulls me closer until my chest is pressed against his. "I know it's crazy, and I know it probably scares the shit out of you, but I *have* been dreaming about you and what I would say to you and what I would do if you ever walked back into my life and I got a second chance to make another impression on you."

His hands let go of their hold on the back of my shirt and he moves them up between us, cupping my face in his palms and lowering his voice. "I know it's crazy and I know it's fast, but honestly, I don't give a fuck. As soon as I heard you were back in town, I knew it would be the only chance I'd get to make sure you never forgot who I was again," he admits, running his thumbs back and forth over the skin of my cheeks while he stares into my eyes.

"I'm pretty sure your name is going to be burned into my brain for the rest of my life, don't worry about that," I whisper, while my ovaries crank up the volume on their house party and Leo starts moving his face closer to mine. "I'll totally cover for you, too. Shit, people already think you knocked me up, I can just tell them we spent the night together or something. Boom! There's your alibi! But just in case, I promise to come visit you in prison if this doesn't work out. I'll teach you everything I know about joining a gang and making sure you're always the guy with the most packs of smokes."

Leo stops moving when his mouth is a centimeter from mine, quickly pulling back to look down at me in puzzlement.

"Why would you need to cover for me or visit me in prison? You don't think *I* killed Jed, do you?" he asks, pulling his face back more so he can get a better look at my own, which probably mirrors his *What-in-the-actual-fuck* expression.

"I mean, you kind of admitted it, didn't you? You have those bruises and cuts on your knuckles and you said things got heated between you guys, and then Andrea Maynard told me at The Hungry Bear this morning that Jed had a black eye when you guys found his body, and you got all sweet and mushy when I told you I'd help you. What am I missing here?" I ask.

"You're missing the fact that I didn't fucking kill anyone!" Leo shouts, dropping his hands from my face to step back from me and pace in the small hallway. "When I said things got heated, I meant that I followed behind him to the bar just to get him away from here, and then I punched him in the face as soon as we got to the parking lot and got out of our vehicles. And when you said you'd help me, I just thought you meant covering for me about the bruises on my knuckles, but I already signed a statement about what went down that night. Jesus, Payton, you thought I killed him?"

Oh, shit.

"Um, just kidding?" I reply in a weak, tiny voice.

"Here I've been thinking you were avoiding me all day because *you* had something to do with Jed's death, especially after how fucking insane you and Emma Jo were acting last night. And instead, you just sat around assuming *I'm* the one who killed him!" he complains, throwing his hands up in the air in frustration.

"Hey! We don't *act* insane, we ARE insane. It's a

gift, and it's taken a hell of a lot of years to perfect. Also, I didn't just sit around all day. I spit on a dog, stole some coffee, and started dating Billy Ray. My plate has been entirely too full to avoid you just because I may or may not have thought you killed Jed, thank you very much! And didn't you just get done reminding me that I haven't seen you in over a decade and might not know very much about you? Well, how was I supposed to know you weren't a murderer?!" I argue, leaving out the part about how Emma Jo and I decided to do our own investigation.

"BO JANGLES DID IT IN THE KITCHEN WITH A SHOVEL, MUSKRAT!" Emma Jo suddenly yells from down the hall. "EVERYONE GETS A MUSKRAT WHEN WE SOLVE THE CASE!"

Son of a bitch…

"Please, for the love of God, tell me you two aren't conducting your own investigation…" Leo trails off, looking up at the ceiling in annoyance while he speaks.

"Fine, I won't tell you that," I reply, crossing my arms in front of me and shooting him a sarcastic smile.

He opens his mouth a few times to say something, each time clamping it quickly closed and trying again until his cell phone starts buzzing from his back pocket. He yanks it out, reads the text, and then shoves it back in his jeans without saying a word since I've clearly rendered him speechless, before turning and walking to the door.

"I'll be back. At least promise me you'll leave Bo

Jangles alone while I'm gone," Leo mutters as he yanks the door open and walks out onto the porch.

"I make no promises! That little asshole is at the top of our suspect list!" I shout to his retreating back before closing the door behind me and locking the deadbolt.

CHAPTER 22

Recorded Interview
June 4, 2016
Bald Knob, KY Police Department

Chrissy Lou Smith: Where is Sheriff Hudson?
Why isn't he doing this interview?

Deputy Lloyd: He's otherwise detained,
ma'am.

Chrissy Lou Smith: He's shacked up with
that murderer, isn't he?

   Crying, sniffling, nose-blowing

Deputy Lloyd: Ma'am, I was told you have
some information about Jed Jackson's
murder, is that true?

Chrissy Lou Smith: Do you think it's
serious? I mean, do you think they'll
really get married?

Deputy Lloyd: Ma'am, I need you to focus,
okay? One of the deputies said you left a

message about Mayor Jackson, which is why
I called you in here today.

Chrissy Lou Smith: Did you know Payton owes
over $150 in library fines? What kind of
an animal keeps a copy of The Outsiders
for twelve years and never returns it? A
murderer, that's who. You should arrest
her.

Deputy Lloyd: Ma'am, I can't arrest someone
because of library fines. Especially when
we're trying to solve a murder.

Chrissy Lou Smith: Stealing books is a
crime and no one is doing anything about
it! You should arrest her, but make sure
it's tomorrow after five o'clock.

Deputy Lloyd: And why should I wait until
after five o'clock?

Chrissy Lou Smith: Because I have a facial
peel scheduled at four, and I want to look
my best when Sheriff Hudson needs a
shoulder to cry on. Do you think I'd look
better as a blonde? The sheriff seems to
go for blondes these days…

CHAPTER 23

*Let's take a moment and think if I'm a
morning person...NO.*
—Coffee Mug

"SWEET MOTHER OF pearl, how many green bean casseroles does one person need?"

Rubbing my tired eyes with my fists, I stand in the doorway of the kitchen, blinking rapidly and vowing to never drink wine again, especially when I can't get rid of my hangover with coffee the next morning. I've officially started hallucinating and I think I see Bettie standing in front of Emma Jo's open refrigerator, shaking her head while she lifts the foil covering a baking dish, scrunches up her face in disgust and turns to look at me.

"Jesus, you look like shit. One little murder accusation and you let yourself go."

My eyes widen in shock when I realize I'm not seeing things and Bettie really is standing in Emma Jo's kitchen, looking me up and down with a wince.

"I've had a rough couple of days, I guess," I admit with a shrug.

"Don't worry, Mommy is here and I brought help," Bettie informs me, lifting her arm and pointing to something on the counter I didn't notice when I first walked in here.

"Oh, my God! You brought Baby Cecil!" I shout, racing across the room and throwing my arms around the smaller version of the Cecilware Venzia espresso machine that I have in my house. "My baby, I've missed you so much. You have no idea how hard it's been here without you."

I rub my cheek against the cool metal of the machine and pepper the top with kisses, my eyes filling with tears when I turn away from Baby Cecil and smile at Bettie. A flash of fear covers her face right before I race across the room, throwing myself into her arms. She awkwardly pats me on the back while I cry into her shoulder until she finally has enough and pulls out of my tight hold.

"Alright, you're creeping me out. We're not huggers. We've never been huggers. What did I miss since our last phone call?" she asks, moving back against the kitchen counter and pulling herself up on top of it while I busy myself making both of us a cup of coffee with the Kona beans Bettie also brought with her.

It's been…shit, three days since I spoke to Bettie on the phone, and I can't believe I forgot all about how she never called me back and told me who left her that voice mail. I've been a little preoccupied trying to figure out who else in this town could be responsible for murder, aside from me and Emma Jo. I've also been a little distracted by Leo, not that I've seen him other than from a distance in town while I attempted to get people to talk to me. At least he's been sending me texts. Mostly just one-word ones like *STOP, DON'T,* and *PAYTON,* sent to me each time he saw me in town trying to get people to stop pointing their fingers at me. I mean, what does he expect me to do, sit around and wait for him to solve this case? As if. Not that I don't think he's a smart guy and could do it, I just think he's *too* smart and I'd much rather find someone else to blame before he gets those stupid autopsy reports back and has to do something about all that pesky gossip floating around about me.

Gossip my mother has kindly kept me up-to-date about since Franny Mendleson is a secretary at the sheriff's department and Franny Mendleson and my mother play Bridge together every week. I guess according to Bald Knob, you really can't outrun your past, since everyone in town has been talking non-stop during their interviews about what a horrible teenager I was and how it only makes sense I'd gravitate from underage drinking to first-degree murder.

I ramble all of this to Bettie in one long, run-on sentence, not stopping to take a breath until I get it out and start crying all over again when Baby Cecil spits out the most delicious smelling liquid I've ever been in the presence of and I bring the cup up to my lips.

"Alright, seriously, suck it up. All this crying and

snotting all over the place is giving me hives. It's not like you *actually* killed the guy. Who cares if a few people think you did?" Bettie asks, ripping a paper towel off the roll and handing it to me so I can blow my nose. "And you've got a hot piece of man meat who practically professed his undying love to you. I don't see what the problem is."

I wipe the tears from my cheeks, moving over to the fridge and opening the door with my cup of coffee hugged tightly to my chest, refusing to ever let it go.

"Wow, we really do have a lot of food in here. People have been bringing it by non-stop for the last couple of days. I could go for some macaroni and cheese, how about you?" I ask Bettie, keeping my back to her and my head shoved in between trays of cold-cuts and pans of mystery casseroles.

"Payton Marie Lambert, what are you not telling me?" Bettie asks, jumping down off the counter and walking over to me to yank me out of the fridge and slam the door closed.

She takes one look at my face and smacks me on the arm. "Holy shit, did you really murder the guy? Damn, bitch! I didn't think you had it in you!"

"This is not funny," I argue when she laughs. "Before we get into all of that, how about you tell me what you're doing here. Oh, my God, what happened to Liquid Crack? Did it catch on fire? Did the health department shut us down? Did the investors find out about what's going on here in Bald Knob and change their minds about the franchise?"

Bettie grabs my arm and pulls me over to one of the kitchen chairs, shoving me down into it and then pushing the coffee cup back up to my mouth.

"Drink, Payton, drink. Liquid Crack is fine. The news from this bustling metropolis hasn't yet reached Chicago, you're fine," she replies sarcastically. "I left Brad and Amy in charge of the store for a few days. That voicemail the other day was from some guy named Deputy Lloyd and he said he had a few questions to ask me about you. I figured it was best if I flew into town and saved him the trouble of repeatedly calling my phone and me not answering it because I didn't recognize the number."

"You left Brad and Amy in charge of my baby? The two potheads who keep trying to convince me that pot coffee is the wave of the future and take three hours to make one cup of coffee?!" I screech.

"Slow your roll, psycho. Do you honestly think I'd leave the shop if I thought they couldn't handle it?" Bettie explains. "They know what they're doing, it's fine. Also, I love how you're more concerned with Liquid Crack than you are about the possibility that you might seriously go to prison for murder."

"Oh, good, you're awake!" Emma Jo says as she walks into the room with a tray of cookies in her hand and gives me a smile. "I was going to come up and wake you, but then someone came to the door with more food and I got delayed."

She sets the cookies down on the table in front of me and Bettie takes a handful before flopping down next to me in a chair.

"This one's a saint, I tell you," Bettie announces, pointing at Emma Jo with a cookie. "I've been listening to her deal with bullshit condolences since I got here an hour ago. All those people saying how wonderful your husband was and how big of a loss his death is. Give me a break!"

I look back and forth between Bettie and Emma Jo nervously, not quite sure how Emma Jo is going to feel about me spilling the beans about Jed's abuse to someone she doesn't know.

"It's fine," Emma Jo reassures me, taking the last empty chair on the other side of me. "Bettie and I talked a little bit in between knocks on the door. I like her."

"You *should* like me. I'm awesome. So, what are we going to do about Payton beating this murder rap? Has she tried sleeping with the sheriff yet?" Bettie asks, spitting cookie crumbs across the table while she speaks.

"Sadly, no. I've tried pushing her in that direction as well, but the last three days they've been like two ships, passing in the night," Emma Jo muses, grabbing a cookie from the tray and taking a bite.

"Well, he's busy trying to gather evidence against her, I can see how that would make blackmail sex a little tricky. We need another plan," Bettie nods.

"Hello? I'm sitting right here," I complain, waving my hands in front of both of their cookie-stuffed faces.

"We know. And yet, you're still the town's number one suspect and not even a twelve-year-long wet dream is going to stop the sheriff from arresting the responsible party. Although, with the way Benjamin won't disappear, I'm assuming you have a magical vagina, so that sex thing needs to stay on the table for now," Bettie says with a point of her cookie at me.

"She's had a very eventful couple of days," Emma Jo explains, patting the top of my hand.

"Yeah, I heard all about you throwing down with Bo Jangles when Starla accosted me in the driveway as soon as I pulled in. That little ball of fur is adorable. I can't believe you were mean to him," Bettie chastises.

"You are officially off my Christmas card list."

"I'll be back on it when you hear what I have to tell you," Bettie replies with a smile, turning to look at Emma Jo. "Who's Roy Pickerson? I was told this Roy guy got into a fight with your dearly departed husband a few weeks ago."

"Roy owns Pickerson's Bar. How in the hell did YOU hear about this fight?" I ask in annoyance.

"I stopped at the Gas N Sip on my way here to get a Pepsi and the guy who owns the place told me about it," Bettie explains with a shrug, grabbing another cookie and taking a sip of her coffee, like it's no big deal Mo Wesley opened up to a complete stranger just passing through town.

"Seriously? I was born and raised here and no one will give me the time of day. You're here for five minutes and Mo is spilling secrets," I complain, drinking more of my coffee before my head explodes.

"Well, you shouldn't steal coffee from him, he doesn't like that very much. Also, I was quite pleasant and smiley and that makes people want to talk to me. You should try it sometime," she mocks. "Plus, it probably helped that I pretended like I didn't know you and said I was an old friend of Emma Jo's. Everyone loves Emma Jo in this town. When I told him this Payton Lambert character sounded kind of sketchy, I couldn't get the guy to shut up."

"You are the worst friend ever," I grumble, glaring at Emma Jo when she laughs.

"Do you want me to tell you the rest about Roy or not? Apologize and tell me I'm pretty," Bettie demands, folding her hands together on top of the table and staring me down until I begrudgingly comply.

"I'm sorry and you're really pretty," I mutter.

"There, that wasn't so hard now was it?" Bettie asks, grabbing her coffee cup and leaning back in her chair. "So, Roy Pickerson of Pickerson's bar has a son who will be turning sixteen at the end of the summer, correct?"

Emma Jo and I nod and she continues.

"Right, so I guess Caden has been applying to take college courses next school year. He needed a letter of recommendation and good old Roy took it upon himself to ask everyone's favorite mayor, since Caden has been mowing your lawn and pulling your weeds for the last few years," Bettie explains with a nod in Emma Jo's direction.

"Yes, he has. He does such a great job, too. He's always here first thing in the morning, every three days like clockwork, even during the school year when he comes on the weekends," Emma Jo explains.

"Right, well according to your husband, Caden didn't mow the lawn in the correct direction and that doesn't show good work ethics, so he refused to write the letter. Roy Pickerson was NOT a happy man," Bettie finishes.

"You have got to be kidding me?" Emma Jo complains with a shake of her head.

"Are you really shocked at this point that you were married to a douchebag?" Bettie questions her.

"No, I guess not."

Bettie smacks her palms down on the table.

"Alright, bitches, Bettie is here, and it's time for me to work my magic. The entire town is crying in the streets like Jesus died and pointing their fingers in Payton's direction because she's like a stranger to them and they don't trust her," Bettie states. "Your to-do list now includes *Make Nice with the Townsfolk*."

"How in the hell am I supposed to do that when no one will talk to me?" I question in irritation.

"Try not abusing any more dogs or complaining about the town you grew up in. You've been telling me since I met you how much you hate this place and how you never wanted to come back. Well, now you're back, and as you've always said, word travels fast in Bald Knob," Bettie reminds me. "These people know you don't want to be here, and they can sense how uncomfortable you are being back here. Instead of grilling them on the streets, try being nice. Ask about what they've been doing since you were gone and get to know them as people and not as suspects on your murder list."

I want to be offended by Bettie's words, but she's absolutely right. I've been miserable since I got here because I felt like I'd outgrown this town and the people in it. Then I rekindled my friendship with Emma Jo, hung out with my parents, kissed Leo, and had hours and hours of dirty thoughts about him. I kept complaining about all the things I missed and left behind in Chicago, when I should have been concentrating on all the things I missed *here*, where I grew up and where all of my best memories came from.

"Fine, you're right. I'll do better at being nice to people," I reply with a sigh.

"I'm sorry, I couldn't hear you. Can you say that again, maybe a little louder?" Bettie requests, holding one hand up by her ear and leaning over the table toward me.

"Don't make me have Emma Jo bake you a blueberry pie," I growl under my breath.

"Okay, I'd like to add something to the to-do list,"

Emma Jo says in a quiet voice. "I'm going to come clean about my marriage and tell everyone about Jed's abuse so people finally know that he wasn't as good of a guy as they thought he was."

"No! Not even *no,* but HELL-TO-THE-NO!" I argue.

"Payton, she has a good point. If people find out what Jed's been doing to her all these years, they're going to be sympathetic to that and stop trying to throw you in prison," Bettie adds.

"I said no, and that's final. I love you Emma Jo, but I'm not going to let you do that. You hid it for all of these years for a reason, and I'm not going to stand by and watch you spill all of your secrets and humiliations and relive all of those horrible memories so everyone will have something else to gossip about."

Emma Jo's eyes fill with tears and I reach over and grab her hand, giving it a squeeze.

"I wasn't a very good friend to you for twelve years. Let me at least have this so I can stop feeling like such an asshole, okay?"

We sit staring at each other silently for a few minutes until Emma Jo finally nods and swipes away the tears that fell down her cheeks.

"Okay, fine. You give me no choice but to bump your magical vagina up to the top of the to-do list," Bettie informs me, pulling out her phone from the front pocket of her cut-off jean shorts and tapping away at the screen.

"What are you doing?" I ask while she bites her bottom lip and concentrates on whatever she's doing.

"Give me a minute. Genius takes time."

After a few more taps on the screen, she puts the phone on the table and slides in across to me.

"Hey! That was MY phone! What did you do?" I ask in a panic, opening up all of my apps to see what I can find.

"Calm down, sweet tits. I booked a night at a spa in Louisville for me and Emma Jo tonight so you can have some alone time with the sheriff and rub that voodoo vagina magic all over him without worrying about being interrupted. Cast your spell and maybe he won't arrest you," Bettie suggests with a smile. "Don't worry, I already sent a text to that fine man and told him what's up."

I quickly open up the text messaging app and groan when I see the outgoing text Bettie sent to Leo from my phone.

"Bring your sweet ass over tonight at seven. Clothing optional," I read out loud.

"Hey, leave your phone unattended without a lock code and suffer the consequences," Bettie shrugs, pushing her chair back from the table and crooking her elbow for Emma Jo to take.

"Come on, Emma Jo, we've got a night of pampering to pack for, and Payton needs at least seven hours to shave her pits and weed whack her legs."

Emma Jo giggles and gives me a sheepish smile

when she stands up and grabs Bettie's outstretched elbow, letting Bettie pull her out of the kitchen.

"YOU ARE BOTH DEAD TO ME!" I shout.

"Then this is me, speaking from beyond the grave when I remind you to trim your bush while you're at it. No man needs to choke on a hairball!" Bettie yells back from down the hall.

CHAPTER 24

Recorded Interview
June 5, 2016
Bald Knob, KY Police Department

Deputy Lloyd: Have you been in contact with
Payton Lambert since the night of May
31st?

Benjamin Montgomery: Of course I've been in
contact with my fiancée.

Deputy Lloyd: Your fiancée?

Benjamin Montgomery: Yes. We're getting
married!

Deputy Lloyd: So you've spoken to her since
she arrived in Bald Knob?

Benjamin Montgomery: Yes, of course. She's
my fiancée and we've been planning our
wedding. Do you happen to know where the
Brooks Brothers is in Bald Knob? I need to
get a pair of pants tailored while I'm
here.

Deputy Lloyd: Um, we don't have a Brooks Brothers.

Benjamin Montgomery: You don't have a Brooks Brothers?! What kind of a third-world town is this?

Deputy Lloyd: Sir, can you tell me how Payton behaved when you spoke to her? Was she angry? Did she say anything about an altercation with someone in town?

Benjamin Montgomery: She was deliriously happy, obviously, because we're getting married.

Deputy Lloyd: Yes, you said that already.

Benjamin Montgomery: What about sushi? What's the sushi situation here? I haven't had a decent tuna roll in two days.

Deputy Lloyd: We don't have any sushi restaurants in Bald Knob, we just have The Hungry Bear. They make a great meatloaf on Mondays and you can't beat the omelets for breakfast.

Benjamin Montgomery: Do they make kale-and-egg-white omelets?

Deputy Lloyd: Uh, I don't think so. What's kale?

<u>Benjamin Montgomery:</u> What's kale? How do you people even survive here?!

<u>Deputy Lloyd:</u> Mr. Montgomery, can you tell me anything else Payton might have said to you in the last few days about the town or people who live here?

<u>Benjamin Montgomery:</u> We only discussed our wedding. And she clearly left out the fact that this town is on the verge of falling apart. No Brooks Brothers, no sushi, and no kale? This is what Hell is like, isn't it?

CHAPTER 25

My plan for today? Same as always. Drink coffee and be sexy.

—Coffee Mug

"YOU LOOK FINE, stop fussing with your hair," Bettie scolds, leaning against the wall, watching me check my reflection in the hallway mirror for the tenth time.

"I look stupid. This is stupid. I'm going to text Leo and tell him I'm sick," I state, pulling my phone out of the back pocket of my short jean skirt, that I've wisely added a lock code to since this morning.

Bettie lunges for me and snatches the phone out of my hand.

"If you tell him you're sick, I'll tell him it's with herpes. You are not cancelling," she warns me.

"Give me back my phone!" I demand, holding my hand out to her.

"Promise me you won't cancel or you're getting herpes ALL over the place. In every nook and cranny and even in your ears. SAY IT!"

"Ugggh, FINE! I won't cancel. But this is still stupid," I complain when she hands me back my phone.

"It's not stupid. I'm an evil genius and my plans always work," she informs me when Emma Jo comes out into the hall and whistles.

"Wow, you look hot!"

I nervously run my hands down the front of the tattered jean skirt that Bettie brought with her and forced me to wear, telling me all of the clothes I packed were too stuffy and not "Bald Knob" enough. She wouldn't even let me put on heels, grabbing the teal pair of strappy stilettos that perfectly matched my top out of my hands and tossing them across the room, informing me barefoot and casual was the way to a man like Leo's heart.

"I hope there isn't a need for me to bend over at any point tonight or this short scrap of material will ride up and put my lady bits on display," I mutter, turning around and looking over my shoulder at my ass.

"I think that's kind of the point, isn't it?" Emma Jo questions.

"You'll have to forgive Payton, she's not very experienced when it comes to the art of seduction," Bettie laughs.

"Hey, I take pride in the fact that I didn't lose my virginity until college, and I can count on one hand how many men I've slept with," I reply indignantly.

"You only need half a hand to add up that list," Bettie reminds me.

"I only need one finger," Emma Jo adds sadly.

"Jesus, you two need to get out more. You're so lucky you have me," Bettie says with a smile.

Seriously, if there's a list somewhere of worst ideas in the history of the world, trying to seduce Leo and distract him from the things I haven't told him and keep him occupied with something other than digging deeper into this case is probably right there at the top of it. I've slept with exactly two and a half men. The guy I lost my virginity to in college who lasted five seconds and then rolled over and went to sleep, a guy I drunkenly let go down on me right after college who *I* then rolled over and went to sleep on, and Benjamin. Who wouldn't have sex unless both of us showered immediately beforehand and refused to get sweaty during the act, which always had to happen in bed, before eight o'clock when Anderson Cooper came on. Let's just say hot, wild, spur-of-the-moment sex is something I have zero knowledge of. Not that tonight is spur-of-the-moment since it's sort of planned and I've had entirely too much time to freak out about it, but going by how Leo kisses and talks and touches me, I'm pretty confident in the fact that hot and wild will be included on tonight's menu.

If I don't screw it up, start thinking about goat anus, giggle, or dwell on how much of an awful person I'll be by doing this. He's flat out told me he's had a thing for me for twelve years and that he only went into law enforcement because of me, and now I'm going to use him for sex.

It's official. I'm going to hell.

"Are you sure this top is okay? It's a little tight," I complain, tugging up the low-cut neckline of my ocean blue tank top with the Liquid Crack logo right over my boobs. "I didn't realize when I ordered these to sell at the store that they were so…slutty."

Bettie smacks my hands away from fiddling with the tank top, grabs the hem and pulls it down until there's so much of my cleavage showing that I'll have a nip-slip if I sneeze.

"Bend over and pull those puppies up higher," she instructs, pointing at my chest.

With a sigh, I do as she says, bending at the waist and sliding my hands into the cups of my bra to pull my boobs out more. When I stand back up and hold my arms out, Bettie studies me for a minute, fluffs up my hair I let air-dry in long beach waves, takes a loop around me, and stops when she's back in front of me.

"You'll do," she says with a nod.

"Gee, I feel much better now."

Emma Jo comes over and pats me on the back.

"You look sexy and gorgeous. Leo isn't going to be able to keep his hands off you, which will make your job much easier. And really, it's not like it's an *actual* job. You like him, right? You think he's hot, his kisses turn you into a puddle of goo, and he really, really likes you, Payton. This is going to be a good thing. I just know it."

I smile at Emma Jo's encouragement and start to feel a little calmer until there's a knock at the door. Bettie and Emma Jo grab their overnight bags and Bettie pauses with her hand on the doorknob.

"By any chance have you checked Facebook lately?" she asks innocently.

"No, not in about a week, I guess. I've been a little busy," I remind her with a pointed glare.

"I might have updated your status with a tag in Bald Knob that says *Barefoot and pregnant and ridiculously in love in Kentucky*," she informs me.

"You didn't!"

"Good luck tonight! Kisses!" she exclaims without answering, blowing me a kiss as she opens the door, the devious smile on her face immediately falling when she comes face-to-face with Leo on the front porch.

"Sweet Jesus, I think *I* just got pregnant," she mutters as she looks him up and down.

"I'm sorry, what?" Leo asks, leaning in to try and hear her better.

"Nothing, they were just leaving," I speak through clenched teeth, quickly moving forward to open the door wider and gesture with my arm for Emma Jo to leave as Leo moves to the side to give her room.

With Bettie's eyes still glued to Leo's body, she stumbles over the threshold when I shove her out the door right behind Emma Jo, pausing behind him to make hip thrusting motions and throw up a few fist pumps.

Leo whips his head around when he sees me staring behind him and Bettie quickly stands up straight and gives him a salute.

"The name's Bettie Lake. Don't let the tats fool you. I'm not as sweet and innocent as I look. I'm a raging bitch and I will cut you if you hurt Payton. Too-da-loo!" she says with a wide smile, giving Leo a finger-wave as she grabs Emma Jo's arm and pulls her across the porch and down the steps.

"Have fun, kids! No wild parties and lights out by midnight. Mommy and Mommy will be back tomorrow!" Bettie adds with a wave over her shoulder, Emma Jo looking back to give me a smile and a thumb's up.

When they get into Bettie's rental car and she starts it up, I move back into the house and hold the door open for Leo. He's wearing his usual non-work uniform of jeans and a t-shirt and just like every time I see him, my heart flutters in my chest and I want to get down on my knees and thank his parents for passing down those excellent genes. You know, after all those awkward teenage years.

"I'm glad you messaged me. I was going to stop by tonight anyway if I didn't hear from you," Leo tells me when I close the door behind him and lean my back against it.

"In the spirit of full disclosure, I should probably let you know I didn't send the text, Bettie did. And she was drunk. She drinks a lot. I think she might have a problem and need an intervention," I ramble nervously.

Leo moves to stand in front of me, leaning closer to press his palms against the door on either side of my head, caging me in. My heart thunders in my chest, and I'm suddenly thankful Bettie wouldn't let me wear shoes. I would have toppled over and made a fool of myself by now.

"I think *you* were drunk and now you don't want to admit you said I have a sweet ass," he retorts, one corner of his mouth tipping up in a smile as he looks down at me.

"I have no problem saying that," I scoff, rolling my eyes and laughing uncomfortably.

"So you DO think I have a sweet ass."

He's giving me the full power of his smile now, and all I can do is stare at his lips while the smell of his woodsy cologne surrounds me and makes my knees weak.

"You're annoying," I whisper, tipping my head back to look up at his eyes.

He brings the lower half of his body forward until its pressed right up against me, and with his arms still pinning me in against the door, I wouldn't be able to move away if I wanted to.

"And you've been avoiding me. Again. We need to talk about what's going on, Payton. If you know something about what happened with Jed, you need to tell me. I can't let you keep going around town questioning people," he speaks softly.

There's no bite to his voice; it's just calm and sweet and it doesn't raise my hackles when he tells me he can't *let* me do something, like it normally would. Without overthinking it, I grab the front of his shirt, push up on my toes, and pull his mouth down to mine. He immediately takes charge, slipping his tongue past my lips and I moan softly into his mouth when his tongue moves against mine.

His hands slide down the door next to my body and then he wraps his arms around me, pulling me up and against him as he deepens the kiss. The way he works his mouth against mine is magical and perfection, and it makes me forget the world around me. I lift one of my legs and wrap it around his thigh, drawing his hips closer to mine as I slide my hands up his chest and twine my arms around his neck.

Leo keeps an anchoring hold on my body with one arm, pulling his other hand forward around my waist. I gasp into his mouth when he moves his palm upward and it glides over my ribcage, so close to my breasts that they start to tingle and ache to feel his hands on them. He keeps moving his hand up, pausing with it right over my heart, then continues up across my neck until he's holding my cheek in his palm, keeping my head in place while he tortures me with his kiss. I match each swipe of his tongue through my mouth, throwing all my nerves out the window as I kiss him back until it's his turn to groan in pleasure.

Suddenly, he jerks his mouth away from mine and a

quiet whimper of need and frustration escapes me. His hand is still holding my face as he looks down at me, both of us panting like we just ran a marathon.

"Question. Are you trying to distract me with sex?" he asks in between breaths.

I wait for the guilt to overwhelm me as I look up at him, but it never comes, because I realize I *don't* want to use him for sex. I don't care about distracting him or keeping him busy, I just really, really want to have sex with him. Because of *him* and how he makes me feel, not to avoid possible jail time. But I don't need to tell him that. No need for me to give him the upper hand too soon.

"I don't know, is it working?" I ask in a breathy voice I don't recognize, nothing at all like the sarcastic one I imagined using in my head.

Leo brings his head back down and teases me, the feel of his lips like a breath of air as he just barely touches them against mine and moves them ever so slowly back and forth, until I'm so out of my mind with wanting him to kiss me again that I almost scream.

"I don't know," he whispers. "Are you going to get a case of the giggles again when I touch your ass?"

I smile against his mouth and remove one of my arms from around his neck, reach behind me and grab onto the hand of his arm that's wrapped around my waist. I tug it down and smack it against my ass, keeping my hand over top of his to hold it in place.

Taking my other arm off his shoulder, I reach up to

his hand that's still holding my cheek, place mine over top of his again and slide it down my neck and collarbone until he's cupping my breast in his palm. Leo lets out a groan and presses his forehead against mine.

"Ass, check. Boobs, check. All systems go with no signs of giggling in the near future," I reassure him softly, arching my back and pushing myself harder into the palm of his hand when he starts swiping the pad of his thumb over my nipple.

He moves his head back to look down at me once again and I wonder if he can hear how loudly my heart is beating against my chest. I wonder if he knows that no one has ever lit my body on fire the way he does and how no one has ever made me want something so badly that my body literally aches with it.

"Remember that comment I made the other day when I first kissed you, about ruining you for any other man that comes after me?" Leo asks, his hand moving out from under mine against my ass to slide down my thigh, and then come right back up under my skirt until he's palming my cheek with his bare hand.

I nod, unable to speak when he's squeezing and rubbing my naked ass and his thumb is still sliding back and forth over my nipple, driving me crazy even through a thin layer of cotton and the lace of my bra.

"Don't forget the words I said, because I wasn't fucking kidding," he growls, slamming his mouth against mine.

CHAPTER 26

Recorded Interview
June 5, 2016
Bald Knob, KY Police Department

Deputy Lloyd: I don't feel comfortable
doing this.

Sheriff Hudson: Too bad. I already typed up
my official statement, but you still need
to interview me and make sure nothing gets
screwed up with this investigation. We
don't need a lawsuit on our hands on top
of everything else.

Deputy Lloyd: Fine. Well, I had Franny make
another copy of the questions the County
Commissioner's office faxed over since it
came through kind of dark, so we should be
able to wrap this up pretty quickly. First
question, in your written statement, you
stated you had an altercation with Mayor
Jackson on the night he died. Is that
true?

Sheriff Hudson: Yes. We were outside
Pickerson's Bar after I escorted him from
the Jackson's property, where I witnessed
him assaulting Payton Lambert. I was angry
and it was unprofessional, but I punched
him in the face and told him if he ever
went near Payton or Emma Jo again, I'd
make sure he spent the rest of his life in
prison. We parted ways, I went back to the
Jackson's residence to keep an eye on the
house, and I didn't see Jed Jackson again
until his body was discovered the next
morning.

Deputy Lloyd: You were in your department-
issued vehicle the entire night?

Sheriff Hudson: I got out a few times to
take a piss, but other than that, yes. I
was in my vehicle the entire night until I
left at seven the next morning to get
coffee.

Deputy Lloyd: Is it true you… Oh, my God.
What the hell?

Cursing, shuffling papers

Sheriff Hudson: Just ask the question,
Buddy.

Deputy Lloyd: I… shit! I can't ask you

these. I just…what the hell?

Shuffling papers, more cursing

Sheriff Hudson: Buddy, just ask the questions! Jesus…

Deputy Lloyd: Fine! Is it true you knocked up Payton Lambert and you've already applied for conjugal visits when she goes to prison?

Sheriff Hudson: Are you kidding me right now?

Deputy Lloyd: That's what it says right here! I'm just asking the questions on the paper.

Sheriff Hudson: No comment. Next question.

Deputy Lloyd: Is it true you were going to ask Chrissy Lou out on a date before that home-wrecker came back to town and ruined everything? Oh shit…

Sheriff Hudson: There's no way that's a question from the County Commissioner's office.

Deputy Lloyd: It's right here on their official letterhead!

<u>Sheriff Hudson:</u> Give me that thing…

Shuffling papers, cursing

Buddy, you need glasses. This isn't the County Commissioner's Letterhead. It says "County Gossip by Franny"

Shuffling papers

<u>Deputy Lloyd:</u> Shit. Maybe I shouldn't ask the rest of them then, huh? Although, I'd really like to know the answer to question 27B - Is it true you've been in love with Payton Lambert since high school?

<u>Sheriff Hudson:</u> This interview is officially over.

CHAPTER 27

*Men are like coffee. The best ones are hot, rich and can
keep you up all night long.*
—Coffee Mug

"**K**EEP YOUR ARMS above your head and don't
move," Leo orders as he kisses his way down
my naked body in the spare bedroom.

After his reminder about ruining me downstairs in
the hallway, Leo got to work pretty quickly on making
that statement a reality. Clothes were shed and strewn
all through Emma Jo's house as we kissed our way to
the stairs, and then he scooped me up into his arms
and carried me up here, tossing me down on the bed in
the dark room and covering my body with his huge,
hot, muscular one.

My hands wrap around the spindles on the headboard above me, gripping them so tightly that I hear
them creak, and silently promise Emma Jo I'll buy her a
new headboard if I happen to rip a few of these things
out.

With the light of a full moon shining through the
bedroom window, I can perfectly see Leo as he moves

down my body, kissing every inch of my skin as he makes his way between my thighs. He glances up at me from under his long lashes after each kiss and the hungry look in his eyes skyrockets my desire until I can feel the wetness pooling between my legs, an inch away from where is mouth currently hovers.

"Hold on tight, Payton," he whispers, his warm breath puffing against my sex.

I barely have time to do what he says when the sound of a spindle cracking in my hands echoes around the room as soon as I feel his mouth on me.

"Holy shit…" I moan loudly, my back arching and my thighs dropping open wider when he immediately goes to town on me, licking, sucking, and swirling his tongue in just the right spot.

His fingers join his mouth between my legs, pumping in and out of me in sync with the flicking of his tongue. Leo instinctively knows how to touch me, where to touch me, and how fast or slow I need him to move that glorious mouth between my legs, like he's been going down on me all of his life. Or he studied oral sex in college. Got a master's degree in Pleasuring Payton. Graduated top of his class with a Diddling Doctorate. His expert lips and tongue and fingers and the sight of his head between my thighs when I manage to lift my head and look down at him is so damn hot, that the slow tingling build of my orgasm quickly switches gears into an explosion of epic proportions.

The wooden spindle in my right hand finally gives

up the fight, breaking in half with a loud *crack* when my release rushes through me with the speed of a freight train. Leo moans his approval, the sound vibrating against my sex as my head flops back down to the bed and I shout his name while he continues to lick and suck every last drop of my release from my body.

Before I can catch my breath, and without any time to recover from the current ringing in my ears and the pulsing ache between my legs, Leo crawls back up my body, grabs the broken spindle from my clutched fist and tosses it across the room.

"That was a good start. This time, I want to hear you scream my name," he tells me, settling his hard body between my thighs while he laces his fingers through mine and pins my arms to the bed above my head.

I open my mouth to demand he stop ordering me around and try to get back some sort of upper hand since I feel boneless and unable to form a coherent thought, but the only sound that comes out of me is a loud moan when he slams his lips to mine and thrusts himself inside of me at the same time. He's big and he's hard, and even with my recent orgasm, it's a tight fit and it takes a few pushes and pulls before he finally gets all the way in, and then, I give up any idea of trying to get the upper hand with Leo. He can have it all he wants if it feels this good.

His tongue battles mine, he moves his hips slow, he pushes in deep, and I'm so lost in the pleasure of having him inside me and feeling the weight of his body on top of mine that I don't care about anything else. Just like when his mouth was between my legs a few moments ago, he moves in and out of me with the perfect rhythm and hits the perfect spot with each slam of his hips until I'm clutching so tightly to his fingers that still hold my arms above my head that now I'm afraid I might break one of *those* things off, just like I did with the spindle of the headboard.

He keeps kissing me, his tongue swirling deeper the faster he moves between my legs, and I let out a shocked gasp into his mouth when another rushing wave of an orgasm explodes out of me without any warning. No tingling in my toes, no slow traveling up my legs, or quivering in my belly, it hits hard and fast and my body rockets off the bed as I push my hips up to meet Leo's. My sex pulsates and squeezes around him and he rips his mouth from mine so I can follow his orders, screaming his name until my voice gets hoarse.

Leo finally releases my hands as I move the lower half of my body faster and harder against him, wanting nothing more than to feel and hear him reach his own release. He slides his arms under my body and wraps them around me, holding me tightly against him as he buries his face in the side of my neck, drilling himself inside me so hard and fast that he inches us up the bed with each powerful thrust. My hands smack against his back, my fingernails dig into his skin, and I wrap my thighs around his hips and hold on tight until he slams against me one last time, holds himself deep, cursing and moaning my name against the side of my neck as he comes.

Aaaaaand it's official. I'm ruined.

For all other men, women, and most definitely vibrators.

"THIS IS AMAZING. What's it called again?" Leo asks, digging his fork back into the pile on his plate and shoveling in a mouthful.

"It's called slop. I know, not a very appetizing name for breakfast food, but my mom used to always make it and I haven't had it since I moved away. Sounded like a good idea when I woke up," I shrug as I drink my coffee and watch him finish off his second plate.

Slop was a staple in our house growing up and my mom made it every Sunday morning before church. It's basically scrambled eggs, cheese, bacon, sausage and hash browns, all cooked together in a pan and "slopped" onto your plate. After I moved away, I was too busy with school and opening Liquid Crack to have time for anything more than take-out, and then when I met Benjamin, he was a health food nut and dragged me down into *that* pit of hell with him, making me feel guilty any time I so much as looked at a pizza delivery menu or walked by a McDonalds. I didn't realize until I woke up starving this morning just how much I missed greasy, unhealthy food that clogs your arteries and lowers your life expectancy.

Damn, it's good to be home.

"It's fucking amazing, Payton. Not the most delicious thing I've had in my mouth in the last twelve hours, but it'll do," he winks, causing a blush to spread out over my cheeks.

After the first two orgasms Leo gave me, something I'd only read about in books and assumed was a myth like unicorns and leprechauns with pots of gold, we passed out in a tangle of arms and legs until a few hours later when he woke me up by sliding into me from behind and proving another myth true – it's possible for a man to recover quickly and go all night long. Hence, waking up starving and feeling like I could eat a horse. Or two dozen eggs, a slab of bacon, pound of sausage, bag of fried and buttery hash browns, and enough cheese to feed a small country.

I also woke up with enough guilt for that same small country, realizing before the first time we had sex and through all four times after, that I am not a woman who can sleep with a man and keep secrets from him. That fact was made clear when Leo woke me up an hour ago with his head between my legs again. I almost confessed to everything right then and there. Shit, when he kept teasing me with that tongue of his and holding off my orgasm until I thought I was going to black out, I almost confessed to killing Kennedy and knowing where Jimmy Hoffa's body is buried.

I didn't just make slop because I was hungry and knew Leo would like it, I did it to suck up to him in the hopes that a full stomach would make him a little less angry when I told him about the pie and how the rumors and interviews people were giving to the sheriff's office weren't necessarily false.

"Although I will say, I'd enjoy this home-cooked breakfast a little more if you were sitting across from me naked," he says with a smile around another mouthful of food.

"That's just what I need, for a neighbor to walk by and accuse me of breaking another law with public indecency. What I'm wearing is probably cutting it close anyway," I state with a roll of my eyes, thankful I had enough brain activity this morning to at least throw on a pair of tiny black cotton shorts that I usually wear to work out in when I'm in Chicago and a matching black and hot pink Nike t-back tank top.

"Luckily, I'm the sheriff and can make up my own laws. Those shorts are hot and make your ass look amazing, but from now on, it's illegal for you to wear clothes. Go grab my handcuffs from the car, you're under arrest."

I have to rub my thighs together under the table when he brings up the cuffs, and really, he's the one that should be under arrest for wearing nothing at the kitchen table but last night's jeans that hang low on his hips and no shirt. Touching and kissing that massive chest and those cut abs of his the previous night with nothing but the moonlight to guide me is nothing compared to seeing it on full display in Emma Jo's kitchen with the bright morning sun streaming through the windows. Unfortunately, my desire for Leo to use those handcuffs on me is short-lived when I remind myself that if I don't come clean with him right now, he'll be really pissed when he has to use them on me in an extremely boring, non-sexual way.

"Leo, I-"

"Knock, knock, anyone home?" a voice shouts from the front door, cutting me off right when I'd gotten up the courage to talk.

Leo pushes himself up from the table and I follow his lead, suppressing my groan of annoyance when Starla waltzes into the kitchen with Bo Jangles in one hand and a glass baking dish in the other.

"I see someone finally got you coffee," Starla states with a nod of her head in the direction of the mug I'm holding in my hand. "Does that mean the crime rate in this town will go back down?"

Leo laughs and I do my best not to vault around the table and break one of Starla's arthritic hips by remembering what Bettie said yesterday: I need to be nice to the people of Bald Knob if I want them to like me. Instead of assaulting the old woman, I paste a tight smile on my face and keep my mouth shut before I say something I'll regret. Like, "Fuck off, old woman. And take your ugly ass dog with you."

"What brings you by this morning, Starla? Can I get

you a cup of coffee?" Leo asks, taking the baking dish from Starla when she holds it out to him.

"Just bringing by one of my pineapple upside down cakes for poor Emma Jo. You make sure she gets that. I heard she went to some fancy spa with a friend of hers last night. It's good for that girl to get out of the house and get some pampering after the sadness of the last couple of days," Starla says with a sorrowful look on her face that makes me want to scream because people are so upset over the death of a woman abuser and all-around asshole.

But again, I keep my mouth shut like a good girl. Damn Bettie and her stupid ideas to keep me out of prison.

"That's very kind of you, Starla. I'll make sure Emma Jo knows you stopped by," Leo tells her, setting the cake on the counter next to the sink.

Starla stands in the kitchen staring between Leo and I and when I move to go to Baby Cecil and top off my cup of liquid courage to deal with this shit, Bo Jangles growls and tries to lunge at me out of Starla's arms. I immediately stop and put my hands up in the air until Starla can get the damn dog to calm down.

"Bo Jangles, that's enough, now. I know you don't trust that woman, but there's no need to make a spectacle of yourself in the sheriff's presence," she admonishes the stupid dog, cuddling him to her chest and kissing the top of his head.

Leo pushes away from the counter to stand next to

me, sliding his hand around my back and pulling me against him. I didn't realize how much I needed the comfort from him until I feel the warmth from his body and the strength of his arm around my waist, not afraid to show Starla Godfrey that he's on my side in his own quiet way. And that just makes me feel like more of a jerk for not telling him about the pie yet.

"I see the rumors are true and you're shacking up with *her*," Starla huffs, glaring at me before moving closer to Leo's side and lowering her voice. "Are you sure you feel okay sleeping next to a murderer? Are you being held here against your will? Do you need one of those safe word things?"

Leo chuckles softly again and I bring my cup of now-cold coffee up to my lips to once again hold my tongue.

"Now, Starla, you know better than to listen to gossip. Payton grew up here. She's part of Bald Knob even if she's been gone a while, and I'd appreciate it if everyone would try to be a little nicer and give her the benefit of the doubt," Leo explains in a kind, soft voice that makes my heart go all-aflutter and want to throw him down on the kitchen floor and straddle him right in front of Starla and her damn dog. *That* will give the little shit kicker something to growl about.

"Of course, Sheriff Hudson," Starla replies with a fake smile in my direction. "Well, I best be going. Just wanted to drop off that cake."

She turns to leave and stops in the kitchen doorway.

"Oh, I almost forgot. Smells like something died outside. Don't know what it is, but it's awful. Might want to check that out. And while you're at it, make sure *that* one was accounted for last night, you never know," she says with a jerk of her chin my way, forgetting all about her agreement to be nice to me.

Leo removes his arm from around me and walks Starla to the front door, while I race to Baby Cecil and start drinking enough coffee to calm my nerves and think about the best way to inform Leo that he probably slept with a killer last night and he might just need the use of one of Starla's safe words.

CHAPTER 28

Recorded Interview
June 5, 2016
Bald Knob, KY Police Department

Deputy Lloyd: Ma'am, this is very
unprecedented.

Starla Godfrey: A citizen of this town
wants to give his statement and you're
going to deny his civil rights? I thought
better of you, Buddy Lloyd, this is such a
shame.

Deputy Lloyd: Mrs. Godfrey, Bo Jangles
isn't a citizen, he's a dog, and he can't
speak.

Bo Jangles: RUFF!

Starla Godfrey: That's right, love muffin.
You tell him. See? He can speak and he's
telling you he doesn't like Payton
Lambert.

Deputy Lloyd: Ma'am, I don't mean to be

rude, but we're in the middle of a murder investigation and I don't have time to waste interviewing your dog.

<u>Starla Godfrey:</u> You won't think it's a waste of time when he tells you he was a witness to a crime this morning. Go on, Bo Jangles, tell him.

<u>Deputy Lloyd:</u> Ma'am I don't-

<u>Starla Godfrey:</u> Quiet down and let him speak! Go ahead, baby. Mommy's right here. I know it's scary and I know you're traumatized, but you need to tell Deputy Lloyd the crime you saw this morning.

<u>Deputy Lloyd:</u> Ma'am, how about YOU just tell me this alleged crime he witnessed this morning.

<u>Starla Godfrey:</u> The crime is that we caught Payton Lambert red-handed taking advantage of Sheriff Hudson. I'm pretty sure he's being held in Emma Jo's house against his will. He wasn't wearing a shirt. I bet she took it and burned it in the backyard just like she did with the evidence of her killing Mayor Jackson.

<u>Deputy Lloyd:</u> Wait, what? What evidence? How do you know she burned evidence?

<u>Starla Godfrey:</u> Well, I don't know exactly, but I saw her carrying a white garbage bag out to the yard the night after the mayor was killed and she burned it in the fire pit at the edge of Emma Jo's property. Seems a little suspicious if you ask me.

<u>Bo Jangles:</u> RUFF!

<u>Starla Godfrey:</u> See? Even Bo Jangles agrees.

CHAPTER 29

*My morning coffee makes me feel like I've got my shit together. I
don't, but it feels like it.*

—Coffee Mug

"SO, YOU LIVE out on your parents' farm now?" I
ask Leo, standing next to him at the kitchen
sink while he helps me wash the breakfast dishes.

Yes, I know I'm stalling, but give me a break. Confessing to a murder takes time and finesse, and I'd
much rather stand shoulder-to-shoulder with a shirtless
Leo when he's sated and happy after a quickie on the
kitchen table right after Starla left, then watch his face
scrunch up in anger and annoyance.

"Yep, I've been living there for about six years. The
farm got to be too much for them to handle after a
while, so I bought it from them and helped them move
into a smaller home right in town. It's hard work, but I
love that house, and I love running the sweet corn
stand every summer.

Leo's parents owned Hudson's Sweet Corn, the
best and only place to get fresh corn starting in July,
and one of my favorite memories growing up was
going out to the stand by the road on their property to

buy sweet corn for dinner. Leo's dad always had a bunch of vintage candy he got from a place in Louisville that he sold at the stand as well. Bottle Caps, Turkish Taffy, Candy Cigarettes, those little wax bottles with the liquid in them, and a whole other assortment of awesome things that my dad always let me buy an entire brown paper lunch bag of whenever we'd go there. Mr. Hudson would throw in a few free extras for me and he'd give me a wink, much like the ones his son always gives me now. I loved the huge, old farmhouse out on Bald Knob road, and I love that Leo took it over, as well as the sweet corn business instead of selling it when his parents retired and that staple of Bald Knob will still be around for many years to come.

As Leo's hand slides over mine to grab a dish from me to dry, a sudden picture flashes through my mind of me standing next to Leo at the roadside stand, just like this, helping him bag up sweet corn for buyers while also selling them my coffee. Everyone is happy and smiling and Leo leans down to give me a quick peck on the lips, the vision so clear and perfect that it brings a tear to my eye.

"Hey, are you okay?" Leo asks, bursting the bubble of my daydream.

"Yep, just got some soap suds in my eye," I reply quickly, rubbing my eye against my shoulder instead of using my soap-covered hands.

Stupid daydream making me all girly and emotional. I live in Chicago, not out on a sweet corn farm with a man who can give me more orgasms than I can give myself in one sitting. My life is in Chicago. Liquid Crack is in Chicago, and I'll be going back to that life and my business as soon as this whole Jed mess is over, as long as I'm not convicted of his murder.

Sure, my business is going to be franchised and technically I could open up a Liquid Crack here in Bald Knob since my contract states I get first choice of all potential locations. But there's no way anyone in this town would be all happy and smiley if I was trying to sell them coffee. They'd still hate me and be angry if I laced it with Xanax, wrapped a diamond bracelet around the cup, and gave it away for free. And let's not forget the hot guy part of the daydream, standing next to me at the roadside stand kissing me. Just because he had a thing for me all these years, doesn't mean he wants to *keep* having a thing for me for years to come. Maybe now that he's slept with me and knows what it's like instead of just dreaming about it, he realizes it wasn't all he thought it would be.

Shit. Now I'm being emotional, girly, AND feeling sorry for myself.

Leo's phone rings from next to him on the kitchen counter and he glances down at the screen.

"Sorry, I need to take this really quick," he apologizes, drying his hands on the towel and then draping it over his should before he grabs the phone and brings it up to his ear. "What's going on, Buddy?"

I finish washing the last few dishes and leave them

to dry on another towel on the counter, listening to Leo's end of the conversation that only consists of a few *uh-huh's,* one *yep,* and ends with a "Be up there soon."

Leo disconnects the call and I turn to face him.

"Let me guess, Buddy was calling to tell you Starla left here and raced up to the station to give an interview about how slutty I am?" I ask him with a small laugh.

"Who knows," he chuckles. "He just said there's something I need to look at and to get down to the station as soon as I could."

He slides his arms around my waist and pulls me against him, reaching up to tuck a strand of hair behind my ear that escaped the messy bun I threw it up in after we christened Emma Jo's table.

"You're beautiful and sexy, and sleeping with you was better than any dream I've ever had. You're far from slutty," he reassures me, running the tips of his fingers softly down the side of my face.

His words make me feel giggly and not sorry for myself at all anymore, which causes me to put my guard down and blurt out something stupid.

"I should hope not, considering you're only the third-and-a-half man I've slept with in my entire life."

Leo's hand drops from face and I slap mine over my mouth, staring up at him with wide eyes. There's never a good time to tell a man how many other men you've slept with, especially fifteen minutes after you *last* slept with him, and when your number is so alarmingly low that he's going to wonder how you even knew what to do.

"How exactly does one sleep with half a man?" Leo asks, a grin twitching at the corner of his mouth.

"It has a little something to do with that thing you did last night. And first thing this morning. And you know what? I don't feel very comfortable talking about this. The half-thing is a very technical numbering scale that requires a lot of math, vodka, and poor decisions that I don't have time to explain right now," I inform him when I remove my hand from my mouth and try to pull out of his arms so I can hide under the kitchen table and enjoy my mortification in peace.

He tightens his hold on me and refuses to let me go.

"So what you're saying is, after all that math, vodka, and poor decisions, I'm only the third guy you've technically slept with?"

I glare up at him and give him my best *I'm not happy with you right now* look.

"Wipe that cocky smirk off your face or I'll go down to the station and give my own report confirming that the sheriff of Bald Knob does indeed likes to sleep with a murderer."

And once again, I say something stupid which completely kills the mood. For me. Leo is too busy still smiling down at me all proud of himself to worry about the chaos and guilt going on in my brain. He leans his head down to kiss me and I quickly bring my hand up between us and press it against his lips to halt his progress.

"Leo, there's something I need-"

"PUT YOUR CLOTHES ON! MOMMY AND MOMMY ARE HOME!" Bettie yells from the hallway as the front door slams closed.

"Son of a bitch. What is this, Grand Central Interrupting Station this morning?" I mutter under my breath when Leo drops his arms from around me and we turn to face Bettie and Emma Jo as they walk into the kitchen.

"My, my, don't you look...satisfied this morning," Bettie says with a smirk, crossing her tattooed arms in front of her while she leans her hip against the kitchen table.

"How was your Brazilian wax last night? Did they have to call in reinforcements and order a cement truck mixer of melted wax to remove the jungle between your legs?" I ask sweetly.

"I wouldn't know. The entire state of Kentucky now has a wax shortage and the spa workers have PTSD after dealing with *your* vagina wilderness," Bettie lobs back with her own sweet smile.

"Alright, that's enough, you two," Emma Jo scolds, moving to stand between us. "What Bettie meant to say is that we're sorry we interrupted you guys."

"Nope. Pretty sure I said exactly what I meant to say," Bettie states.

"Suck it," I tell her, with a flip of my middle finger.

"Are you two really friends or arch enemies?" Leo asks, pulling me against him, probably assuming I'm going to launch myself at Bettie and punch her in the face.

"She's one of my best friends, and I love her more than anything, duh," I reply with an eye roll.

"I love her *more* and let me just remind you, if you hurt her, I will slit your throat," Bettie adds, emphasizing her statement by sliding her finger across her neck.

"I'm so confused," Leo mumbles as I pat my hand against his chest sympathetically before moving away from him to pour Bettie a cup of coffee.

"Anyway, as I was saying," Emma Jo continues, "we didn't want to interrupt and we planned on sitting out on the front porch for a little while when we got home, but there is a God-awful smell outside and we couldn't take more than a few seconds out there. It smells like something died."

Bettie moves next to me while I wait for Baby Cecil to spit out some golden goodness.

"She's not kidding. It's really bad out there," she whispers in my ear while Emma Jo and Leo are busy talking about whatever is outside stinking up the neighborhood. "What did you do last night, aside from ride the hot sheriff like a wild bull? Do I need to club him like a baby seal so you can dispose of more evidence?"

"Alright, counting Starla, that makes three people

who've complained about a mysterious smell," Leo announces, making Bettie and I turn around to look at him. "You ladies stay here while I go out and see what it is."

"Fuck that, we're going with you," Bettie informs him, waving her arm for Emma Jo and I to follow along as Leo leads the way out of the kitchen and down the hall.

"I've got a tire iron in the trunk of the rental car. Just say the word..." Bettie whispers in my ear again as we head outside, down the front porch, and make our way around the side of the house.

The four of us traipse through the back yard, the smell getting stronger and more horrible the closer we get to the back of Emma Jo's property, until we all have to cover our noses as we walk.

"IF YOU FIND ANOTHER DEAD BODY BACK THERE, SHERIFF, I CAN SEND OVER BO JANGLES TO STAND GUARD AND MAKE SURE PAYTON DOESN'T TRY TO FLEE THE SCENE!" Starla shouts from the other side of her fence.

That damn woman must have had her face plastered to the window of her house, just waiting for something to happen, with how quickly she got out to her back yard to see what was going on.

Leo gives her a quick wave over his shoulder, otherwise ignoring her as our little group continues walking until we get to the edge of the woods that run behind all the houses on Emma Jo's street. We don't get more than five feet into the tree cropping and thickets before we find the source of the smell. Leo quickly puts up his arm to stop the three of us from coming any closer while he continues walking a few more feet and then stops.

We ignore his outstretched arm and move right up next to him, gasping in one collective breath when we see what Leo is staring down at: a yellow pie plate that's been licked clean, with two dead raccoons lying on their sides next to it.

"So THAT'S where it went!" Emma Jo exclaims.

Leo looks back at her in confusion and I quickly wrap my hand around her arm and give her a squeeze of warning to shut the hell up, but she doesn't take my subtle hint and just makes things worse.

"I mean, that's where THEY went. The raccoons being the *they* in question. I haven't seen them in a few days and I got worried. Because RACCOONS in the wrong hands could be dangerous. RACCOONS in the wrong hands could kill people," she rambles.

Leo looks back and forth silently between us with a raise of his eyebrow while I quickly try to fix her word vomit.

"Dangerous on account of the rabies. You know, raccoons having rabies and all that and rabies being deadly," I add with a nervous chuckle, not fixing her word vomit AT ALL.

"So, you've seen these raccoons before?" Leo questions Emma Jo.

"Our Emma Jo is just like Snow White! Animals from all over the land flock to her and want to be friends with her, even rabid raccoons," I reply lamely while Leo turns away from us and squats down by the raccoons.

Jesus, STOP TALKING, PAYTON!

"Until they eat one of her pies and realize she poisoned them," Bettie whispers from the other side of me.

I give her a quick jab to the ribs with my elbow right before Leo stands back up and turns to face us with the pie plate in his hand.

"Emma Jo, isn't this one of yours? Looks like they ate whatever was in it and then just keeled over," he states, bringing the plate up closer to his face to inspect it.

"What? No! That's definitely not one of mine. It's yellow, and I hate the color yellow," Emma Jo quickly replies. "All of my pie plates are in my kitchen and accounted for, and I definitely don't have any yellow ones!"

Leo flips the plate over in his hands and then tips the underside in our direction with another raise of one eyebrow, and we can all see clear as day an engraving stamped on the bottom of the plate that says *Property of Emma Jo Jackson*. I see Bettie shake her head and bow it out of the corner of my eye, and I wait for her to toss her hands up in the air and call us idiots.

"What Emma Jo meant to say is that she hasn't *always* hated the color yellow, isn't that right?" I ask, turning my head and widening my eyes for her to fix this before it gets more out of hand than it already is.

"Right!" she quickly pipes up. "It was more of a recent decision, actually. I read an article in *Good Housekeeping* that yellow dishes cause cancer, so I threw out every dish I owned that was yellow."

"And these raccoon friends of yours just pulled it out of the trash and dragged it into the woods so they could bake their own little raccoon pies?" Leo asks, narrowing his eyes at Emma Jo and then sliding the same questioning glare in my direction.

"Right! Exactly! And look at that, they probably died from cancer. I feel so much better now about throwing out all of those yellow dishes, don't you, Payton?" Emma Jo asks.

I just nod my head like an idiot, already feeling like the lowest of the low for not telling Leo about the pie, quickly feeling much worse about the whole thing the deeper and dumber I go with more lies, especially with the way he's looking at me right now. Like he doesn't believe a word out of my mouth and he doesn't know whether to be hurt or pissed after what happened between us in the last twenty-four hours.

"Sheriff, if you'll excuse us, we need to make sure all of the yellow dishes have definitely been removed from the kitchen, just in case. Also, I'd greatly appreciate it if you could get rid of those poor raccoons for me," Emma Jo tells Leo with a smile as she grabs my arm and pulls me quickly toward the house.

Bettie takes one last glance at a pissed-off-looking Leo and then makes a run for it, jogging to catch up with us.

"PAYTON!" Leo roars from the woods when we get to the side corner of the house.

"SORRY! CAN'T TALK NOW! I'VE GOT CANCER TO CURE!" I shout back to him over my shoulder, watching him stand there by the dead raccoons with his hands on his hips and a scowl on his face, until Emma Jo yanks harder on my arm to get me to move faster and we disappear around the side of the house.

"Jesus God, how have you two not been arrested yet?" Bettie complains when we get to the front of the house.

"Shut your face, do you know what this means?!" Emma Jo asks her excitedly when we stop at the top of the front porch.

"That you probably won't get the death penalty because you'll fail the psych evaluation?" Bettie replies dryly.

"No, this means we officially didn't kill my husband with a poisoned blueberry pie!" she answers, clapping her hands together like a toddler while jumping up and down happily.

Her words take a few seconds to sink in and dig their way past all the guilt and when they do, I forget about feeling bad for keeping things from Leo and I join Emma Jo in her happy dance, grabbing her hands and bouncing up and down with her.

I quickly put an end to my squeals of delight when something else occurs to me.

"Wait, but that means we're still responsible for killing two innocent creatures," I remind Emma Jo sadly.

She immediately stops bouncing around and her arms fall to her sides.

"They were really cute and cuddly, too," she adds with a frown.

"They were two rabies-infested, fly-covered, rotting carcasses who were dumb enough to steal a poisoned pie from your kitchen windowsill, drag it into the woods, and inhale it!" Bettie reminds us.

A slow smile spreads across Emma Jo's face as she turns to Bettie.

"Yes, but they gave up their sweet, cuddly lives to prove our innocence, and Payton and I need time to mourn them. Also, they were not a thirty-two-year-old abusive man and former mayor of this town, which means Payton and I aren't murderers!"

We give each other a high-five and Bettie sighs loudly, shaking her head at us once again.

"So, that means there's still a killer out there, walking the streets of this Podunk town. I don't know what scares me more, thinking you two idiots could have killed someone or not having any idea if some random stranger I met in town did it. I need a drink," Bettie grumbles, moving away from us to open the front door.

"I'll get the wine!" Emma Jo announces as we follow Bettie inside the house. "Every time someone says the words *dead raccoons*, everyone drinks!"

CHAPTER 30

Recorded Interview
June 5, 2016
Bald Knob, KY Police Department

Deputy Lloyd: Franny, you can't just go
around changing official documents from
the County Commissioner's office. Do I
need to remind you this is a murder
investigation?

Franny Mendleson: And do I need to remind
you there are thirty-seven questions the
good people of Bald Knob deserve to know
the answers to?

Deputy Lloyd: About Sheriff Hudson's love
life?

Franny Mendleson: It's the most horrible
thing to happen to this town in my sixty-
seven years!

Deputy Lloyd: The murder of Mayor Jackson
wasn't horrible?

<u>Franny Mendleson:</u> I meant, horrible for the single women of this town, obviously.

<u>Deputy Lloyd:</u> Franny, Sheriff Jackson and who he may or may not be seeing has nothing to do with our investigation, and I can't have you messing things up with your need to know all the happenings in this town.

<u>Franny Mendleson:</u> It has everything to do with this investigation since he's seeing a murderer! Or is it murderess? I can never remember which one.

<u>Deputy Lloyd:</u> Nothing has been confirmed and Payton has not been charged with any crime. You know that, since you work here and have typed up all the interviews, notes, and paperwork. We need to be focusing on the crime, not pointing fingers or wasting time with something that has no bearing on this case. I'm completely shocked that you would do something like this and not see the seriousness of the situation.

<u>Franny Mendleson:</u> Of course what happened to Jed Jackson is serious and terrible, but I have complete faith in the competence of this wonderful law enforcement agency that has employed me

for forty years. With only one raise. And two measly weeks of vacation. I'm sure I won't make the same mistake again, or do something silly like contact the County Commissioner's office and tell them what's going on.

<u>Deputy Lloyd:</u> I'll speak to the sheriff about getting you a raise and another week of vacation time.

<u>Franny Mendleson:</u> While you're at it, make sure he answers those questions. The people of Bald Knob need to know.

CHAPTER 31

*I love people who make me laugh, make me think, and
make me coffee. Not necessarily in that order.*

—Coffee Mug

M Y EYES FLY open when I hear a noise, immediately regretting that decision when the morning
sun blinds me and my head starts to pound, reminding
me I once again drank too much wine last night. I've
officially corrupted Emma Jo and turned her into a
wino, bringing me down with her.

I groan in pain as I roll from my stomach to my
side and turn my head away from the window.

"HOLY FUCKING SHIT!" I scream, bolting upright when I see Leo sitting silently on the edge of the
bed, staring at me.

I bring my hand up to my aching head that hurts
worse after being startled, sitting up too fast, and the
ear-piercing sound of my own shout.

Thankfully, after Bettie, Emma Jo, and I disap-
peared into the house yesterday morning and started
down the dark path of celebratory day drinking, Leo
disposed of the dead raccoons and left without coming

back in the house. He sent me several texts throughout the day and last night about how we were going to talk first thing in the morning, but I didn't think he actually meant *first-first* thing in the morning. I thought he'd be nice enough to let me wake up first, grab some coffee, and get rid of my hangover like a decent human being. When I didn't reply to any of his texts because…day drinking, which led to afternoon drinking, which then led to night drinking, followed up by a return of my guilty conscience, he sent one last cryptic text. Right before I dragged my drunk ass upstairs and passed out and after Bettie, Emma Jo, and I went over our murder suspect list and added a few more names now that we knew we weren't guilty, I got a message from Leo that just said, "Know where I can get a good piece of pie?"

Let's just say, it's a good thing wine makes me sleepy and Emma Jo said the words "dead raccoon" enough times that the three of us went through an entire case of the stuff, otherwise I would have tossed and turned all night worrying about that damn text.

And now, here Leo is, sitting on the edge of the bed looking way too edible in his crisp, clean sheriff's uniform, staring at me without saying a word until it starts getting uncomfortable.

"Were you watching me sleep?" I ask, trying to be annoyed so he doesn't know I'm two seconds away from shitting my pants.

"Would it creep you out if I said yes?" he asks in his deep, baritone voice that makes my insides all melty and my ovaries start handing out invitations for another party.

"Probably," I confirm with a nod, pulling the sheet up to cover my chest since I feel too exposed sitting this close to him wearing nothing but a black lacey bra and matching thong.

Which is stupid, considering this man has seen me naked several times, but not in his sheriff's uniform and not when he was acting like a sheriff. He was just Leo then. Now I feel like I'm in trouble with the way he's looking at me all seriously in that uniform, and at least with a little bit of cover from the sheet I don't feel so powerless. I know, it's stupid, but sheets have power, trust me. The only reason no one has been attacked by the monster under their bed is because they were covered up with a sheet. It's science, people.

"Then no, I wasn't watching you sleep," Leo finally responds. "I was listening to you TALK in your sleep."

I scoff, tucking the sheet tighter around my chest.

"I do NOT talk in my sleep."

"You talk a lot about pie in your sleep," he confirms with a grin, making my stomach flop nervously. "Should I be concerned you're dreaming about pie instead of me?"

The only thing that stops me from breaking down into a puddle of tears across his lap and begging him to forgive me is the cup of coffee I spot in his hands that he's holding down by his knees.

"You should only be concerned if that cup of coffee in your hands isn't for me," I speak with false confidence, nodding in the direction of the cup instead of meeting his eyes.

He laughs softly, handing over the coffee. I forget about my need for sheet protection, letting it drop to my waist as I greedily grab the warm cup from his hands, moaning with satisfaction when I take my first sip.

"I know, it's delicious. But don't go falling in love with me just yet. I have to come clean. Bettie tried to show me how to work that machine, and I screwed it up so many times that she finally shoved me out of the way and made it herself. She scares me," Leo admits with a shudder.

I don't hear a word he says because I'm too busy focusing on the whole "falling in love with me" comment, wondering why in the hell I'm not making a run for it and jumping out of the second-story window to safety. I don't want to fall in love again. Love is dumb. Love makes you do stupid things like spend five years with a man who doesn't understand your passion and then won't take no for an answer when you try to end things. I don't want to be in love again and it should be the funniest idea in the world that Leo would suggest such a thing, even if he is joking.

Why isn't it funny? WHY ISN'T IT FUNNY, DAMMIT?! And why does my heart start beating faster when I think about how easy it would be to fall in love with him?

"That really is the best coffee I've ever had. I'll get

the hang of Baby Cecil, don't you worry. We'll get to know each other, build some trust, and he'll be pouring out your Liquid Crack for me in no time," Leo reassures, making my inside do that melty thing all over again because he understands Baby Cecil's temperament and understands the importance of using him for decent coffee and he just plain understands *me*. Benjamin used to roll his eyes whenever Bettie and I referred to the coffee machines by their names, refusing to use them himself because it was "juvenile".

"Speaking of Bettie, where is she? I usually hear her banging around and screaming about being up at an ungodly hour whenever she has to help me open Liquid Crack," I tell him with another sip of coffee when I notice how incredibly quiet the house is.

"Beats me," Leo says with a shrug. "Emma Jo opened the door and then dragged Bettie outside after she let me in saying they had something important to do. They looked like they were up to something, but I didn't have time to chase after them and demand answers. I'm too busy doing that with *you*."

I slowly lower the coffee cup from my mouth guiltily and lean over to place it on the nightstand, realizing the time has come to spill the beans. Well, the pie, if you want to get technical.

"Before I say anything, can you please remove the Taser from your utility belt and place it a safe enough distance away?" I ask him.

He laughs, but quickly stops when he sees the serious look on my face.

He sighs, looks up at the ceiling quietly for a few minutes, probably praying to God for more strength to deal with my crazy, then removes the Taser gun from his belt and slides it onto the nightstand next to my coffee.

"Good?" he asks.

"It's still within reach, but you'd have to lean forward and that will give me at least a few seconds head start," I shrug, staring over at the Taser like it's going to jump up from the table on its own and attack me.

"Payton, look at me. What's going on?"

Taking a deep breath, I force my eyes to his. He scoots closer to me on the edge of the bed, grabbing both of my hands from my lap and tugging me toward him.

"Talk to me. I know something is going on with you. No more avoiding me. Talk," he orders in a soft voice, letting go of one of my hands to brush a few strands of hair out of my eyes and tuck them behind my ear.

"So, the pie plate you found in the woods by the dead raccoons yesterday really was Emma Jo's, but you already know that since her stupid name was stamped on the bottom of it," I explain with a roll of my eyes, remembering how ridiculous we behaved yesterday in the woods.

Taking another fortifying deep breath, I spit out everything else in one never ending sentence before I lose my nerve and try to distract him with sex again. Something tells me it might not work this time. Leo is in uniform and he means business.

"We baked a blueberry pie in it the night Jed was killed, but not just any blueberry pie. It might have had an entire bottle of Lysol Toilet Bowl Cleaner mixed in, and we had a lot of wine that night and left it on the kitchen windowsill to cool, and the next morning it was gone, and then Jed's body was found in the backyard, and we freaked out thinking *he* took the pie and ate it and then died in the backyard, and then Buddy came over and said it smelled like someone had baked a blueberry pie, and we freaked out even more, and then the whole town started blaming me for the murder, and we heard some rumors about people in town getting into arguments with Jed, so we made a list of other possible murder suspects in case it turned out we didn't *really* kill him with a poisoned pie, but I couldn't get any of the suspects or anyone else in town to talk to me because they hate me, and then you found the dead raccoons and the pie plate, and we were so happy to find out we didn't kill Jed with a poisoned pie that we drank way too much wine last night while going back over our murder suspect list," I finish, taking in a gasping breath of air and letting it out with a whistle. "Whew, so, that's that. Want me to make you some breakfast?"

I look at him hopefully, realizing quickly when I see a muscle tick in his jaw that I won't be able to distract him with sex OR slop. He's back to staring at the ceiling and he does it for so long that I start to worry his head exploded or his heart gave out, going by how silent and still he is.

"Really, the one to blame in all of this is the wine. It's all cool and yummy and then it forces you to make poor life choices, like keeping important things from the guy you're-"

"Stop talking," Leo cuts me off in a low, gruff voice, his eyes still up to the heavens.

He sounds a little scary right now, but I'm too busy being grateful he cut me off when he did, because I almost said something completely insane like "Keeping important things from the guy you're falling in love with."

And I couldn't even blame the wine for *that* almost-slip.

Leo continues staring up at the ceiling in Emma Jo's spare bedroom until I can't stand the silence anymore and I have to say something.

"Are you having an aneurism? Your eye is doing a funny, twitching thing."

He gives me the silent treatment for a few more minutes before doing something completely unexpected.

He laughs.

And not just one of his usual, low chuckles. This one is a head tossed back, full belly roar of amusement and it goes on a lot longer than the uncomfortable ceiling stare.

"It's not *that* funny," I complain, crossing my arms over my chest.

"Oh, believe me, it's not funny at all. Nothing about this situation is funny but if I don't laugh, I might be tempted to throw you over my knee and spank the hell out of you for keeping this shit from me," he replies, the laughter finally dying out. "I'm the sheriff, Payton. I was elected to keep this town safe, and the people here have been counting on me to solve Jed's murder, and while I was busy working my ass off to do that and working my ass off to get close to you, you were busy covering up a murder and lying to me about it."

I bite my bottom lip nervously and have to swallow a few times to stop myself from crying.

"Well, when you put it that way, it *does* sound kind of bad," I reply sheepishly. "Can we go back to the spanking thing? I'd like to know more about that."

My attempt at lightening the situation doesn't work. Leo pushes himself up from the bed and starts pacing in the middle of the room, running his hands through his hair while he curses and grumbles under his breath.

"Okay, now it's your turn to talk. I don't like all of this pacing and mumbling. It's making me nervous," I tell him.

He finally stops his manic movement, sighs deeply and comes back over to sit down next to me on the bed.

"Payton, Jed wasn't poisoned."

I laugh and roll my eyes at him.

"Yeah, I know that. Did you already forget about the dead raccoons and the missing pie?" I reply.

"No, I mean, I've always known he wasn't poisoned. Like, as soon as Billy Ray rolled his body over," Leo informs me. "Maybe if you would have trusted me and told me about what was going on a lot sooner, you could have avoided all the freaking out, wine drinking and poor decisions."

I throw my hands up in the air with a huff and glare at him.

"How in the hell was I supposed to know? You haven't said anything to me *or* Emma Jo about the autopsy or what's been going on with the investigation. We've had to hear everything through gossip and rumors around town. And then you got all weird, giving us those knowing looks and winks and bringing up pie all the time, so we thought you knew and it turned us a little crazier than normal. And I'll have you know," I say, poking my finger into his chest. "It made me feel like absolute shit to keep it from you, especially after we slept together, and I've been trying to tell you since then but we kept getting interrupted, and then the mystery of the pie was solved."

"And then wine happened," he adds.

"And then wine happened," I agree with a nod. "Fucking wine."

We're both quiet for a few minutes until Leo finally

reaches over and takes my hands in his again.

"I'm sorry I didn't tell you what was going on, but I'm not sorry you felt like shit for keeping this from me. You *should* feel like shit for that," he sighs. "And I only brought up pie around you all the time because I knew it made you act weirder than usual, and I was just trying to get you two to tell me what was going on. I seriously had no idea it was because of something like *this*. You honestly thought this entire time that *you* were the one who murdered Jed?"

All I can do is shrug. The more I think about it, and actually saying it out loud to Leo, made me realize just how stupid the entire thing was and how dumb Emma Jo and I acted. Did we honestly think we could get away with murder if it turned out Jed really had died from eating the poisoned pie we made?

"I should have kept you guys up-to-date with the investigation and the autopsy and I'm sorry about that and for whatever part I played in the two of you losing more of your minds," he apologizes, his voice going quieter. "I'm out of my element here, Payton. The first murder that happened in this town, happened under *my* watch, and I don't know what the hell to do."

I quickly scoot closer to him, letting go of his hands to wrap my arms around him and rest my chin on his shoulder so I can be near him and still look at his face.

"Don't apologize to me for anything. I know this has been hard on you, and I know you're probably not allowed to tell anyone certain things about the case and it was wrong of me to expect that from you," I admit softly. "I was just freaked out and things got a little out of hand trying to cover it up."

Leo pulls his face back a few inches from mine and stares down at me.

"Cover it up?" he repeats.

"Ummmm, did I forget to mention I also bagged up the pie baking mess from the kitchen while you were busy outside that night with Jed's body, hid it in the hall closet, and then snuck out of the laundry room window later that night and burned it in the back yard?" I ask.

He leans forward, pulling out of my arms to rest his elbows on his knees and put his head in his hands.

"I swear on Baby Cecil, that's the last thing I haven't told you," I promise, patting his back and making soothing circles with my palm.

More cursing and grumbling under his breath comes from Leo until I grab his arm and haul him back upright.

"Oh, stop being so melodramatic and tell me how Jed died," I demand.

"You're lucky you're cute and I really like you," he replies, shaking his head before continuing. "Like I said, as soon as Billy Ray rolled Jed's body over, I knew the preliminary cause of death, and that it wasn't poison."

He gives me a pointed glare and I give him one right back, waving my hand at him to speed it up and tell me the rest, without all the glaring and annoying sighs.

"Up close, I could see the blood all over the back of his head and it was pooled right under it in the grass. Someone jammed something into the back of Jed's skull that night," he finishes.

A sudden flash of a memory hits me from the other night, when I answered the door for Buddy the night he Tased me. I reached for something to use as a weapon just in case, grabbing for that damn award of Jed's that was always on the small table by the front door, but it wasn't there. And now that I think about it, it hasn't been there since then either.

"What's wrong? You've got that pie look in your eyes again," Leo states, dipping his head down to catch my eyes that were in a daze, staring at the buttons on the front of his shirt.

"It's nothing," I reassure him with a smile. "I was just wondering who could have done something like that. And you know, what kind of weapon they would have used."

Shit. I just promised him I didn't have anything else to hide, and here I am keeping things to myself again. See? This is why it's not safe for me to ever fall in love again. I suck at it.

"Not sure yet," Leo replies with a shrug. "The medical examiner in Louisville is still running tests. Right now all we know is that it was something sharp and pointy, but we'll know for sure after he makes a mold of the wound and analyzes it. Hopefully any day now."

Sharp and pointy...just like the tip of that award.

"Alright, as fun as this morning has been, I need to get to the station and see if he called." Leo kisses me on the cheek before he gets up from the bed. "Just to let you know, I'll be expecting you to distract me a whole hell of a lot with sex when I get off work tonight to make up for keeping this shit from me. And for torturing me through all of that by wearing a tiny scrap of lace over your tits that I want to rip off with my teeth."

I laugh nervously even as my body heats with the imagery his words bring, giving him a smile as he walks backward to the door.

"Oh, and I left you a present downstairs on the kitchen table. Don't bake any more poison pies when you get in there," he adds with a wink, and then he's out the bedroom door and I can hear his boots thumping down the stairs.

Hopefully, by some miracle, he left the award and possible murder weapon on the table for me as a present. That way, I won't have to worry about what he'll do when I have to come clean with him. Again.

CHAPTER 32

Recorded Interview
June 5, 2016
Bald Knob, KY Police Department

Justine Pickerson: This is horrible. Just
horrible. I'm such a horrible person.

Deputy Lloyd: Ma'am, are you okay?

Justine Pickerson: I'll never be okay
again! When I think about the things I
said… I had to come into the station as
soon as I heard so I could change my
previous statement.

Roy Pickerson: Me too. I just can't believe
what we heard and I feel awful about it.

Deputy Lloyd: Mr. and Mrs. Pickerson, what
did you hear? I've already told you, we
can't use rumors and gossip to arrest
anyone.

Justine Pickerson: Where in the hell have
you been all day, Buddy Lloyd?

Deputy Lloyd: Um, I've been here at the station. Trying to solve a murder.

Justine Pickerson: Well, I've been down at the square with the rest of the town and I have seen the light of my wrongdoings. There's no need for you to continue this investigation. I'd like to confess to the murder of Jed Jackson.

Deputy Lloyd: Wait, WHAT?

Roy Pickerson: Yep, me too. I helped her kill Jed Jackson.

Door opens and slams shut

Starla Godfrey: Oh no you don't, Justine. I'M confessing to the murder of Jed Jackson.

Door opens and slams shut

Mo Wesley: Excuse me, is there where I confess murder?

Door opens and slams shut

Andrea Maynard: Sorry to interrupt, Deputy Lloyd. I just wanted to tell you that I killed Jed Jackson.

Door opens and slams shut

<u>Teresa Jefferson:</u> Oh, hello everyone! Is now a bad time to confess to killing Mayor Jackson? My husband Frank would like to confess too, but he had to go to work, so I'll just do it for him.

Door opens and slams shut

<u>Andrea Maynard:</u> Wow, it's a tight squeeze in here. Move over a little, Starla, I need room to write down my confession of murdering the mayor. I brought some meatloaf from The Hungry Bear and left it out at the front desk if anyone is hungry.

<u>Mo Wesley:</u> Mmmmm, meatloaf. I could go for some meatloaf. Confessing to murder makes me hungry.

<u>Deputy Lloyd:</u> What in the hell is happening right now?

Door opens and slams shut

<u>Franny Mendleson:</u> Hi, I just-

<u>Deputy Lloyd:</u> Let me guess, you want to confess to murdering Jed Jackson?

<u>Franny Mendleson:</u> No, I was just coming in here to tell you there's meatloaf out at my desk if anyone wants a piece. But now that you mention it, yes, I'm the one who

killed Jed.

Door opens and slams shut

<u>Sally Plunkett:</u> Oh, good, you're all here.
My poor baby girl.

Crying, sniffling, nose blowing

I did it, Deputy Lloyd. I killed Jed
Jackson, that lowlife piece of dirt.

<u>Andrea Maynard:</u> Scum of the earth!

<u>Teresa Jefferson:</u> I can't believe that
rotten man was our mayor!

<u>Justine Pickerson:</u> I always knew there was
something wrong with him.

Door opens and slams shut

<u>Caden Jefferson:</u> Oh, hey Mom, hey Dad.
Please don't ground me, but I killed Mayor
Jackson.

<u>Deputy Lloyd:</u> Jesus Christ… I should have
been a doctor, like my mother always
wanted.

<u>Starla Godfrey:</u> You should always listen to
your mother, Buddy. I know you need to
arrest us, but that's going to have to

wait. We've got food to make and deliver, isn't that right, everyone?

Cheering, clapping, laughing, loud undistinguishable voices

<u>Andrea Maynard:</u> You should come with us, Deputy. I know Emma Jo wouldn't mind you stopping by. I've seen the way she looks at you.

Cheering, clapping, laughing, agreements from loud undistinguishable voices

<u>Deputy Lloyd:</u> Well, what's everyone standing around here for? Someone grab the meatloaf and let's go!

CHAPTER 33

A good friend knows how you take your coffee. A great friend adds booze.

—Coffee Mug

"YOU WERE ALWAYS such a sweet girl. That lasagna just needs to be popped back in the oven at 350 degrees for thirty minutes."

Justine Pickerson hands me the plate in her hands, gives me a pat on the cheek, and a smile and then walks out of Emma Jo's kitchen.

"I'm so glad you came back to town, Payton. It's a much better place with you in it, isn't that right, Bo Jangles?" Starla says, handing me a plate of chocolate chip cookies while at the same time, holding her rat dog out for me to pet.

I nervously reach my hand over to him and my mouth drops open in shock when he licks my hand and then nudges it with his nose, requesting a pat on the head.

Starla moves out of the way to make room for Frank and Teresa Jefferson, both of their arms piled with plates of food while they lavish me with similar words of praise as everyone else.

It's already been a strange enough morning, and I was already on the verge of tears when I came downstairs to the kitchen and found the gift Leo said he'd left for me. Having the entire town traipsing in and out of Emma Jo's house all afternoon, piling me with food and compliments has thrown me for such a loop that I haven't been able to do anything but smile, take the food from their hands, and put it with everything else currently covering all the available surfaces in the kitchen.

After the train of people finally comes to an end with Buddy as the caboose, handing over a pan of meatloaf from The Hungry Bear and then leaving dejectedly when I tell him Emma Jo isn't home, I flop down in one of the kitchen chairs, staring in a daze at the pans of cheesy potatoes, spaghetti, chocolate cake and fresh sweet corn that Andrea Maynard said Leo's parents asked her to drop off.

Thirty minutes later, Bettie and Emma Jo finally come home to find me still sitting in the exact same spot, still staring in shock at all the food in front of me.

"Jesus, what's with all the food? Who died this time?" Bettie asks.

Emma Jo laughs and smacks her in the arm as the two of them pull out chairs and sit down next to me.

"I don't…I have…I…"

They both look at me in confusion as I stutter and I try one more time to make the words form and come out of my mouth.

"They…I…people…I…meatballs," I mutter, pointing at the pan of homemade meatballs that I have no idea who dropped off.

"Yes, you *do* have meatballs. You're using your words, very good, Payton!" Bettie exclaims with a pat on my head, which finally breaks me out of my stupor.

I smack her hand away and attempt to glare at her, but as soon as I scrunch up my face, my eyes fill with tears and I drop my head down on top of my arms resting on the table.

"Oh, shit. We've got a crier. Emma Jo, this is all you. I don't do crying," Bettie announces, and I hear her chair scrape against the floor as she gets up from the table.

I feel Emma Jo rub her hands up and down my back and she squats down next to me and asks me what's wrong.

"People brought food. And they were nice. And they told me I was pretty!" I wail, crying even harder now.

"Those animals! I'll kill them!" Bettie jokes as she fires up Baby Cecil and starts making coffee.

Getting up from my chair, I move over to the box on the counter, picking it up and shoving it into Bettie's arms.

"And those. THOSE!" I shout, pointing at the box Leo left for me on the table that I had to move to the counter when the food started piling up.

Emma Jo moves over to Bettie's side as she lifts the flaps on the box.

"Leo gave them to me. I'm keeping secrets from him and he's so sweet, and I'm the worst person in the world and I can't believe he did that," I cry, my tears falling harder and faster when they both gasp and Bettie pulls out one of the items inside.

"University of Kentucky," Emma Jo says, reading the white lettering on the royal blue mug Bettie holds in her hands. "That's where Leo went to college."

Bettie puts the mug back in the box and pulls out another, this one black with the famous Las Vegas sign on one side.

"Ooooh, Vegas! I remember he went there a few years ago for a bachelor party for a guy he went to college with," Emma Jo announces as I swipe the tears from my cheeks and move to stand in front of the box Bettie continues to look through.

With every mug she pulls out, Emma Jo gives us the meaning behind it until we get to the twelfth and final one. A purple mug with the words *Bald Knob* in white, surrounded by a big, red heart.

"He gave you coffee mugs of all the places he's been since you left," Emma Jo whispers, the emotion so strong in her voice that it quivers.

"That guy really *did* pine away for you all these years. He literally thought about you every time he went somewhere over the last twelve years, bought you a mug, and held onto them until you came back. Holy shit," Bettie mutters, moving the box back to the counter and ripping a paper towel from the roll, dabbing it under her eyes. "God dammit. Now I'M crying. I hate all of you people."

Emma Jo sniffles as well, grabbing her own paper towel to blow her nose and wipe her eyes, all of us standing around the kitchen like a bunch of cry-babies.

"Yeah, well I hate you too! You left me here alone all morning to deal with all the crazy people in this town," I yell at both of them. "I found out how Jed was murdered, and I'm pretty sure I know what the murder weapon was, and I didn't say anything to Leo about it, and I feel horrible because I think I'm falling in love with him, and then I find those mugs he left me, and then people start dropping off food and telling me they missed me and all kinds of other nice shit that just makes me nervous, and neither one of you were here to assist me in my time of need!"

Emma Jo wraps her arms around me from my side and Bettie goes back to Baby Cecil to finish making coffee.

"We're sorry, but we're here now. Let's discuss the most important part of what you just said. You're falling in love with Leo?!" she asks excitedly.

"Seriously? That's all you got out of that?"

She shrugs and drops her arms from around me when Bettie hands me a mug of fresh coffee.

"Yeah, I'd like to review that statement as well," Bettie says.

"We're not reviewing anything because I don't want to talk about it. I live in Chicago, remember? My life is in Chicago, not in Bald Knob," I remind them, hating the hitch in my voice when I state the facts that suddenly make me really sad all over again. "How about we discuss what the two of you were doing this morning and why you weren't here when I needed you?"

Bettie and Emma Jo share a look and I wait them out, crossing my arms and tapping my foot until one of them finally gives in. Emma Jo is the first to crack, unable to hold it together under the stare of my irritated glare.

"We called a meeting down at the square and I told everyone that Jed abused me our entire marriage," Emma Jo blurts out, wincing as soon as she finishes when my irritated glare turns into full blown anger.

"WHAT IN THE ACTUAL FUCK?!" I screech.

"Oh, pipe down, nut job," Bettie says with an eye roll. "It was time, Payton. And look what happened? The entire town stopped thinking you were a murderer, and now they love you and want to make you fat with all this greasy food. You're welcome."

"Sure, the town is being good to me *now*, but that's how it always starts. They get you all nice and complacent and then they turn on you like a pack of wild dogs when your guard is down. And look what else is going to happen? Emma Jo is going to be the new suspect and focus of gossip now that the town knows she had a legitimate reason for killing Jed, and she'll never be able to ride off into the sunset with Buddy and have a good life," I complain.

"Sweetie, you need to stop worrying about me so much," Emma Jo says softly, wrapping me in her arms once again. "I love you, and I will never be able to thank you enough for coming home, and taking care of me and making me see just how strong I could be. You've done more than enough, Payton. I won't let you take the blame for Jed's murder and deal with the wrath of this town on top of that. I can't. It's not who I am and you know that."

My eyes blur with tears and I start to wonder where the hell they're all coming from. I've never cried this much in my entire life.

"Also, I'm not riding off into the sunset with Buddy Lloyd. I don't even like him," she scoffs.

"Nice try, asshole. I've seen the way you stare at his ass whenever he's around," Bettie laughs.

When Emma Jo starts to protest again, Bettie claps her hands together.

"Alright, The Crying Game is over. The people of Bald Knob love Payton and again we need to make sure it sticks this time, especially because that lasagna is fucking delicious and I'd like whoever made it to keep dropping it off," Bettie announces, pointing at the foil-covered pan next to her. "Emma Jo, go hunt up some more wine. Payton is going to suck it up, try and convince us of all the stupid reasons why she can't fall in love with Leo, and then we're going to discuss that little murder thing that happened and this murder weapon you seem to know something about."

Emma Jo quickly goes to the fridge to procure more wine.

"Tonight's secret word is *murder weapon*!" she announces, turning from the fridge and holding up two bottles of wine.

Seriously, how did I get so lucky to have friends like these two? Looks like it's another night of drinking and poor life choices.

CHAPTER 34

Coffee before talkie.
—Coffee Mug

THANKFULLY, I MANAGED to keep the wine drinking to a minimum the rest of the day, because being drunk tonight and then hungover again tomorrow is something I don't need right now. Emma Jo pouted when I took her wine glass away and put the wine back in the fridge, but she was mollified when I pulled out the murder suspect list and gave her and Bettie something else to do other than scream, "MURDER WEAPON!" and drink themselves into a coma.

After going over the list for several hours, I started to feel really bad about pointing fingers when these people had showered me with food and compliments all day. Sure, I was still afraid they'd turn on me at any moment, but right now, it felt good to be liked by everyone and very, very bad to be trying to figure out which one of them we should accuse of murder.

When I told Bettie and Emma Jo about the cause of Jed's death and how it was something sharp and pointy, they were as confused as I was regarding the whereabouts of the award that used to sit on the front table. Bettie never remembered seeing it and Emma Jo said she hadn't paid much attention to it, but that the last time she saw it was when I was holding it my hand, shoving the thing toward Leo's chest when he showed up at the house and I didn't know who he really was, assuming he was just the guy from the hospital and he was stalking me. Which of course made me freak out that my fingerprints were all over that damn thing, but Bettie assured me that since we know for a fact I didn't really kill Jed, someone else's fingerprints would be on it too. And if they wiped it cleaned and it turned up somewhere, mine would have been wiped off in the process too.

All of this information did little to calm my nerves, and Bettie was proved right once again when I tried my best to convince myself and them that falling in love with Leo was the worst idea ever, but it didn't work. The more time I spent with him and the more I got to know him, I knew it was a battle of the heart I'd never win, especially after the whole coffee mug present he left in the kitchen this morning. How do you *not* fall completely, head-over-heels in love with a guy who does something like that for you? And how do you choose between him and the business you scarified everything for, and worked your hands to the bone to build from the ground up, and the life you love almost as much in another state?

The answer is – you can't. Which leaves me to wear I am now. Feeling like shit, all alone in Emma Jo's house, curled up on the couch, and staring at the TV I didn't even have the strength to turn on. Bettie and Emma Jo decided to head up to The Hungry Bear to get dinner a little while ago, and I declined their invitation to go with them, which they were far too excited about and okay with, grabbing their purses and practically running out of the house. It was a little suspicious that they felt the need to go out for food when we had an entire kitchen filled with everything you could imagine, and I knew they left and were happy I didn't go with them because Leo would be here any minute and they assumed I was going to profess my undying love for him. They'll find out soon enough that the only profession I'm going to be doing is about the award on the hall table and how I was the last one to touch it.

I hear Leo's car pull into the driveway and I wipe my hands nervously down the skirt of my short, strapless, eyelet white sundress as I get up from the couch and meet him at the front door.

"Hi," I greet him softly, opening the door before he can knock.

"Jesus, how do you get more beautiful each time I see you," he mutters as he keeps walking toward me, scooping me up into his arms in the doorway and planting a kiss on my lips.

He sets me back down on my feet, pulls his mouth

away from mine, and looks down at me with a soft smile.

"Hi," he says, finally returning my initial greeting. "How was your day?"

I move out of his arms and step out of the way so he can come inside, closing the door behind him.

"Oh, nothing too eventful. I got a box of amazing coffee mugs from this hot guy I know, and then the entire town decided to stop by, bring me food, and tell me they don't hate me anymore. You know, the usual," I answer with a shrug.

"A hot guy gave you coffee mugs? Wow, he must be pretty awesome," Leo replies with a grin.

"Jesus, you're just like Emma Jo. Focusing in on the least shocking part of whatever I say," I complain.

Leo laughs, cupping my face in his hands and kissing the tip of my nose.

"I'm sorry, you're right. Having the entire town decide they don't hate you is a big deal. I heard all about Emma Jo's announcement on the town square. How's she doing?" he asks.

"Oh, she's perfectly fine. She couldn't care less that all of her secrets are currently being spread all over town and everyone will be pointing at her and whispering about her for the next fifty years," I mutter in irritation.

"Okay, let me rephrase that. How are *you* doing since Emma Jo told the whole town what Jed did to her?" Leo asks softly, rubbing his thumbs back and forth against my cheeks, and making me feel like a jerk, though I know he didn't mean to.

"I know, I get it. I have no right to be upset about any of this. It's Emma Jo's life, it happened to *her* and it's her choice whether or not she wants one person or five hundred to know what kind of hell she lived through for twelve years. I just never wanted her to put herself out there like that, especially not for me," I admit quietly, looking away from his eyes to stare at the collar of his t-shirt.

"What do you mean, especially not for you? What's wrong with someone doing something for *you* for a change?"

"Why should she do anything for me?" I fire back, bring my hands up between us to pick imaginary lint from his shirt. "I was a shitty friend to her for twelve years, and I had no idea what was going on back here because I didn't *want* to know. I left and I didn't look back, and I didn't care."

Leo sighs, putting more pressure on the hold he has of my face to tilt it up and force me to look at him.

"Just because you think you were a bad friend, doesn't mean you should have to deal with the whole town blaming you for a murder you didn't commit, Payton. It's insane and I'm sorry, but I'm glad Emma Jo told everyone. I know it was hard for her, and I know she'll have a long road ahead of her to heal from all of this, but as you saw today, the people here...they're good people. They take care of their own and they're going to take care of Emma Jo and protect her, just like you did."

For some ungodly reason, it seems like I still have tears left and they quickly fill up my eyes and spill over onto my cheeks, where Leo's thumbs swipe them away one by one as they fall.

"Uuugghhh, I hate crying. Crying is so dumb. Tell me about your day," I demand, pulling away from him so I can stand in front of the hall mirror, wipe my own cheeks and get my shit together, considering I need to prepare myself to come clean about the award.

"Well, you're not the only one who had an eventful day," he says, coming up behind me and watching through the reflection as I dry my tears and wish I could be a pretty crier, like women in movies. "It seems poor Buddy had his hands full after Emma Jo's announcement when the whole town filed into the station and every one of them confessed to Jed's murder."

My eyes meet his in the mirror, and when I see he's not kidding, I whirl around to face him.

"What? Are you serious?"

Leo laughs, but it's not really one filled with humor. It leans more toward exhaustion and frustration, which is evident when he runs his hand through his hair in his signature "I'm about to lose my shit" move.

"Dead serious," he replies, then quickly winces. "Sorry, bad choice of words. So, yeah, everyone rallied around you and confessed to the murder because they felt bad about blaming you now that they know you came home to help Emma Jo and the reasons why. And I can't take any of those people seriously which means I still don't have a prime suspect, a reason for the murder, or a murder weapon."

My heart starts beating faster and my palms start to sweat as soon as he says *murder weapon*. I glance over at the empty hall table and my stomach immediately gets tied in knots.

"Leo, I-"

He moves in the blink of an eye, swooping me back up in his arms and cutting off my words with his mouth. Just like every time he kisses me, I lose all sense of reason and I lose *myself* in him. He deepens the kiss and lifts me up against him, my legs automatically wrapping around his waist as he moves us through the house, stopping at the base of the stairs to break the kiss.

"Whatever you were going to say, can it wait until tomorrow?" he asks, hefting me up higher with one arm and bringing the other one up to smooth his palm down the side of my face. "This has been a shitty day, at the end of a shitty week, and right now, I don't want to think about murderers or the meddling people of Bald Knob. I don't want to think about anything for the next ten to twelve hours but getting you naked as fast as possible, sinking myself inside of you, and forgetting about everything else around us. Right now, I just need *you*, Payton."

Jesus, how do you say no to something like that?

"So what you're saying is, you want me to distract you with sex?" I ask, looking down at him with a smile as I run my fingers through his hair.

He smiles back up at me and I lean down and kiss him while he grabs onto my ass with both hands and carries me up the stairs.

I forget about the secrets I'm keeping when he lays back on the bed and pulls me on top of him so I'm straddling his thighs.

I forget about murder weapons and suspects when I lift up just enough to unbutton his jeans, slide down his zipper, and reach inside his boxer briefs to palm his hardness and pull it out.

I forget about my life in Chicago and how whatever this is that's happening between us will never work out, when he pushes my dress up to my hips, slides my white lace underwear to the side with one hand and clutches my hip with the other to position my body over him.

I forget my name and what day it is when he thrusts his hips up, filling me so quickly and perfectly that his name comes out as a gasp when I almost forget how to breathe.

He holds tightly to my hips, slamming me up and down on top of him until there's nothing I can feel, nothing I can do, and nothing else I care about but taking away his worries and making him forget right along with me.

It's fast and it's hard and it's wild, and somewhere

along the way, Leo rips my dress the rest of the way off of my body and tosses it across the room, pushing himself up to sitting so he can slide a lacy cup of my strapless bra to the side and latch his lips to my nipple, sucking it into his mouth. I move up and down faster and harder in his lap, gripping his hair tightly in my fingers until we're both covered in sweat, moaning and muttering each other's names.

When he pulls my nipple harder into his mouth and moves his fingers between my thighs to rub and slide them against that perfect spot, I come with his name on my lips and he quickly follows, pumping up inside of me and jerking his hips between my legs until we both get lost in blissfully mindless oblivion.

CHAPTER 35

I'm a bitch before coffee. And after.
—Coffee Mug

PULLING EMMA JO'S car into the driveway, I grab the bag of Styrofoam containers from the front passenger seat and head into the house, knowing I only offered to go pick up breakfast so I could butter Leo up and to get out of the house as fast as possible so I could have a little time to collect my thoughts.

Don't judge me. Desperate times call for desperate measures and an omelet from The Hungry Bear would have to do.

As soon as I walk through the front door and head toward the kitchen, I see Leo coming down the hallway and I smile at him as I pause and wait for him to get to me. The fierce, pissed-off look on his face makes my smile drop and I set the bags of food down on the floor by my feet. He walks right by me without saying a word and I quickly turn and grab onto his arm.

"Hey, what's going on? What's wrong?"

He jerks his arm out of my hand and the look he gives me is enough to make any woman want to shrivel up into a ball and go off to cry in a corner.

"First, you keep a secret about the damn pie, then, I can tell you're still keeping something from me even though you promised you wouldn't, but I let it go because I just wanted to be with you and none of that seemed important in the grand scheme of things," he states in a low, angry voice that renders me speechless. "This whole time, I've been busy falling in love with you, and you've been busy planning your fucking wedding."

"Sweetheart, you're home!"

This confusing, Twilight Zone moment is brought to you by Benjamin Montgomery, the dumbass who just waltzed into the hallway from the kitchen.

When I realize what Leo is so upset about, ignoring the minor detail about me still keeping something from him and COMPLETELY passing right over that whole declaration of love thing for the time being, my heart stops trying to beat its way out of my chest and I stop panicking. And start laughing. Which is the absolute opposite thing you should do when a guy you've been sleeping with who thinks he's in love with you, who looks five seconds away from slamming his fist into the wall, and also thinks he just found out you've been lying to him about being engaged.

"Glad you find this amusing," Leo growls at me, looking over at Benjamin and giving him a nod. "Nice talk, Ben. You'll excuse me if I don't feel like staying around to chat more."

"It's BENJAMIN," the dumbass replies as Leo turns and stalks to the door, yanking it open so hard it slams against the wall.

"Fuck you very much, Benny," Leo mutters over his shoulder, giving Benjamin the finger as he starts to leave.

I finally pull my head out of my ass, stop laughing, and lunge after Leo, grabbing his arm again, tugging him to a stop and making him turn around to look at me.

"You, aren't going anywhere," I inform him, still clutching tightly to his arm as I look back at Benjamin. "And YOU are a fucking idiot! We are not engaged, there isn't any wedding, and you need to get that through your head before I ram it in there with a two-by-four!"

Benjamin's face falls and as I stand here looking at him in his three-piece suit and slicked back hair, I wonder what in the hell I ever saw in him. He's a pansy-ass idiot, and I can't believe I never realized just how stupid he was.

"But, mother already booked the country club! It's a fantabulous location for a wedding and I can't just have her cancel it," he whines.

"For the love of God, stop using that word. You sound like a douchebag," Bettie complains, coming into the hallway with Emma Jo on her heels.

"We heard loud voices and came down to see what was going on," Emma Jo explains, looking nervously around the room and the tension flying through the air.

Leo tries to turn away and pull his arm out of my hand again, but I refuse to let go. Quickly moving around to stand right in front of him, I drop my hold on his arm long enough to grab fistfuls of his t-shirt and pull him down so he's forced to look at me.

"Benjamin and I broke up before I came back to Bald Knob. He proposed, I said no and ended things, and I haven't seen or spoken to him in over a month. We aren't engaged, we aren't planning a wedding, and I wouldn't marry him if he was the last man on Earth, standing on a deserted island holding the last cup of coffee," I explain.

"That cuts me deep, Babykins. Really deep," Benjamin sighs.

"Shut the hell up before I punch you in the neck," Bettie threatens. "Get your ass back in the kitchen and stay there until we tell you to come out."

Benjamin does as he's told, knowing better than to mess with Bettie first thing in the morning before she's had a chance to cuddle up with Baby Cecil.

When he disappears from the hallway, Leo's face finally starts to soften and not look so homicidal anymore. I move in closer to him right as his cell phone rings. I take a step back, moving over by Bettie and Emma Jo to give him a little privacy, even though we can hear everything he says.

"Hey, Buddy, what's going on?" Leo speaks into the phone, keeping his eyes glued to mine. "Really, the

M.E. got the report to us already? Right. Yeah. Something in a triangular shape, narrow at the top, and then tapering out?"

My mouth suddenly goes dry and Bettie whispers a curse under her breath next to me. While Leo continues to listen to Buddy talk, his eyes slowly move away from mine and go right to the side table that he's standing next to.

"And he's sure it was something in the shape of a triangle? Something with a point on one end?" Leo asks, staring at the empty table for a few more seconds before his eyes come back to mine.

As hard as I try to not look guilty, it just makes me think about it so much that I start doing everything that will point the blame right at me. I bite my lip, I wring my sweaty hands together, I fidget with my hair, and I bounce nervously from one foot to the other until Bettie finally has to put an arm around me to keep me still.

Leo finally ends the call, his eyes never leaving mine as he slides the phone in his back pocket and stands by the door silently. I can feel his disappointment and hurt like a physical punch to the chest and it almost makes me bend over at the waist, clutching my heart.

"Alright, fine, I admit it! I killed Jed with the stupid award that was on that table," Emma Jo suddenly announces.

My head whips around to her and I stare at her with wide, horrified eyes until she gives me a tiny, barely visible wink and I realize what she's doing. She's trying to cover my ass with Leo and there's no way in hell I'm letting her do that.

"Shut up, no you didn't. I'm the one who killed Jed. I lost my shit in a blind fit of rage and stabbed him in the back of the head with the award," I proclaim, smiling at Emma Jo when she narrows her eyes at me.

"No you didn't! I killed him and that's final!" she shouts.

"You did not! Stop trying to take his murder away from me!" I argue.

"I killed him and then I buried the award back in the woods where no one will find it, so THERE!" she screams at me.

"Oh, yeah? Well, I killed him and then tossed it into Bald Knob Lake where no one will find it, so HA!"

We go back and forth for several minutes until Bettie finally throws her hands up in the air and steps between us.

"For fuck's sake. I'M the one who killed Jed. I actually got into town earlier than everyone thought just for that reason. Bettie Lake did it, in the backyard, with a major award," Bettie says, like she's reading a card from the game Clue.

"ALL OF YOU NEED TO STOP TALKING RIGHT THE FUCK NOW!" Leo suddenly shouts, causing all three of us to shut our mouths and look over at him.

His eye is doing that weird twitching thing again, and now I'm worried this is the thing that will officially throw him over the edge and give him an aneurism.

"Bettie, take Emma Jo and go sit your asses down in the living room. Payton, get *your* ass outside with me. NOW," he orders, pointing to the door with his nostrils flaring.

"What should I do?" Benjamin asks, poking his head out from the kitchen.

"SHUT THE HELL UP!" all four of us shout at him in unison.

Benjamin scurries back into the kitchen, Bettie and Emma Jo go into the living room, and I follow behind Leo as he marches out the door and stomps down the steps. He stops when he gets to the middle of the front yard and turns to face me.

"You have one last chance. What is going on and what are you not telling me?"

I take a minute to think about everything that happened today and over the last couple of days. I think about the fact that if that murder weapon turns up, I don't have an alibi for the night Jed was killed because I was passed out face-down on Emma Jo's living room floor. And then my brain kicks into high gear and I realize, Emma Jo doesn't have an alibi either. Hypothetically, I could have grabbed the award from the table, snuck outside in the middle of the night, and killed Jed without Emma Jo ever knowing because she was upstairs asleep. And the same goes for her. She could have just as easily done the same thing and I never would have realized she'd been out of the house.

My heart drops and my stomach plunges to my toes. Right when everything is finally all out in the open with Leo, I'm standing here in front of him while he waits for me to admit I don't have any more secrets, wondering if my best friend could have been the one responsible for this whole mess. I can't bring myself to tell him this, no matter how much it will kill me not to. I can't hurt Emma Jo like that. I can't put that seed of doubt in Leo's mind and force him to investigate her. I won't do that to her.

"At least answer this," Leo finally speaks when he realizes I'm not going to. "Were you really never engaged to that jackass, and did you really not spend the last week while you were here with me planning your wedding?"

I let out the breath I was holding when he asks me something a hell of a lot easier than what I thought he would.

"I swear on Baby Cecil's life, I was never engaged to Benjamin, and I'd rather shove a rusty fork in my eye and live without coffee forever than plan a wedding with him," I reply.

Leo sighs with relief and I'm so happy the conversation has moved away from murderers that I continue talking without thinking. Something I should never be allowed to do and honestly, I don't understand why someone hasn't assigned me an adult so I can be supervised at all times.

"I'm sorry I didn't tell you about Benjamin, but

honestly, I didn't see the point. We broke up before I came home, and it's not like this thing is serious and we need to tell each other about every person we've ever dated before," I say with a nervous laugh, remembering the whole 'falling in love with you' thing he said inside all over again and suddenly feeling like someone is choking me.

Leo is dangerously quiet for a few seconds, and I quickly realize I should have just kept my mouth shut because every time I open it around him, I seem to say something stupider than the last time.

"Who said what we have isn't serious?" he finally asks.

"Well, I mean, you never said it WAS serious, sooooo…," I trail off, once again ignoring the falling in love with you thing because holy shit! I'm pretty sure my best friend might have killed her husband and all of these monumental things are happening all at once and I'm in a full-blown panic right now.

"I kind of thought I made myself clear when I said I was falling in love with you just a few minutes ago," he replies. "I didn't say it sooner because I knew it would freak you out."

He gets right up in front of me, his body as close to mine as he can get without actually touching me, and I hold my breath for whatever he's about to say next, knowing it's probably going to ruin me all over again.

"I was serious the first time I saw you in that hospital room, even though you didn't remember me. I was serious the first time you found out who I was and couldn't stop picturing me naked."

I want to roll my eyes, but my face is frozen in shock, so I stand here like a mute as he continues.

"I was serious the first time I kissed you, I was serious every time I covered for you and put my job on the line when I thought you might have known something about Jed's death, and I was serious the first time I buried myself inside you and every single time after that. I've been serious this entire fucking time, so now it's your turn. Are you going to freak out, or are you going to tell me you feel the exact same way?"

I can't speak and I can't stop the tears no matter how much I want to. I need to say something; I know I need to say something but I have no idea what the hell to say. I don't know what to do and I don't know how to make such a life-altering decision after a handful of days when my best friend might be going to prison. I know I should articulate all of this, but I can't. I can't do anything but stand here in front of him, ripping both of our hearts in half because I'm scared and I'm a coward.

"That's what I thought. Have a nice life back in Chicago," Leo mutters.

He turns and walks away from me, crossing the street to his car, and I just watch him go. I stand here in the middle of the yard and I let him go, knowing without a doubt that I am now officially and completely ruined.

CHAPTER 36

Coffee: A warm, delicious alternative to hating everybody every morning forever.

—Coffee Mug

"**Y**OU HAVE TO get out of bed, this is very unhealthy," Emma Jo complains, moving over to the window and opening the blinds.

"GAAAAAAAAAAH, CLOSE THEM, IT HURTS!" I scream, covering my hands over my eyes like a vampire being burned by the sun.

I *feel* like the undead right now, considering I've done nothing but curl up under the covers and cry for the last week. Okay, that's not true. I got up a few times, once to take a shower and another time to go down, grab Baby Cecil and bring him up to bed with me.

"Also, this is a fire hazard," Emma Jo scolds, moving Baby Cecil from the top of the bed to the nightstand, pushing aside the twenty or so dirty coffee cups that litter the surface.

"But he loves me unconditionally and never lets me down. I need him," I whine, reaching for the machine as Emma Jo smacks my hand, unplugs it, and scoops it up into her arms instead.

"And if you want him, you're going to have to come downstairs into the kitchen and drink your coffee like a normal person."

I huff, pushing myself up to lean back against the headboard and cross my arms over my chest.

"You're mean, and I don't like you very much right now."

"Yeah? Well I don't like you very much right now either. What in the hell are you doing, Payton? If you're so miserable without Leo, then talk to him," she urges, tucking Baby Cecil under one arm as she sits down next to me on the side of the bed.

She grunts a little sound of pain and quickly gets back up, flinging back the covers and grabbing what she just sat down on.

"Why are you sleeping with a spindle from the headboard? Is this some kind of kinky sex toy? Oh, my God! Did you break this off and use it!" she shouts in horror, tossing it across the room where it hits the wall and falls to the ground.

"No, you sicko! I broke it when Leo and I were…when Leo was…" I can't finish the sentence without crying and Emma Jo sighs, sitting back down on the edge of the bed. "I'm sorry I broke your headboard. I promise I'll buy you a new one."

I swipe the tears off my cheeks and Emma Jo leans forward, putting Baby Cecil on the floor by her feet, sitting back up and turning to face me.

"I don't care about the damn headboard, I care about *you* and what you're doing to yourself. You let Leo walk away because you said you knew things would never work out and you pretended like it wasn't serious, even though you knew damn well it was. You talk this big game about how you have a life back in Chicago and you can't stay here, but yet, here you stay," Emma Jo states.

"I stay because I'm waiting for all of this mess with Jed to get cleared up so I know you're okay. If you want me to leave, I'll leave," I reply indignantly.

"Stop being such an asshole, it's giving me a head-ache," Bettie announces, walking into the room and making the bed bounce when she flops down on the other side of me on her stomach, pushing herself up on her elbows. "Strap on a set of balls or I'm not letting you drive by Leo's house anymore."

"You drove by Leo's house like some crazy ex-girlfriend?!" Emma Jo exclaims in shock.

Okay, so I got out of bed and out of the house one other time in the last week…

"No! I didn't drive by Leo's house like a crazy ex-girlfriend!" I argue as Bettie and Emma Jo both frown at me. "I had Bettie do it while I hunkered down in the passenger seat, thank you very much."

Emma Jo sighs, closes her eyes and shakes her head.

"It was a pathetic display and I was embarrassed to

be a woman that day, but she bribed me with a fifteen percent raise, so what's a girl to do?" Bettie asks Emma Jo with a shrug.

I feel like the biggest idiot on the planet, but there's nothing I can do about it. I know what I did was wrong and I know I made the wrong decision, but I can't take it back now. I can't fix it, even if I knew how, which I don't. After Leo left me standing in Emma Jo's front yard and I finally managed to convince Benjamin to go back to Chicago and never contact me again, I stupidly thought Leo would call or text or come back by the house. I felt worse with every hour and day that passed when he didn't do any of those things. I deserved his silence, but that doesn't mean it hurt any less. I tried a hundred different times to pick up my phone and call him, but what the hell would I say? Everything I said is still true, nothing has changed. My life is in Chicago. I moved away from Bald Knob because I needed to get out of this small town where everyone knows your business and there aren't any opportunities to grow or change or be anything other than a small town girl, living in a lonely world.

Shit. Now I'm using lyrics from a Journey song to justify my life. I've reached an all-time low.

Emma Jo leans over and pulls my arms away from my chest, holding my hands in hers.

"Leo called me last night," she says softly, making my ears perk up and my heart beat double-time. "The mess with Jed is officially cleaned up. I don't want you to go. I've loved every insane minute of having you back home and being your friend again, but it's okay. If you need to go, you can go. I won't stop you. I'll be sad and I'll miss you, but I won't stop you if you feel like that's what you need to do."

I should feel some sort of relief at her words, but I don't. I should be scrambling out of bed, grabbing my laptop and booking the first flight back to Chicago, but I can't.

"What do you mean, the mess with Jed is officially cleaned up. What happened?" I ask, deciding to focus on this mess first, instead of trying to figure out why I'm not more excited to know I can finally go back to Chicago.

"Well, it looks like the medical examiner has officially ruled Jed's death as an accident," Bettie informs me.

"What? How is that possible?" I question in shock.

"There were a hundred and twenty-seven people who confessed to his murder at last count," Emma Jo says, taking up where Bettie left off. "Too many confusing stories and confessions, no witnesses, no viable suspects, and no murder weapon equals case closed. Did you know we have a sprinkler system installed in the yard?"

I shake my head at Emma Jo's question. She nods and continues.

"Yep. We had it put in about ten years ago. A couple of the spigots have pushed up out of the ground a little higher over the years. The medical examiner concluded that Jed must have tripped over something, landed on one of the spigots, managed to pulled himself off of it, and then bled to death in the yard."

My jaw drops open and though the explanation seems plausible I guess, something just doesn't feel right about it. There's still something unaccounted for.

"What about the missing award from the front table?" I whisper.

Emma Jo squeezes my hand, but doesn't say anything for a long while. Finally, she lets go of my hand, gets up from the bed and walks over to the window, staring out into the backyard.

"The first time he hit me, I was so shocked, I actually laughed," she speaks softly with her back to me and Bettie. "I didn't laugh the next time when he broke my nose and I couldn't breathe from all the blood dripping back down into my throat. It became my reality, my way of life. Watch what I say, be careful of what I do, but even then I wasn't guaranteed to walk away without a bruise or something broken, it all depended on his mood or which way the wind blew or something other stupid thing that had crawled up his ass. He kept doing it, because I kept letting him. I had no other choice, nowhere else to go. I didn't have a job or my own money. I was a housewife. That's all I'd ever known. I spent twelve years making up excuses for why I couldn't attend certain functions or why there were marks and bruises on my body that make-up and clothing wouldn't cover when I did leave the house. I made up excuses for the beatings, I made up excuses for him and I came up with a hundred different excuses for why I couldn't leave."

Even though I know Bettie isn't the touchy-feely type, my hand automatically reaches for hers where she's still propped up on the bed next to me, listening silently to Emma Jo speak right along with me. She doesn't pull away when my fingers lace with hers. She squeezes them tighter and holds on for dear life.

"When I was in the hospital and they asked me if there was an emergency contact I could call, I didn't hesitate to give them your information. I needed strength. I needed someone who could make a decision that I hadn't been able to make for twelve years. Someone who was always stronger than me, smarter than me, and would never in a million years let herself get to the point I was at – hopeless and just wanting it to end, however that had to happen."

Emma Jo finally turns away from the window, wiping a few tears from her cheeks that fell while she spoke, giving me a shaky smile.

"I don't know what I would have done if you hadn't gotten on that plane and showed up at the hospital. Actually, yes I do," she says with a humorless laugh. "I knew there was a full bottle of sleeping pills in my medicine cabinet that would do the trick. Finally end all of this bullshit and give me some peace. But you did it. You showed up and you saved me. You kicked my ass into gear, got me out of the hospital, and gave me a reason to keep fighting. So I fought. When you were passed out on my living room floor, I made a decision and I fought and I took back my life. I'm not sorry for what I did, but I am sorry for everything that happened after and how you got caught in the middle of it. I never wanted that to happen."

She stops speaking and the silence is so thick in the room I can almost see it clouding the air. I'm in shock at what she just sort of admitted, but then again, I'm not. There's only so much a woman can take before you push her too far. Emma Jo was pushed far beyond her breaking point and like she said, she just wanted it to end. She just wanted some peace.

"Jesus Christ, and I thought *I* was a scary bitch," Bettie mutters. "Remind me to never piss you off."

Emma Jo smiles, a little less sad this time.

"I killed him, and then I buried the award back in the woods where no one will find it," I whisper, repeating the words Emma Jo shouted when the two of us were fighting back and forth, when I thought Emma Jo was trying to cover for me knowing about the murder weapon with Leo, and I refused to let her do it. "You weren't just shouting whatever you could to protect me, were you?"

She doesn't say anything for a little while and then she shrugs.

"It was an ugly, stupid fucking award."

I can't help it, I laugh. It's sick and it's fucked up

and if I were a different person, I would be picking up the phone and calling the police, but I'm *not* a different person. I'm strong and I'm stubborn, and if you're my friend, I will do everything I can to protect you and I will take your secrets with me to the grave.

It doesn't take long for Bettie to join me in laughter, and then Emma Jo comes back to the bed, curls up next to us, and the three of us laugh until tears are streaming down our cheeks. Happy ones, instead of sad ones, for the first time in a long time.

"Alright, bitches, that's enough nonsense. It's time to get serious," Bettie suddenly announces, pushing herself up to her knees. "Payton, we need to fix you. You're broken and it's too late to return you and get our money back, so who has any ideas?"

"I'm not broken, I'm just sad. I'll get over it once I get back to Chicago and things get back to normal," I reply, the urge to cry when I say that out loud so strong that it almost chokes me.

"Have you realized she just says *Chicago* now and doesn't call it home?" Emma Jo asks Bettie.

"Oh yeah, I totally noticed. She's not fooling anyone," she replies.

"I love her, but she really is kind of an idiot about some things. What should we do?" Emma Jo questions, tapping her finger against her lip in concentration.

"First thing we need to do is drag her out of bed and hose her off. She smells like regurgitated milk and bad decisions," Bettie complains, plugging her nose.

"Stop talking about me like I'm not sitting right here, assholes," I complain. "And I don't smell *that* bad."

Pulling my tank top up to my nose, I take a whiff and cringe.

"Okay, so maybe I do need a shower, but still. I'm not an idiot, and just because I didn't call Chicago home means nothing."

Emma Jo and Bettie both share a look and then they laugh.

"Didn't anyone ever tell you it's not polite to laugh at someone? Were you raised by a pack of wolves?" I grumble in annoyance.

"We'll stop laughing *at* you when you stop saying stupid shit that makes us laugh," Bettie informs me. "Sorry, babe, but survey says – Chicago is no longer home. *This* is your home. It's always been your home. I didn't believe it until I got here and saw it with my own two gorgeous eyes, but you belong here, Payton. These crazy people are *your* people. Sure, they're always all up your ass and in your business, but it's not that annoying when they're doing it to protect you."

She's right. In my head, I know the words she's saying are true, but I can't get my head and my heart on the same page right now.

"Sure, they like me now, but what happens when they turn on me again and think I'm out to corrupt all the innocent people who live here?" I question.

"Then you'd have a hulking, beast of a man who

fucks like a God and loves your crazy ass for some strange reason, to stick up for you and protect you and tell everyone to mind their own business," Bettie fires back.

"I screwed it up. He'll never forgive me," I whisper.

"You don't know that unless you try. You taught me how to be a fighter, and now it's my turn to return the favor. Get your ass out of bed and fight for what you want, Payton," Emma Jo says.

"But...what about Liquid Crack? I mean, I can't just stay here and forget about my shop and leave it to someone else to run," I argue.

"What the fuck do you think you're doing by franchising it?" Bettie asks in annoyance. "Other people are going to be running Liquid Cracks all over the U.S. You can't be in a hundred places at once, and hello? Give me a little credit here. I'd run that place much better than you anyway," Bettie smirks.

Suddenly, my sad and broken heart starts to heal a little bit at a time as I think about what Bettie is saying. She's right. There are going to be Liquid Cracks all over the place and it's not like I ever planned on being at all of them. I put my faith in the investors and the lawyers to help me choose the right people to open up and run my babies in whatever state they want, and I need to trust those people to run them how I would. I need to trust this town I grew up in to take care of me when I need it and do the same for them. I need to let go of the idea that I can't grow here and I can't be who I want to be here. And I need to let go of my fear of falling in love. I already fell, I was just too stupid to admit it to the one person who needed to know it.

I hear a knock at the door downstairs and a huge smile spreads across Emma Jo's face when she jumps up from the bed.

"The cavalry is here!" she announces.

"Finally," Bettie sighs. "Any more of this After School Special bullshit and I was going to slit my wrists."

She gets up from the bed and stands next to Emma Jo, the two of them looking down at me expectantly.

"What's going on? Who's here?" I ask when we hear another, louder knock at the front door.

"Just a few neighbors and friends I invited over. They've heard some rumors about how you have this amazing coffee machine that makes delicious coffee and they're pretty excited about trying it. Some of them have even started up a petition that you should open up a Liquid Crack, right here in Bald Knob, can you believe that?" Emma Jo asks slyly.

I can't believe it. Not at all. Which is why I'm still sitting in bed, staring up at her like she has two heads.

"Now would probably be a good time to get out of bed and get cleaned up. No one will want your coffee if they're too busy being disgusted by your atrocious appearance," Bettie states, yanking the covers off of me, grabbing my hand and pulling me out of bed.

"I'll go get the door and get everyone comfortable

while you get ready. While you're busy making coffee for the good people of Bald Knob, we'll come up with a plan for how you can grovel at Leo's feet, profess your undying love to him, and show him that you aren't really a crazy person, you just play one on TV," Emma Jo informs me as she hurries around the bed and leaves the room to answer the door.

"And while she's doing that, I'll call the spa. Leo will never want you back if he has to bring out the hedge trimmers and chop shit down between your legs. That's too much work for any man," Bettie states, pulling her phone out of her pocket and tapping on the screen as she too leaves the room.

"YOU'RE AN ASSHOLE, YOU KNOW THAT?!" I shout after her.

"LOVE YOU TOO, BUSHY BEAVER, MEAN IT!"

CHAPTER 37

I'm sorry for what I said before I had my coffee.
—Coffee Mug

"**Y**OU GUYS DIDN'T have to come with me."

Emma Jo takes one hand off the wheel and reaches over to the passenger seat to pat my arm that's currently wrapped around baby Cecil resting in my lap.

"Of course we did. We're here to support you. Right, Bettie?" she asks, glancing up to the rearview mirror.

"You're the moral support chick. I'm just here to watch her walk into the danger zone and crash and burn."

Turning around in my seat, I glare at Bettie in the back.

"What? I'll make sure you're okay first before I point and laugh, like any good friend does."

She holds her hand out for a fist bump and I ignore it, shifting my body back around to face forward, looking out the front window at the passing landscape of farmland, my leg bouncing nervously in my seat.

"You're lucky I'm not sitting back there with you,

or I'd open up the door and shove you out into oncoming traffic," I mutter.

"See? That's the spirit! But FYI, we're literally in bum-fuck nowhere. We haven't passed another vehicle or human being since we left Emma Jo's house," Bettie reminds me.

"Fine. I'll push you out in front of a tractor, you cow," I grumble.

"Alright, children. Don't make me turn this car around. It's going to be fine, you'll see," Emma Jo reassures, giving me another pat on the arm before putting her hand back on the wheel to turn down Leo's road.

"Maybe this wasn't such a good idea. I should have called first. Given him some kind of warning," I mutter, adding my second leg to the nervous bouncing until Baby Cecil is flopping around on my lap.

"Never give a man a warning. If he can see what's coming, that just gives him a chance to run. A sneak attack is always the best maneuver," Bettie states.

The next few miles pass in complete silence, aside from Bettie singing the song "Danger Zone" under her breath, making my nerves skyrocket and I contemplate asking Emma Jo to turn the car around.

If you would have told me when I first got back to Bald Knob that I'd never want to go back to Chicago and actually wonder why I left in the first place, I would have called someone to have you committed. There is no one more shocked than me that I'd come to that conclusion long before Bettie and Emma Jo kicked my ass out of bed the other day, I just hadn't realized it until they called me out on it. My decision was cemented when I got out of the shower and joined my friends downstairs to find out that Emma Jo wasn't lying. Half the town really had shown up to her house to try my coffee.

I spent the rest of the day showing people how Baby Cecil works, making everyone coffee, letting them see pictures of Liquid Crack that I had on my phone, talking about the franchise and just getting to know the people I'd grown up with all over again. When the gathering got to be too crowded for Emma Jo's house, Starla invited everyone over to her backyard saying, *"It's probably best we don't go out to Emma Jo's yard and party on top of the spot where Jed was whacked in the head. Even if dancing on his grave does sound like a fine idea."*

There was a tense moment of silence where everyone looked at each other nervously. Then, Emma Jo laughed and everyone else joined in, making comments and jokes about someone finally putting Jed out of Emma Jo's misery and how everyone should have been given a chance to punch him in the face one last time before his body was carted away.

This is a town full of sick assholes, but they're *my* sick assholes and I'd never been happier to claim them.

Roy Pickerson ran to his bar and brought back a few cases of beer, Andrea Maynard had the owners of The Hungry Bear shut down early and bring over some food, Bettie lit a fire in Starla's fire pit, and we all sat around listening to Caden Jefferson and his garage band play for us all night. They actually didn't sound too bad after a few beers, and we all had a great time together. Well, until Buddy was called to the house because after a few beers, Starla thinks she's a stripper. He stopped by at the end of his shift and it took him twenty minutes to convince her to put her clothes back on, go in the house, and sleep it off.

The best part of the whole night, was when the party disbanded and Buddy stayed behind to help Emma Jo clean up the mess. When I got up around three in the morning to go to the bathroom, I looked out the window and saw the two of them still sitting by the fire talking.

The worst part of the whole night was me constantly looking over my shoulder, hoping Leo would walk into the yard. Buddy tried to explain that he was swamped at the station with all of the paperwork from the murder investigation, as well as getting the farm ready for sweet corn season, but I could see it written all over his face that he didn't come because I was there.

I startle out of my thoughts when the car slows and turns into Leo's driveway. We pull off into the grass on the right, parking next to a whole row of cars that have pulled in to buy their sweetcorn for tonight's dinner.

On the left side of the drive is a long white tent lined with a few strands of large clear bulbs, that were just turned on since the sun is starting to set over the fields on either side of the farmhouse a few acres away. A couple of long tables are lined up under the tent, one holding a cash register and a pile of plastic grocery bags, and I smile when I see the table next to it still holds row after row of boxes of vintage candy. Behind the tables are several huge bins, filled to the top with sweetcorn that was just picked fresh today.

The stand and the land it sits on, as well as the huge white farmhouse off in the distance takes my breath away, but not as much as the man I see walking down to the stand from one of the fields. Our car is parked in between two other cars on the opposite side of the yard where he is and his attention is focused on the stand, which is a good thing. I can take a few minutes to stare at him without him knowing, and boy, what a nice few minutes it is. He's wearing a pair of tan cargo shorts and a white t-shirt, his hands in his front pockets as he walks until he gets up under the tent and starts shaking hands and greeting the people in line for corn.

"Alright, looks like he's distracted so now's our chance to grab everything and get over there," Emma Jo states, opening her car door.

"Hold on, let me make sure I have video ready to go on my phone. If Payton bites it, I want it documented for future enjoyment," Bettie says.

I curse at her and she laughs while getting out of the back seat. With one last deep breath for courage while Bettie and Emma Jo get everything out of the trunk, I quickly open my door and get out with Baby Cecil in my arms.

The two of them lead the way and I hide behind them because I'm too much of a chicken shit to face Leo first. I'm hoping that by the time he sees them and says hello, it will be too late and too awkward in front of all these people for him to order me off his property.

I hear his voice speaking to people the closer we get and it brings tears to my eyes. I've missed him and his voice so much that it hurts and it almost makes me want to turn back around and go hide in the car because I'm so afraid that low, baritone voice that I adore so much is going to turn hard and angry when he sees me.

"Don't you even think about going back to the car," Emma Jo mutters under her breath to me, reading my mind.

"Ladies," I hear Leo greet Emma Jo and Bettie with a smile in his voice when we get close enough for him to notice them. "How are you doing this ev-"

He comes to an abrupt halt when the two of them part, and I watch his smile disappear when he sees me, his face a mask of complete nothingness.

I swallow over the lump in my throat, remind myself that I'm a strong woman, and continue to move forward between Emma Jo and Bettie. His eyes stay locked on me as I move under the tent and behind the tables, but I look away to concentrate on what I'm

doing before I break down into tears from nerves. One
of his workers starts to take orders and fill up bags of
sweetcorn for customers while Leo continues to stand
there perfectly still where I can see him watching me
out of the corner of my eye as I set Baby Cecil down
on the table with sweaty hands and plug him into the
extension cord connected to the strands of lights.

Emma Jo and Betty busy themselves on the other
side of me, setting up the paper cups, lids, cream and
sugar, and the other items Emma Jo brought with us.
When we're all finished I power up Baby Cecil while
Leo continues staring at me without saying anything.

Sliding a mug I brought with me that says "I love
coffee" under the nozzle of Baby Cecil, I press a few
buttons and watch as liquid gold comes pouring out of
him, filling the cup with steamy goodness, the smell
perking me up and giving me a little extra courage.
When it finishes, I slide the mug out, turn and hand it
to Leo without saying anything, my eyes meeting his
briefly before I quickly turn back to the machine. Just
that one glance into his eyes was enough to make my
hands shake and my knees almost give out, but I forge
ahead. Grabbing the other mug I brought with me, the
one Leo gave me that says "Bald Knob" with a giant
red heart around it, I fill up my own cup of coffee,
grabbing it and turning back around to face him with a
deep breath.

Leo takes a sip of coffee and I almost want to
chuck my cup at his face for looking so casual and

relaxed when I want to throw up. I refrain from doing that, though, since I really like his face and don't want to mess it up.

He leans to the side to look around me, nodding at Emma Jo.

"I see you brought pies," he states.

I try not to let it get to me that he hasn't said anything to me yet, but again, I deserve this and I'm just happy he hasn't called Buddy to haul me away in cuffs.

"Yep! I've got some apple and cherry to sell," Emma Jo exclaims brightly.

"What, no blueberry?" he asks with a twitch of his lips, raising one eyebrow.

"I decided to retire from the blueberry pie making business. They cause cancer, didn't you hear?" she replies sweetly.

Leo chuckles softly, the sound making my stomach flop as he turns his eyes toward Bettie.

"Emma Jo's selling pies, what are you selling?" he asks her.

"Oh, I'm not selling anything. I'm just here to watch Payton make an ass of herself. Got any popcorn?" Bettie asks.

I remove one shaking hand from around my mug of coffee and flip her the middle finger over my shoulder without taking my eyes off of Leo. I watch as the smile he gave Emma Jo and Bettie slowly slips away when his eyes finally land back on mine.

"So what are you doing here?" he asks in low voice

that gives me goose bumps and makes my heart beat faster.

"Just sharing my coffee with the town of Bald Knob," I reply, my voice sounding shaky and high pitch in my ears.

"I heard your coffee has been a big hit."

He speaks with absolutely no emotion, taking another sip from the cup in his hands.

"What can I say, my coffee is very loveable," I tell him with a shrug, feigning nonchalance.

He stares at me quietly for a few minutes before sighing and setting his cup down on the table next to him and then slides his hands into the front pockets of his shorts.

"It is, but it's also stubborn and a giant pain in my ass," he retorts and I immediately realize he's not talking about coffee anymore.

"But my coffee can also be really sweet, and knows when it made a huge mistake, and will do anything to make it better, because the customer is always right."

I finally see the corner of his mouth twitch as he looks down at me, and my courage goes up a few notches knowing he's trying really hard not to smile and the chances of him kicking me out have lowered extensively.

"Even though you returned your cup of coffee because it was bitter, is there any chance you'd take it back and love my coffee again?" I whisper, setting my own cup down and taking a step toward him.

I hold my breath until he slowly pulls his hands back out of his pockets and takes his own step to me until we're toe-to-toe.

"I never stopped loving your coffee, I was just mad at it for burning me," he replies, his eyes staring deeply into mine.

"I'm so sorry it hurt you. My coffee sometimes does things without thinking and then regrets everything immediately," I admit with a choked voice filled with emotion as my eyes cloud with tears.

Leo points to my coffee cup that I set down on the table.

"Do you really love Bald Knob?"

I smile up at him through my tears and nod my head.

"I think I fell in love with Bald Knob the first day I came back. It just took me a while to realize it and not be so afraid of loving it," I explain.

"I always thought coffee and Bald Knob made a great pair, but it really sucked when some people didn't agree. How can I be sure you won't change your mind and stop loving Bald Knob?" he asks softly.

Bringing my hands up between us, I place my palms on his chest, one resting right over his heart and I can feel it thumping rapidly, just as fast as my own.

"The same way I can be sure that you won't change your mind about loving coffee. Because I trust you. And my coffee is fucking delicious," I state with a smile.

He finally laughs deeply and aside from just the sound of his voice, it's the best thing in the entire world to hear. Shaking his head at me, he slides his hands around my hips and finally touches me, clasping his hands at my lower back and pulling me against his chest.

"Most delicious thing I've ever had in my mouth," he whispers with a cocky wink as I push up on my toes and he lowers his head, pressing his forehead against mine. "I really, really love your coffee."

Sliding my hands up his chest, I press them to either side of his face.

"Good, because my coffee loves you more than anything, and would like to stay here in Bald Knob forever and ever, live on this farm, and someday make little cups of baby coffees with you," I inform him.

"Sweet mother of pearl, will you two kiss already? All this coffee talk is confusing, and I need to get home and take my arthritis pills."

Leo and I look back to see Starla standing on the other side of the table, surrounded by half the town, looking at us expectantly.

"Yeah, can we hurry this up? I need some coffee," Mo Wesley complains, getting a smack in the arm from Andrea Maynard.

"That coffee is Leo's, weren't you paying attention? He'll kick your ass if you touch his coffee," she reminds Mo.

"What a waste of perfectly good battery life," Bettie

mutters, pressing a button on her phone to stop recording and tossing it onto the table in irritation. "You could have at least put up a fight or thrown a few ears of corn at her."

"Alright, everyone, who wants coffee and pie?!" Emma Jo asks loudly, turning the attention away from Leo and I as everyone starts shouting and moving closer to the table.

Leo takes that opportunity to walk us backward until we're out of the tent and away from the crowd of people scrambling to get a piece of Emma Jo's pies and a cup of my coffee.

"One last question before I kiss you. I know it was ruled an accident, but we both know that's not true. Are you ever going to tell me what you know about Jed?" Leo asks, his arms still wrapped tightly around me and no trace of anger in his words.

Twining my arms around his neck, I hold onto the back of his head and pull him down closer to me.

"I promise, I will never, ever keep anything from you again, but this isn't my secret to tell."

Leo looks into my eyes for a few seconds, moving them away from me to look back over my shoulder when Emma Jo laughs loudly at something someone said.

"Son of a bitch..." he mutters under his breath, which makes me start to panic just a little bit.

"She's happy, Leo. For the first time in her life, she's happy and she's free. I know it's your job and I know-"

He cuts me off mid-sentence, quickly dipping his head and pressing his lips to mine. I immediately open for him, moaning into his mouth when his tongue touches mine, wondering how I managed to survive for a week without his kisses, let alone my entire life before I came back to Bald Knob.

Leo ends the kiss much too soon, but considering we're out in his yard in front of half the town and we're both panting heavily just from that one, short kiss, it's probably for the best that he stopped before we went too far and gave the town an X-rated show along with their corn, coffee, and pie.

"If Emma Jo is happy, you're happy, right?" he asks, bringing his hand up to tuck a strand of hair behind my ear.

"Yes," I reply quickly, nodding my head.

"Then that's good enough for me."

I smile so big that I'm afraid my face might crack, launching myself against him and tightening my arms around his neck. His arms band around my body as he lifts me up until my toes leave the ground.

"My coffee really, really wants to pour itself all over your body," I declare happily.

"Jesus, get a room, you two, before I puke from all this happiness!" Bettie shouts over to us.

Leo kisses me with a laugh. He lifts me up higher into his arms, and turns to head toward the house, doing exactly what Bettie demanded – getting us a room, in a big white house, on a sweet corn farm, in Bald Knob, Kentucky…my home.

EPILOGUE

One year later...

"I HEARD THEY had to have it out here on the farm because she tasted the coffee they were going to serve at the Bald Knob VFW, chucked her cup at the president, and was kicked out."

"Yeah? Well, I heard she was running late earlier because she spent the night in jail after Buddy caught her stealing booze from Pickerson's again."

"No, no, no. I heard they *had* to do this because she's pregnant."

I let out a little squeak of surprise and jerk away from the huge oak tree where I've been standing, when Leo comes up behind me and kisses the side of my neck.

"Are you hiding behind a tree listening to gossip, Mrs. Hudson?" he asks, coming around in front of me and pulling me into his arms.

"How else am I supposed to know what I've been up to lately?" I question with a smile, wrapping my arms with a bouquet of white roses in my hand around his neck.

Today, I became Mrs. Leo Hudson, in a small ceremony on the farm. We set up white tents in the front yard and said our vows in front of our family, friends, and the entire town, as the sun set behind the house in the distance.

I promised to never keep secrets from Leo again, make slop for him every Sunday, give him advanced warning if I'm going to do something crazy, and distract him with sex as much as possible, for the rest of our lives (I whispered that last part in his ear. No need to give the town anything *else* to gossip about.)

Leo promised to cherish Cecil and Baby Cecil, not die from an aneurism if I do something crazy, bring me back a coffee mug if he ever goes out of town without me, use his handcuffs on me for fun, and not to arrest me (he whispered that part in my ear) and to love my coffee forever and ever.

The last year has been insane, but I wouldn't change anything about it. After I groveled at Leo's feet and he forgave me, Bettie went back to Chicago to take over running the original Liquid Crack. I didn't let myself get sad about her leaving, because a few days later, Leo took a week off of work and flew back there with me so we could pack up my things and ship them to Bald Knob. I thought I would be sad saying good-bye to Chicago, but I knew I'd be back to see Bettie and to check on Liquid Crack from time to time. And I knew there was nowhere else I'd rather be than at home in Bald Knob, with Leo.

In the last twelve months, Bettie has done an amazing job running the flagship Liquid Crack, just like she said she would. There are now twenty Liquid Cracks throughout the U.S., including the one right on the town square in Bald Knob, with more coming soon.

When Leo and I got back home from Chicago after packing up my things, I moved in with Emma Jo, much to his annoyance. When I explained to him that I couldn't move in with him until we at least went on our first date, he stopped being annoyed and immediately booked a reservation for us to go into Louisville for dinner that night. Where he proposed, by having our server put the ring at the bottom of my after-dinner cup of coffee.

Sadly, poor Leo didn't think this plan through too much, and he quickly realized the error of his ways when I took one sip of the coffee and spit out on the white table cloth, refusing to drink another sip. After ten minutes of arguing and trying to get me to finish the coffee, he finally grabbed the cup, stuck his fingers in the hot liquid, and pulled out the ring.

Like Bettie told me, the people of Bald Knob welcomed me back with open arms as soon as I stopped hating the place I grew up and the people who stuck their noses where they didn't belong. They continue to meddle in my business, but at least they do it behind my back like normal human beings. And they continued their crusade of good will when Leo and I officially got engaged by throwing us an engagement party and striking the words "home wrecker" from their vocabulary.

"Everything hurts, nothing is good, and I'm so hot I think I lost one of my toes when it melted off," Emma Jo complains, walking up next to us with one hand on her stomach and the other on her lower back.

"Honey, why aren't you sitting down? Do you need some water? Are you hungry? I can fix you a plate of food if you're hungry. Here, sit down," Buddy tells Emma Jo, following behind her with a white folding chair, opening it up, and gently pushing her down into it next to the tree.

He gives her a quick kiss on the cheek and then he's off, in search of food, water, and whatever else he can think of that Emma Jo might need.

"I can't believe how much I love that man," she says softly, staring after him as he moves through the crowds of people milling about the yard, drinking, talking, and listening to the music of Caden Jefferson's band.

"I can. It's been a year and you're still staring at his ass all the time," Bettie laughs, coming up to us with a bottle of beer in her hand.

As much as Emma Jo tried to deny it last year, she liked Buddy Lloyd. A lot. And the entire town knew how much Buddy liked her right back and did everything they could to pry into their business and push them together. Buddy understood the kind of life Emma Jo had lived for twelve years and he didn't rush her. He taught her how to trust someone not to hurt you, he treated her like a princess, and he showered her with all the love and compassion that she'd never had with Jed. Even though they wanted to take things slow, the universe had other plans.

"How am I only seven months pregnant? I feel as big as a house," Emma Jo complains, rubbing her hand in circles around her huge stomach.

"You should see your ass," Bettie snorts, which earns her the middle finger from Emma Jo and a smack on the arm from me.

As much as this town loves gossip, no one batted an eye when Emma Jo's stomach started expanding, nor did they put up a fuss when Emma Jo told everyone her and Buddy wouldn't be getting married until after the baby came, because there was no way in hell she wanted to be pregnant and unable to drink wine at her own wedding. Everyone in town knew Emma Jo had lived through enough hard times, and they were just too happy for her to bother with gossip and rumors.

Not only did Emma Jo finally have someone who loved her the way she deserved and they had a baby on the way, she was no longer a housewife without any money of her own. As soon as I made the decision to open a Liquid Crack in Bald Knob when I returned from packing up my things in Chicago, I hired Emma Jo as my manager, and the first Liquid Crack to have a pastry chef. She runs the business when I'm not there or helping Leo on the farm, selling her pies alongside my coffee. The night I offered her the job, she broke down in tears, finally blurting out everything that happened the night of Jed's murder. This obviously happened after several bottles of wine, and it wasn't my intention when I started pouring the Moscato down her throat. I just wanted her to finally admit she was in love with Buddy, not come clean about killing her husband.

From what I could understand through her slurring and crying, Jed started blowing up her phone with calls and text messages after he'd been punched in the face by Leo in the parking lot of Pickerson's Bar. Since I was passed out in her living room, Emma Jo decided to take matters into her own hands and tell Jed to come over so they could talk. She never had any intention of killing him, she just wanted to finally stand up to him and tell him it was over. She grabbed the award from the front table for protection and snuck out into the backyard to wait for him. Jed met her out there and immediately started threatening her. As he charged in her direction, she wasn't fast enough to pull the award out from behind her back and hit him with it. He wrestled it from her hands and tossed it to the ground behind him. When he laughed at her attempt to overtake him, she kicked him in the balls and shoved him as hard as she could, which resulted in Jed tripping over his own feet and falling backward...right onto the award that pierced his skull. She panicked, yanking it out of his head, and ran deep into the woods, burying it where no one would ever find it. Since he was still breathing when she came back from her trek to the woods, Emma Jo really was just as shocked as me when we saw his dead body in the back yard the next morning. She honestly thought he'd wake up and crawl away after she locked herself back inside the house that night. Still in shock and not wanting to believe her shoving Jed to the ground was what killed him, she took hold of the poisoned pie theory and ran with it, until *that* idea was blown out of the water after the whole dead raccoon's incident.

Her drunken ramblings then led to even more crying and her apologizing to me for hiding the truth and letting me take the blame, never thinking in a million years that all fingers would point to me. She was scared and she freaked out, and she lied to me and everyone so well that I couldn't be mad at her. I could only be proud that she'd finally found her strength and used it for evil.

"I love you assholes," I state from the comfort of Leo's arms.

"I love you guys more," Emma Jo replies softly.

"You're both a bunch of idiots, but I guess I'm stuck with you," Bettie complains, tipping her bottle of beer in our direction.

The three of us share a look, one filled with friendship, love, and the silent promise that we will keep each other secrets for the rest of our lives.

"This has been a good chat, but if you'll excuse us, I'd like to dance with my husband," I tell Emma Jo and

Bettie, grabbing Leo's hand and pulling him a few feet away.

When we're away from the girls and away from the small group of people on the other side of the tree who are still standing around gossiping, I wrap my arms around Leo's neck again. He holds me tightly against him and we sway gently to the soft music playing across the yard.

"So, you chucked a coffee cup at the VFW president's head, did you?" Leo asks, repeating the gossip I'd been listening to from behind the tree a little bit ago.

"Oh, totally. Gave him a concussion and everything," I smirk. "I was also a few minutes late for the ceremony because Buddy threw me in the clink for stealing booze again."

Leo laughs, squeezing me in a hug and kissing the tip of my nose.

"Then I guess it really *is* true that we had to get married because I knocked you up," he laughs again.

When I don't answer him and just continue staring up at him, his laughter immediately stops and he stares down at me, his eyes wide and his mouth dropped open in shock.

"Seriously?" he whispers.

"I wasn't late for the ceremony because I was in the clink. I was late because I was puking up my guts in our bathroom. Congratulations, Mr. Hudson. We're going to have a little baby cup of coffee!" I exclaim with a nervous smile, not entirely sure how he's going to take this news.

I should have known better than to be nervous. Leo immediately drops to his knees with one hand on my hip and the other pressed gently to my stomach. He looks back and forth from my still-flat belly up to me, and the wide-eyed shock disappears. His bright blue eyes fill with tears and a huge grin stretches across his face from ear-to-ear.

"Amazing," Leo whispers. "The nerd knocked up the hottest girl in school."

Wrapping my hands around his arms, I tug him back up onto his feet, sliding my arms around his waist. He brings his hands up to my face and cradles it as he stares down at me.

"Promise me you won't teach our child about cow insemination or goat testicles," I beg him.

"Only if you promise to never, ever bake me a blueberry pie," he replies with a grin.

"I promise. Just as long as you don't do anything to piss me off, Sheriff Hudson," I tell him with a wink, pushing up on my toes and sealing my promise with a kiss.

The End

Acknowledgements

As always, thank you to my beta readers – Jessica Prince, Michelle Kannan, Stephanie Johnson, and Valerie Potjeau. Jessica, thank you for saying, "Just have them talk to each other like *we* talk to each other." I love you, fuck truck. Valerie, thank you for your Chicago knowledge and teaching me how to hate Ugg-wearing DePaul girls.

Thank you to all the awesome people in Tara's Tramps for your continued support, pimping and love.

Thank you to my agent, Kimberly Brower, for loving the idea of this story and actually making me excited to write it. Thank you for putting up with my 10,000 emails and text messages and talking me down from the ledge. Weekly.

Thank you to Scheva Hurn for your help with small towns in Kentucky. We'll always have Philpot.

Thank you to my husband for helping me come up with excellent names for this book. Jethro Snell will always be the best.

Thank you to my spawns for only asking 100 times if Jed was dead yet while I was writing. I know it could have been 200 times. I appreciate your restraint.

Last but not least, thank you to every single one of my readers who continues to support me with every crazy new book I put out. I love you all to the moon and back.

CPSIA information can be obtained
at www.ICGtesting.com
Printed in the USA
BVOW06s1550231116
468777BV00027B/498/P